CIVIC CENTER

AMERICAN SPIRIT

Also by Dan Kennedy

Rock On

Loser Goes First

AMERICAN SPIRIT

Dan Kennedy

New Harvest
Houghton Mifflin Harcourt
BOSTON • NEW YORK
2013

This edition published by special arrangement with Amazon Publishing

For information about permission to reproduce selections from this book, write to Permissions, Houghton Mifflin Harcourt Publishing Company, 215 Park Avenue South, New York, New York 10003.

www.hmhbooks.com

Library of Congress Cataloging-in-Publication Data is available.
ISBN 978-0-544-03204-0

Book design by Brian Moore

Printed in the United States of America
DOC 10 9 8 7 6 5 4 3 2 1

Maria, Trish, and another long-distance dedication to Milton.

AMERICAN SPIRIT

1

If You Lived Here You'd Be Alone by Now

TEN YEARS AGO when someone asked Matthew the question, "Where do you see yourself in ten years?" he remained silent and tried to look like he had an answer and was only considering how to phrase it. Inside the head, however, the only answer he could hear was, *Those days will eat me alive,* and Matthew knew that probably wasn't what you were supposed to say. It's ten years later and if he can swing this storm of time that's standing still in front of him, fortune will smile like it never has. But it is hard to find a hint of promise in a calendar found suddenly blank; Monday through Friday wiped clean against one's own wishes or plans, a wide-open grid of Valium-and-Heineken-kissed dead end days with a horizon way past the weeks on the page. Maybe thirty-five now, maybe forty, close enough any-way — in America these days, one's forties seem to start at twenty-five.

So this morning, west of the house and on the wrong side of thirty, Matthew Harris is sizing himself up to see how things are going; looking at his reflection in the mirror, in a men's room, in a gas station, on Post Road, a mile or two into Norwalk. The mirror is right next to a wall-mounted vending machine offering up condoms and small packets of knock-off designer cologne, which speaks volumes, really, about how things are going. If you were a camera tracking left to right in here, things would look like this as you drifted along making sense of it: empty paper towel dispenser with just a tiny torn tag of why-bother hanging from the stoic slit of its chipped metal grin; then the scratched-up, dented, bereft vending machine offering up second-rate items for the neck and penis; then the mirror offering up the reflection — long, lanky, slightly underweight now, hungover, semi-moneyed, tall, and medium slim, with no evident interest in shaving. A man with only semi-decent winnings in life's genetic lot-tery, but with enough patrician features in the face to have landed somewhere better than a Norwalk service station men's room, one would have imagined.

Living in Westport, Connecticut, seemed like a good idea at the time; lately most of Matthew's life falls into the cat-egory of having seemed like a good idea at the time. Letting a decade and change slip by working at New Time Media in Manhattan seemed like a good idea at one point as well. But let's commend him for at least having avoided the sartorial trap most men in Westport fall into, the one where it looks like they dress only in clothes from the in-flight catalogs one browses up in business or first; clothes that look paid for with membership rewards points from the platinum American Express, which is how Matthew shopped and dressed until recently—until that last day, the day all of this shit started basically, a day heretofore only referred to as the Incident. That was the day Matthew made his way into the closet at work and switched things up a bit. The closet was actually a room on the twenty-eighth floor at New Time, an office without a desk, and instead stacked wall-to-wall and floor-to-ceiling with clothing in stacks, sacks, boxes, and racks. The closet is where thin people made politely droll by fame were routinely allowed to rummage through and take away free designer clothing that they could've never afforded when they were broke anonymous people, and had no reason to be taking for free now that they were wealthy. From the so-called closet, Matthew took what he thought he might look good in. Or more specifically, what he thought he might look strong and able in, fashionably casual armor to weather the days in front of him, days that would bury the sensibly dressed, steadily employed, soft, agreeable man he had been before this day came.

It was the moment in any epic myth when the warrior chooses the armor that will allow him to undertake the journey in front of him, or in less noble terms, it was the moment when the doctor's bad news, and the subsequent beer and

Vicodin, urge one to finally take from life what has not been given. Take it, and then slouch off in a golden haze, defeated by bosses who don't understand what it's like getting the X-ray that leaves one no choice but to start living like today is the first day of the rest of one's life. Defeated, sure, arguably, but at least he was making the exit like a champion, in a long slow-motion walk that felt like the whole thing was being shot through a soft amber pill-and-lager lens — a foggy but determined, low-spirited stroll with arms bear-hugging the big stack of clothing not intended for him, holding it close to the chest and clutched up under the chin. In the blurry background, the colleagues that noticed were just shaking their heads in the same slow motion that Matthew was walking with.

The digression of bad news and bad habits and bad attitudes aside, hats off to our hero! His new look seems to borrow a page from nineteen sixties European motorcycle racing fashion, albeit a type geared toward hungover, fatigued, lonely, careless, lazy motorcycle racers with a couple of days of stubble; if only on the outside, he's doing great. Matthew leaves the restroom like a major league pitcher mustering what it takes to go out there and give life 110 percent for just one more inning, even though the game has already been decided and fans are trickling out of the seats to get to the parking lot before it's a madhouse scene, heading into traffic jams on the surface streets in order to get home a little early and make a wife happy.

He musters what it takes to leave the gas station restroom

and buy his coffee inside the little market attached to the gas station by the expressway like he always has on weekday mornings like this one. And a gas station market a mile or two outside of Westport, Connecticut, is as close to honest as Westport is going to get. Evidence of the human condition thriving here no matter how hard these people try to deny it; a little concrete hut that seems to be saying, *While I am just an ugly little bunker of a store, and while I may sit just outside your well-scrubbed, exfoliated, moisturized, leafy, conspicuously status-laced suburb, my profitable inventory lays bare the secret of what you people crave beneath your stainless veneer: pornography, cigarettes, tabloid magazines, diet pills, and beer.* Matthew walks up to the cash register and pays for his cup of coffee, trying to affect the usual bored, dull, lithe stroll meant to telegraph a dependable stream of fat and steady checks that has not dried up suddenly; which is to say, he approximates the gait he had before last Friday happened.

On the rack is one of New Time Media's magazines, and on the cover is an actor wearing the same outfit that Matthew is wearing, the same narrow, lazy gray designer tee shirt, the same gray canvas pants with articulated knees, the black boots, the reissued nineteen seventies Italian watch. The head does the production calendar math and, oh, wait, right: Actually, those are in fact the exact same clothes that were on the second stack on the right when he walked in to the closet at work to steal clothing that fateful day, the clothes that were shot back in March for the May cover of the magazine here on the magazine rack. Matthew nods the same silent hello-and-good-bye to the same clerk that he's nodded to weekday mornings for years. As far as the clerk can tell, Matthew will drive into the city like he always has, and go to work like he always does — because as far as anyone can tell, nothing has changed, except, fine, yes, the way he dresses, and maybe the way he isn't shaving as much, and maybe the rest of the shit that's going down the drain weekdays between the hours of nine and seven.

The key goes in the ignition like it always has. The upholstery is trying hard to act like summer; to do that thing where it stays cool in the morning even though the weather is already getting warm outside; but it's only the end of spring, so it hasn't really got the swing of it. The key is turned like it always is, the dash beeps the fast little beeps, the tiny orange lights on the console wake and wink, and the Bavarian Motor Works are started.

While the car idles, Matthew looks in the rearview mirror, reluctantly presses a bit on his cheeks and under his chin in a forfeited negotiation with time that always ends with the half-assed determination to soldier on: *Fuck it, I'm not old. Unless you're, like, nineteen, and sober, and looking right at me from a few inches away in natural light.* It's clearly evident that this is exactly what Matthew is thinking, mostly because he picks up his phone/email/everything device and starts typing the very phrase on the tiny keyboard. He emails this little maxim to himself. Lately, he prefers doing this late at night, fairly or full tilt into a decent buzz after killing another ten-hour workday in his parked car; this way he can be pleasantly surprised on mornings like this one by email containing his moments of insight and words of encouragement. As if one morning, the little life maxim he receives from himself will jump-start things, as if somewhere out there in the ether is the perfect slogan waiting to get his life back on track again. The coffee is in the beverage holder like it's always been. Yesterday's half-spent nest of free community newspapers is on the passenger floorboard, and triplets of Heineken empties have left the nest; rolled under the passenger seat to find their own place in the back and make a go of it on their own in this world, as we all must at one point.

Therapy has not been officially canceled, but now with no paycheck coming in, let's be honest: How long can it last, really? It's a cruel irony that when one has a job, a life, a paycheck, and is relatively on track, there is money for therapy and even sometimes insurance to cover it. Another fine practical joke from the universe, because the days ahead, to put it mildly, are the ones that will probably require a little navigational assistance. But to be clear, the man that we're referring to as a therapist is really, basically, a licensed social worker, and one who has taken up amateur stand-up comedy at age sixty-five, which can be a little awkward in sessions. This is an important clarification — the credential, not the comedy — since the practice of a psychotherapist brings to mind visions of the fortunate lying on a couch and complaining about luxury problems to someone getting paid to nod and not act on their instinct to physically strike the com-

plainer. Milton Mills, C.S.W., is a sixty-five-year-old Southern gentleman, lanky and long, almost always in a well-worn
and frayed suit from about September to late spring, and
those are the only few things you really need to know about
Milton. Lately Matthew suspects that Milton is teaching
him how to release himself from the mandible of the serially
unfaithful land mammal he snared and married as if there
was a bounty on Connecticut game so unwieldy.

Here in the car, the coffee hits blood, the blood races its
commute through veins, the veins lead it to the brain, the
brain realizes it's awake and decides to join the race. Fits
and starts, first spitting a few images; tripped and triggered
memories of largely anonymous sexual encounters that
Kristin — the briefly aforementioned, unfaithful, unwieldy,
retired fashion model wife (wholesale winter-coat catalogs,
but she's been very clear with Matthew that this qualifies as
fashion and modeling and, by definition then, fashion modeling) — would certainly not approve of. Little score-settling
trysts in the car that never manage to provide distraction
from remembering the fact that Kristin always had the house
to herself during the day to undertake her relatively normal
scenario of minor adulterous moral bankruptcy. Managing
one's score-settling trysts in a leased car you can instantly
no longer afford, in parking lots, carries a certain stigma if
you're looking at it from a high horse, or even a normal-sized
horse, really.

Matthew prefers to stick to the outlying sections of the
animal-themed lot at Stan Leland's Grocery Emporium, each

section's designated letter decorated with a corresponding animal to form a convenient mnemonic to jog a shopper's memory as to where they parked — W for Whale; Y for Yak; Z for Zebra, for Zealot, for Zero, for Zoloft. The brain kicking in, and reminding, even insisting this: For the record, any colleague (former) or neighbor (the faceless strangers to the left and right of your home) would tell you that you are sane; that you are a normal man and an upstanding member of this community.

Matthew grabs a piece of it, runs with it: I am normal, normal I am, I am la norm, moral man. The brain aborts this little anagram seizure; sends a synaptic signal that says to hit the numbers and the accelerator. Eleven hundred. Fifteen hundred. Two. Three. Forty.

Eleven hundred. This is the number of people in the company that by now, Monday at 9:00 AM, have certainly received an official piece of corporate email notifying them that Matthew was fired from the job he held for eleven years up until last Friday. They maybe even know the circumstances by now — which is essentially more than Matthew knows, since he fainted as far as he can figure.

Fifteen hundred. Probably the number of dollars that it costs monthly, all told, to drive a leased BMW 745 around Connecticut trying to find something to do until 7:30 PM so that the seasonal-outerwear-model wife, as well as the neighbors, as well as the guy at the gas station minimarket, will still be under the impression that there has been no loss of a job, no loss of a check, no loss of leafy suburban status, no hint of foreboding doom. It's probably fifteen hundred, but it could be more, or less, because Matthew never sees a bill. All of it — the lease, the gas, the insurance — hits the American Express and the platinum program lets you carry a balance, and the balance swells; it should come with a gun, this program.

Two. Number of years married. Matthew chose poorly. In fairness, they both did. Matthew has only ever chosen women who would be certain to start off very sweet then sneak up on him slowly and cause great pain, like those amateur hour drinks that taste like candy and leave you in a grave; the kind that have an energy drink and a few different kinds of booze in them. They wait in the glass to drag one's ass to the floor, the heart toward stroke, the face and neck halfway to permanent nerve damage. Drinks with names like the Mind Eraser, Dead Bull, Cherry Bomb, the Kristin Edwards-Harris. And Kristin has made the same wrong choice, obviously, believing she could find a man who is both stable and not without an edge; who is somehow at once content, staid, predictable, driven, contentious, and restless. She was trying to find the best of both worlds, or five or six, and she's tried to find this combination in a man too many times. And so if she's a lethal drink, he's essentially a candy bar designed to appeal to everyone, and of course, one that lands in the benign middle, ultimately appealing to no one. He is something that's supposed to be light but dark, mild but strong, rich but not, a nut and, at the same time, never one. A candy bar like this never works out. A candy bar like this may as well be called a We Tried Our Best Bar, or a Mutual Disappointment Cup.

Three. This is the number of what could be described as mostly minor parking lot hand-job (more or less) situations. Matthew drinks himself into the idea of it. And anyway, he is convinced he's quit. The score-settling trysts, that is, not the drinking, he needs the drinking these days, thank you very much.

Forty. This the age he used to be nowhere near. Matthew was nineteen about a month ago, just like you, just like everyone else in America.

There is usually a time in life when one wakes up wondering where life is leading, the future still a rushing brace of questions and ambition and opportunity. Lately for Matthew, waking up feels like one thousand rhetorical questions asked without urgency, in sleepy disbelief. The one currently wedged into the head like something parasitic with spiny little fins or teeth to anchor in with is this:

Am I living in a Goddamn Steely Dan song?

Matthew will insist he is not a fan. There are several bands with a much more current supply of boozed and pained urbane pathos; New Time Media has a murder of them locked into record deals and shotgun-patterned across the full field of magazines and cable shows they own. For every nineteen seventies steely measure of moping around, there's a dozen more recent bands to bring you down; The National Death Cab, A Dead Horse for Cutie, His and Hers Morning Suicide Jackets, whatever you need, really. But the head finds it hard to start the cataloging process all over again with a new downer band. The head is all etched up with every Steely Dan lyric and everything there is to know about these songs and tracks and albums and the men who made them; the brain, a gray wall, its every carved and scraped graffito a fact about Walter Becker, about Donald Fagen, about every single member, former member, quasi member, and guest musician — Dias, Hodder, Purdie, Gadd, Feldman, Carlton, you name them. This is only because the fear has long been that Matthew might wind up one of the marginalized beautiful losers in these songs' lyrics and so the head studies the songs and band since age nine or ten, like a cautionary tale of how Matthew could wind up if things get bad, like a schematic of what might go wrong eventually or suddenly, at any minute. There's the older guy dating a teenage girl — "Hey Nineteen." There's the guy in "Deacon Blues" who complains that they have a name for the winners in the world, and who says he wants a name when he loses, which, lately, seems fair enough.

The other thing is this: the brain has probably confused the words *loss* and *loser* for as long as it can remember. Matthew has never told anyone but Milton this, but here it is: He lost his biological parents early on. All he has said about this is that they saved a considerable amount of money on airfare; two deeply discounted round-trip tickets to Florida. Evidently the deal was that by having the pilot slam the plane violently into a swamp at the end of the journey — as opposed to using a costly, fancy airport runway — the airline was able to offer significant savings on fares compared to other full-price airlines. So, at the age of nine years, the brain heard the word *loss* about seven thousand times in one year, from people wearing the kind of sad faces that bad television actors wear, and that might have been when and why the brain latched on to Mr. Becker and Mr. Fagen's songs about losers and tales of suburban failure. The little head swam in the lyrics on the radio copped from a box of foster home donations and stuck under the pillow that never felt like his own, the lyrics of these steely siren songs of the modern and downtrodden swooned their way in as the heart pondered and feared fate beyond its nine years.

This many years later, thirty-one of them, it is now around 10:20 AM, and Matthew clings to routine, piloting the BMW, the Bavarian Mother Womb, speaking softly but aloud. This might suggest to anyone motoring along next to him that he's talking into the car's speakerphone, or maybe calmly repeating a daily affirmation of the successful and spiritually fit.

"No, damn it. No, damn it. No, damn it. No, fuck, no."

And apparently the way to punctuate a mantra like this on one's fake morning commute is to spit casually — with poor, lackluster aim — out the driver's-side window.

The majority of the spit lands inside and runs down the leather interior that can't really be afforded right now, then onto the forearm and elbow resting on the leased armrest. At first, Matthew looks upset, then deflated, and then, fuck it, he'll spit again, and again, spitting, spitting, spitting, and making so Goddamned sure it all lands on the inside of the stupid door. And even spitting and spitting and spitting at the passenger-side window and onto the inside of the windshield. The mouth becomes as dry as it does on the days he got bad news. The breath starts to taste like fear and regret. The mouth's spat saliva is the color of the convenience store coffee, and all of it is inching slowly downward across the car's black interior so that the gray interior of the head will start to curse. At first, the gray deals up a sensible assortment of three- and five-syllable profanities, and then both the profanity and the car accelerate. The same one-syllable profane word is repeated over and over in a short and fast staccato. Maybe six or eight times and then it seems that Matthew is about to either cry or punch something. He hasn't cried since he was nine. He has never hit anyone or anything. And that's when the fit stops and the lull of recent memories begins.

Last night was beautiful; the kind of beauty that doesn't seem to get much mention. This was the last (probably, most likely, ideally) situation involving entertaining a young lady in the car instead of the home. These girls in these bars around here, they've all had twenty-five or thirty years of fine living in good houses and they are eager to make one wrong decision. But Matthew wants to believe that last night was more than just good skin dying to do something bad, but he was probably simply the body double for a professor this girl spent New Haven days dreaming of fucking in a summer house. But for now, try to forget that part of it, and just think about the dark suburban horizon and the calm of it; the sub-divided patterns of rooftops that any number of betrayals, or struggles, or joys, or highly experimental sexual encounters, could be happening under. Think about the symmetrically white-lined and well-lit calm of the night's ample parking — everything clean, vast, and finally, after all of those daylight hours, so sparsely populated. But in the middle of the calming, very recent memories comes a cautionary lyric, worming into the ear, continuing to map everything finally going according to Steely Dan's terrible and seductive F Major 7th plan. The one about crawling like a viper through suburban streets to basically have sex with folks who live on those streets, and then it rhymes words that are all too close to home right now; words like "languid" and "bittersweet" and then the guy starts waxing poetic about dying behind the wheel. Jesus, it's all happening.

Matthew drives along, parsing the lyrics on the car stereo that killed the daydream, and by the time they play the solo, he is reduced to a man catching his reflection in a fifteen-hundred-dollar-a-month rearview mirror; paranoid eyes framed by an expensive haircut with another week or two of mileage left in it, sitting atop a head that has been jerked about by swearing and spitting. But if the head has told the heart one kind thing this morning, it is this: Nobody has the right to act like they'll never have to face days like these; there are probably only two paychecks and a very modest savings account between almost anybody in America and days like these.

2

Brand-New Man

THE GOOD NEWS IS, when the spitting and angry jerking about finally stops, the serenity starts. Matthew tries to type this one down as soon as he thinks it, tries to split his attention between driving and getting the thumb of one hand to type and send it to himself. But he can't, there's swerving, and it's the kind of swerving that evidently frightens oncoming motorists who honk horns that form passing Doppler fades as Matthew misses them by feet and inches then swerves back into his lane. Okay, on second thought, can't type it right now. So the idea is to repeat it instead, to try and remember it, and it works, this mantra. Serenity washes over the Bavarian cockpit like the calm of generic Valium, mostly because Matthew has eaten some generic Valium. But one can't just drive around eating pills and waiting for things to change. Wait, or can they? No, one can't, probably, one must make things change. One must decide what's next! Jogging! Jogging is next. Period.

"This, I don't just talk about. This, I do. Starting now."

And then a pause while Matthew already recants by thinking: *Well, maybe not today. Starting soon, anyway.*

"No! Jesus! See how that almost slipped away in that same Goddamned hot minute that it came? Starting now, I am the jogging type. Just do it, like the ads say."

And just like that, the arms steer the car over to a place where the equipment associated with jogging can be purchased. The brain takes minor issue here. *Jogging sounds strange — a dated word? Jog. Jogger. The joggers went jogging. What are you going to do today? Oh, I'm going to go jogging. Oh, are you a jogger? Yes, I jogged here.* And the decision made inside the head is that the word is probably not dated, it's probably just Scandinavian. So with confidence, Matthew decides that if it's Scandinavian, it's evergreen, as they say, and okay to keep in one's vocabulary forever, really. Jogging is already making Matthew feel good, and he's not even doing it yet, so how could it lead to anything bad? More of this sudden confidence allows Matthew to holler above the din of the car stereo, seemingly without provocation, "*Boom!* It's like that, everybody!" It's a phrase he thinks kids say, but in the moment right after exclaiming it, he wilts again, certain he's gotten the phrase just a bit wrong.

A right turn, a 1.1-mile straightaway, a left turn into this shopping plaza's driveway, proceed along the right, along past the Cineplex (fatties who never jog), along past the place that takes family portraits (terrible families that refuse to jog), farther still past the computer store (you people, you customers in there, you sit inside in front of computer screens all day, never jogging), and now turn down the row of parking that lines up quite nicely with the store called Fuel Feet. *Bing!* Destination on the right; you have arrived. Matthew is on target, in action, goal oriented, calm, focused. He parks the Germanic sedan situation, locks it, and strolls away. The car's windows are all marked from the inside with gobs of spit, the early part of the day lighting it like a safety-glass cage where some endangered creature wakes at dawn to violently spit and craft its brown saliva into webs. The gait becomes a bit more languid and loose as the trio of Valiums kicks in, and Matthew thinks: *This kind of buzz is probably the total fucking sweet spot; right where you want to be for getting into something like jogging.*

The door is pushed, as the sticker on it advises, a small electronic bell sounds, and this dispatches a great spindly geek from the stockroom, a praying mantis with a handsome head, a man creature who has spent the majority of his estimated thirty years running, indeed. Running to anything that might be out there for him, one would imagine; running away from a job like this that forces him to be so suburban and pleasant. Or maybe running away from a marriage or relationship that isn't what he expected. Matthew stares a long, slow pharmaceutical-and-silent hello, realizes he was projecting all of that stuff about running away from things, and is startled when the tanned and sinewy geek mantis speaks through a giant smile.

"Hi, there. How can I help you?"

"Jogging shoes. Jog. Jog. Jogger." Oh, no. Inside the head, words sound odd. Speaking sounds like the dentist's office after the hygienist has been away from the chair for fifteen minutes and something has kicked in, the head hearing itself a split second after speaking, so there's the delay effect, and a stereo hollow to whatever is said.

"O . . . kay. Well, what do you usually look for in a shoe?"

Matthew looks around him slowly and then, pointing, says, "Those ones?"

The blood has talked the brain into the terrible decision to fall back on some improvisational acting classes that New Time Media made Matthew and the rest of the middle and upper management take at a corporate retreat last year. Improvisational acting skills were supposed to make the New Time executives more successful in business, the idea being that they would be able to think quicker on their feet in meetings and dealings and things. That was the big idea. But the big idea didn't make Matthew any quicker on his feet in business dealings. He is, in fact, convinced that maybe these classes are what led to his problems at work to start with, and ultimately to what is still only being referred to by Matthew's brain and Matthew's former employer as the Incident. None of these creative retreats are good situations, one knows this, but one attends and participates, regardless. Fact: There was an exercise that paired people up to feel each other's faces. Fact: Matthew used his left hand, sober as a nun in the light of day, to feel the president of marketing's face for three minutes straight. And from that point forward, even long after the so-called retreat, Matthew would be trying to go about his office dealings at just the normal speed, Steve Timmel would walk by in the hall, and suddenly the brain would torture Matthew. It would essentially say to him, *There is Steve Timmel, president of marketing. You have touched every inch of his face.* And Matthew would immediately stumble and slowly stammer over whatever he was trying to say to the person he was talking to and doing business with. So falling back on the so-called improvisational skills he was taught, while falling into the warm confidence that three little friends, all named Val, have brought on, is not going to end well today. But it starts smoothly enough.

"Firmness. Firm soles, I guess."

"But, like, do you know if your feet have a tendency to roll in, to pronate?"

"They were pronating when I was outside, but they're level now."

"O. Kay. Well, the easiest way to tell is to just look at your current pair of running shoes, and just see how the heels are worn down. Like, if it's to the left or to the right."

Matthew does a degenerate ballet, a sort of slow-motion roadside sobriety test, one leg planted, one leg lifted with a terribly hesitant grace and uncertainty, and offers a look at the soles of the black leather Alexander McQueen cap toes he's left the house in this morning.

After this odd balancing act, there's a fast flurry of words offered up about shoes, socks, blisters, hot spots, ankle roll, impact, posture, and form. Matthew absorbs it all like a sponge. The entire moment is shadowed with a warm haze; one that carries the overwhelming discovery that folks in the retail sector are fundamentally good people with a strong spiritual foundation.

3

W Is for Whale

T HE CAR IS ONCE again parked in the Stan Leland Food Emporium lot, almost at the very edge of this tarmac horizon. The heater is on, like in an athletic warmup kind of way. Pants are off, shoes have been bought and changed into, minimarket Heinekens have been procured, everything is ready for warming up and stretching. It's about a quarter to noon now, Matthew's coffee is empty in the beverage holder; a dead soldier tossed to the back and replaced with a couple of green Dutch private reservists stocked into the center console. Rest in peace, coffee, you've advanced the battle but now we're going to need some real firepower to win the war. There's no reason to beat oneself up about switching to beer a little early, as the prospect of getting back into jogging is daunting, and something is required to take the edge off. Drinking before noon seems like an okay thing when it's clearly fueling a man in an athletic way or in a way that lets him realize his dreams.

You might be thinking that being of a certain age and drinking alone in one's car while "warming up" for one's first physical exercise in fifteen years is not the portrait of a man realizing his dreams, but maybe you've got pretty lofty ideals. Matthew has pushed the seat back as far as it will go to accommodate the athletic warm-up stretching/drinking. And it almost seems like when the leg is stretched in a certain way up onto the dashboard, beer and coffee flow down into the muscles. Same when the arms are pushed up against the glass of the sunroof. One can feel the body coming to life. This is what athletes probably feel like right before they do Olympic jogging or a World Series or something. Matthew seems to be radiating this message: Welcome to the first day of the rest of my life, fuckers. He kicks over the open beer but doesn't beat himself up about it, because these are tight quarters for stretching, even with the seat all the way back. The personal listening device is powered up. The headphones are not really running headphones, since they're the older, very large noise-canceling headphones that were used for business travel. But people used to roller skate with headphones this big, and one assumes roller-skating and business travel are harder on headphones than jogging, so let's hit it. All systems go, let's do this mother. Jesus.

When was the last time any jogging like this happened? By the looks of how this is already going, the answer must be that jogging hasn't happened for Matthew in a very long time. It's supposed to help fight depression, but all one can picture while jogging are the guts — red and shiny, heaving and contracting. It looks near impossible to breathe in this case. The ground is pounding the feet, which are connected to the legs, which lead directly to the knees. Matthew tries to focus on something, and can come up with only a question to focus on: *Fuck, am I old enough to have a heart attack?* Answer: Yes. A difficult answer to face, but it's the truth. Time races by all of us, time creeps along slowly like something playing dead, and then it turns and jumps our ass like we were walking down a block we shouldn't have gotten so far down to begin with.

The stupid music thing is shuffling songs randomly into the ears and head, and Matthew keeps pressing the button hoping that some good jogging song will come up next. One cannot jog to these anthems of downtrodden men and desperado women. And one cannot jog to the stupid slow song by Taylor Swift that New Time Media preloaded every employee's computer with; a slow song that, at some point during the halcyon days of employment, has automatically updated and migrated onto the personal listening device, and now right up the weird coiled cord into the abnormally large headphones on Matthew's head — a head that is bright red, sweaty, huffing. The head of a grown man running to a slow, breathy song for girls about two people becoming one when they kiss. Fuck it, whatever; leave it on, because, well, it is kind of maternal and calming. After all, it is about hearts doing well, so maybe it will keep a heart from seizing and a field of vision from narrowing.

Matthew shifts to a mantra to calm himself: *Fuck jogging.* This simple Zen koan is repeated in his head a few times but then there are good college tries at attitude adjustment shoehorned in: *That's not the attitude, is it?* And also: *That's not how we improve ourselves, is it?* Focus on the positive. Focus on the stupid free song that the former employer shoved onto your computer. Two become one. He tries to start reverse engineering some kind of jogging mantra or message from the benign lyrics. Two really do become one, he tells himself . . . yes, imagine a vision of a healthier, not depressed, brand new you who is finally living a real and authentic life. And now imagine the old you. And now imagine that the versions of you are kissing and becoming one. Excellent. Now just focus on getting around the perimeter of this parking lot at least once and then back to where the car is parked. Throat feels like steel wool. Why are the daytime McMansion housewife jerk-off grocery shoppers staring? Ah, right, still holding the second beer bottle. Bad form, they're right. But still, fucking back off with the judging, you apes. This is the beauty part of never knowing your neighbors. Do you think Matthew cares what any of these people think? He does, sadly, but still, it's not like they know him or know Kristin. Matthew stares ahead, stares back at them, stares at the asphalt below him and thinks: *What are you dirty bats going to do? Tell my wife that instead of being at work I was jogging around the parking lot at Stan's with a beer in my hand with my face all twisted up and red, here atop my weird, sweaty steel wool constricting neck? Go ahead and tell her. I'll just say that I called in sick. I look sick right now, so it fits.*

Plus, these women staring at him, they don't even know Matthew's wife. At this point in her life she's tired of playing nice and having faith that time is on her side. Kristin is a woman who understands that faith without the fucking teeth and fight to take what you want is dead. If these house bots introduce themselves with the idea of ratting Matthew out, she'll shrug to hear the information and eventually screw their husbands if these judgmental monsters give any indication that there's a husband in their house with even a modicum of personality not fraught with struggle or frustrated ambition. Or even just a husband with more money than Matthew has — and they all have that at the moment — so keep your distance if you like your marriage, ladies.

W is for Whale. Now coming up on the *V* section of the parking lot. *V* is for Vegetables, *V* is for the leftover Vicodin one eats in front of the TV when the knees split and their ligaments snap free, after the shins have splintered and made their way through the skin. Goddamn, jogging isn't getting any easier. The eyes start to bulge and water, the face is full of vibration, mostly tonal, because Matthew is now making sounds not unlike the whale on that sign in the last parking section; deep and involuntary primitive bronchial groans. This sound is maybe what the trophy wives are looking at as they saunter from their cars and toward the store without even making the effort to jog. At least find the heart to make an effort at jogging before you pass judgment on how someone is going about it.

Matthew's form is all over the place, hunched and weaving, staggered and wheezing. In a last-ditch effort to right the body's course and form, he throws the beer bottle toward the plants that border the parking lot, but the bottle breaks on the curb, stopping a bit short after achieving — strangely enough — the same off-kilter swerve Matthew is trying to correct in his stride. Now even more of them look and judge and shame, but Matthew finds a resolve in himself that seems to say: *Oh, I see how it is; now I'm the crazy one? I'm the crazy guy wearing makeshift running shorts (boxers that are almost passable and, frankly, probably cost more than most pairs of exercise shorts) and huge headphones, running around the grocery store parking lot drinking and throwing bottles spastically into the concrete?*

Okay, new plan; with the chest tightening a little too fast, it's time to stop this jog short, time to cut across the lot and back to the car for what athletes refer to as the cool-down period. This was far enough for the first one.

Matthew hangs a hard right to cut through the middle section, and the back of a car is suddenly angled right up against him. When it happens, it happens so quickly that one can't figure out why a car would be so close to the hip and waist. It tags him hard, it sends him onto his ass like a cartoon, like slapstick, like grainy blue-and-gray footage from a security camera that has to be slowed down to see what even happened because it happened so fast. The vision blurs for a second and his point of view is instantly that of a man lying on the asphalt looking up at the sky.

The music volume was knocked and jammed all the way on high and the ears are splitting to the sound of a benign melody that speaks of his heart growing strong, of two becoming one. Interrupting his vast and inspirational view of the sky is a hysterical woman, suburban-pretty, stunned, and squawking, in her forties and standing over him looking down and moving her lips without making a sound. Matthew loves the feeling of lying on his back with a woman caring about how he's doing. He remembers this feeling. There's a moment in jogging that the Fuel Feet clerk told him about, it's called "hitting the wall" and it comes with symptomatically irrational thinking and then increased performance levels. He wonders if that's what he's hit. Matthew manages to essentially paw at the large headphones that have been knocked ajar, until they are the rest of the way off of his head.

Staring up, he manages to say something. "I've been . . . I don't usually drink. Fitness is important to me."

What seemed like a fairly polite icebreaker earns him being quickly hushed up and covered with a blanket from a car trunk, thrown onto him by another onlooker who has also rushed over.

"Let's get him covered up. He's talking nonsense, he's going into shock."

And then this man — this half-assed lump of spiritual effect with a 1995 expiration date, whose hair — both receding and long — and Mexican poncho suggest a dicey decision to embrace hippy culture fifty years after it has gone to seed; he continues speaking.

"Okay, let's all just relax for a minute. Let's not panic. Everyone's okay; everyone's right where they need to be at this moment for whatever reason."

There are thanks doled out for this! Thanks are showered on the lumpling instantly! "Thank you for being so calm in the middle of this," the woman says; thank you for keeping us from panicking. Matthew doesn't thank this man. Matthew doesn't want to talk anymore today. He makes his way up and onto his feet to everyone's chagrin, happy to have it in him to shake off the injury like an athlete. But he also wonders if one can, in fact, shake off internal bleeding if it turns out that's what is happening. The two onlookers fuss and follow him and Matthew manages to mumble, "This is probably exactly the kind of shit that makes people quit jogging forever."

4

Wake Up and Get to Sleep

MATTHEW SHAKES IT OFF by walking a couple of cooldown laps around his car, happy to be upright and conscious, but then he looks at his watch. He is certain Kristin has materialized in the house; fading up like a song; growing taller like a shadow trying to block the sun. At 1282 Druxbury, now well past noon, she is with the man she loves. The man vaporizes from the steam of the shower, first a barely darker section in the white, then clearly more than a notion, and then a body in the clear. He seems to dry instantly, or not worry much about being wet, gets back into bed, and kisses her. He appears fine with the luxury of a lazy morning—daily, as far as Matthew can tell. There is no real idea of who this man is, but the eyes picture him wholly in a handful of torturous little scenarios the gray has come up with. Matthew has sensed him for a long while now.

A year ago, or two, or however many, Kristin did little to dissuade Matthew from indulging the worst suspicions he could come up with. He was forthright, he told her that the details in his head were insane, burnished on the brain; he had never been a jealous man, he said, but now the hunches seemed so real that it was hard not to humor them. He said he even knew what they had for breakfast together, that it was like a hotel breakfast, strong coffee in those little silver pots with heavy cream, those little glass yogurts with the foil lid like Matthew and Kristin had from room service in Paris back when the two of them still seemed like a good idea, if only to the two of them. One might argue that Matthew was in need of some kind of comforting from Kristin, in need of some reassurance maybe. That sort of thing isn't unheard of in marriages on occasion. There was a host of things she could have said. She could have said, *Matthew, our love is stronger than these neurotic fits of yours and you need to realize that.* Or even, lovingly, but firmly, *I think you're being a little paranoid, don't you?* These are both just suggestions for things people on earth might consider saying in exchanges like this, and anything along these lines would have done just fine. But the only thing she said was, "Do you know how much fat is in heavy cream?" A long pause hung and answered every terrible question Matthew didn't have the guts to ask. And she broke the silence to seek clarification by asking two questions.

"Did you mean skim milk, maybe?" and "Do you think I'm fat?"

Matthew comes home to this house, this same house, this ghost town, nine or ten hours after leaving it to "go to work" and about seven and a half hours after being hit by a car. The man is gone, but Kristin pops up around every corner about twice an hour and then a little less the later it gets. She's impossible to avoid, even in almost three thousand lonely square feet, well, especially in three thousand lonely square feet. She is upstairs on the phone again, barely heard above a whisper, talking in code to friends or family or worse. She is reflected in the kitchen floor, framed on the walls, embedded like smoke in the drapes, all over the place, just out of sight and range.

Kristin has stuck to saying she's thirty-nine for as long as she can get away with it, she's never in the sun but always evenly tanned, she's sexy but frail and too thin, she's three labels and a watch, and she's also had as many dreams and hurt feelings, holdouts, high hopes, and letdowns as any of us mortal and trying. She was a kid once just like everyone was; she's someone frightened to let the heart believe in second chances, like anyone with a decent heart is. But Matthew was never the man supposed to see any of this in her, and she is not the woman meant to see the same things in him. But they met, then they did what so many people on the 30 percent of the planet not covered by water usually do: They stayed together, determined not to notice what didn't fit, and made relatively small, silent, ostensibly secret, but painfully irrevocable mistakes in a process that will always last longer than it should. And in that process bodies become too fat, bodies become too thin, the result of everything unconsciously becoming reward or punishment for the comfortable mess two people are in when the year on the calendar changes again.

There was a time when the truth came out, a time when both of them were a little bit drunk, drunk enough to talk about making things work. Matthew had been drinking a few alone at home wondering where she could possibly be staying so late most Friday and Saturday nights, and Kristin came home from her Saturday night at about five on Sunday morning. She lay down on the couch, across the room from Matthew, and he gave it his best shot at a better marriage.

"Where were you? And I want you to be honest with me. If we're going to make this work, we need to be honest with each other, Kristin. That's what being married is all about. Just tell me exactly as you would tell a friend. Because first and foremost we're friends, right? Where were you? I was worried."

And then out came the big guns, Matthew adds the phrase he's convinced makes people disappear in a heartbeat: "I love you." This chestnut has left Matthew's lips only a handful of times since age nine, and admittedly, maybe that's part of the problem. Saying it apparently really made Kristin jump at the chance to go back to being friends; back to being two people who weren't locked into it, back before that moment when the plane door closes and you know this is where you're sitting until the very end of the flight, honoring in sickness and in health, forever and ever, amen, and all of that. Kristin warmed to this idea of talking like friends almost immediately.

"I went to Splash with Stephanie, and I met this guy that had a ton of coke, so we did drugs in his car and then somehow I ended up back at his place, sleeping with him and then actually, you know, falling asleep."

Matthew is no longer very interested in talking like friends. Kristin raising the bar to this level of friend-like talking really threw a monkey wrench into the communication exercise.

7:45 PM is the perfect time to come home. It says one has had a full day at the office; even hit some traffic on the way back in from Manhattan; it's early enough to still watch television and consider a way out of the position you're in; it's late enough that dinner won't warrant serious production — it can be eaten alone over the sink, no plate, just a paper towel or napkin. Pants cover the bruises and scrapes and tarmac grind on the legs, though there is the matter of the limp when moving from the kitchen to the couch in front of the television. It's something that Matthew will try to blame on a rigorous visit to the gym, if he has to. There's more blood in the urine, but that was happening before, and the car only aggravated it. The blood is from the pain, and the pain is why there will be an X-ray that anyone in their right mind puts off getting until the pain gets finally too scary. But there has been no X-ray so far, because walking around feeling like you've been kicked in the nuts is a pain that is easy to rationalize when one considers how they've spent so many days in an office feeling like that's what has metaphorically been happening during all of the submitting to superiors under the influence of a heavy mortgage. Nobody knows a thing about it; this business of the blood and pain is between Matthew and God and a sixty-something-year-old Republican doctor that puts his hand in private places on people while he talks about Karl Rove's book being pretty darned good. The brain keeps saying that she knows everything he's trying to hide. A shadowy dart in the corner of his eye is always her and the shadowy dart always knows. And he knows, too; knows everything he's done wrong; everything she thinks of him; everything she did to begin with, how she's the first to admit that maybe she started it. With any luck, sleep will bring a nightly reprieve; Matthew prays in his head to anything that might be listening. He asks that he figure out a way to have fixed what's going wrong inside of him, even though he may not have insurance; he also asks that he never develop a tolerance to the lovely mild opiate called television.

Kristin disappears; the night drifts by, thanks to this lovely oxycontappliance. In the blue glow of this hibernation, grateful for something so powerful that it can make four and a half hours on earth race past without too much time for serious reflection, Matthew figures that maybe what he prays to is, in fact, television; that maybe this is the thing that has taken care of him. The channels dish up an accidental dose of the twenty-four-hour news cycle that Ted Turner invented; the brain is littered with stories of unemployment on the rise, houses in the west going upside down at the bank, banks going sideways down on Wall Street, gunmen storming things, cars piling up in fog, planes crashing in Brazil and Spain, fraud, forced entries, you name it. Matthew uses the remote to set something called parental controls blocking the cable news networks. From now on if he wants this stuff pumped into his head and chest, he needs to enter a five-digit code to allow it in. A few more moves on the remote and he arrives at a string of channels specializing in showing classic reruns that originally aired way back when life made a little more sense. But it might be too late for this sort of nostalgia tonight, because the flurry of news channels that blew through earlier have the brain reeling to think what these old sitcom episodes would be like if they were updated to fit what the cable news anchors say is happening outside every day. The brain crosses wires between the grim news it's already seen on the screen. In an episode of *Seinfeld*, George tries to get Jerry's tax records back after he stops dating a former IRS worker. He approaches her at the diner, not knowing that she carries a knife, and he is stabbed in the chest and thigh. In an episode of *Everybody Loves Raymond*, Ray has a lot of explaining to do to Debra when he is caught hiding a handgun in an oily rag and putting it under their bed, and when the situation is hilariously blown out of proportion by the Barone family, Debra decides to get a gun of her own in case somebody ever tries to break in. In an episode of *Friends,* Joey finally lets the cat out of the bag about his fertility test with Melanie, who was starting to suspect he was gay, then Ross shows up at the café to drop off a birthday present for Rachel. Ross then announces that he's going to China to buy something called a seven-point sword, a rare type of Chinese throwing star that was used as a deadly weapon in the days of warring states and feudal lords. Chandler and Ross secretly arrange for an underground dealer of rare Chinese weapons and torture devices to meet Ross in Shanghai in hopes of Ross being able to also purchase something called a Din Tek Tu Iron Talon.

Moving forward down the line, the television screen dishes up nine women doing these cardiovascular exercises to hip-hop music. The head has stopped its game of polluting everything. The one woman who is leading the exercises, the sort of queen bee in all of this, is beautiful. And she says what one needs to hear when one is in a period of days like this. She has this amazing way of encouraging everyone in a loving way; she's perfect.

"If it starts to burn too much, just ask yourself if you can just do it for one more minute. Hey, nobody's watching. You can struggle as much as you want in your living room, right?"

Yes.

"Feel it?"

Yes.

"Just do your best today and you'll do better, eventually."

I love you.

5

Life: All You Need Is a Gun

THE THING ABOUT the morning after one is hit by a car is that it's a morning of pain; a great deal of it, really, but apparently nothing to waste a small reserve of co-pay Vicodin on. And nothing severe enough to face the sheer humiliation of calling Human Resources to check if getting fired after the Incident leaves one with any continuation of health insurance benefits. So, eventually, a morning snack, a handful of Tylenol 3 — with its little nudge of codeine lying in the liver waiting to be metabolized into morphine. And then one must leave the house on schedule and get one or three miles down the road — which involves getting the coffee, getting onto the throughway in plain view of the clerk, and then exiting three exits away, out of view, and coming back into town on surface streets.

Matthew has settled into the *Z is for Zebra* section of Stan's again. Three sections away from where it all happened yesterday, but there will be no jogging this morning. But choosing the same lot again is important; it feels like one hasn't given up their ground after one bad event. Matthew radiates a casual and positive impression, like an athlete on the bench. Sure, there's an early-season injury, but the athlete still has the focus and spirit to show up at the stadium to sit on the sideline and watch practice.

There is an ad in the free community newspaper that was picked up at the gas station during the morning's coffee purchase. The paper is free, which is a great type of newspaper when there is no job or office; the kind of newspaper or magazine one pays for is the kind of paper taken to an office and read. The large and silent Bavarian land yacht is anchored just aft and to the starboard side of the white-and-black zebra-striped poles of lights that will come on in eight or so more hours for respectfully employed grocery shoppers. This lot, one would basically call it a jumbo lot. Your biggest parking lots in an area like this are going to be in front of big box retailers, or grocers based in shopping centers and maybe flanked by smaller shops. Old money, family-owned super grocers like this one stand alone on tarmac horizons, without the indignity of a strip of smaller shops propping them up or feeding off them. Stan's is a cross between a grocery warehouse superseller and amusement-theme park thing, basically. It's a cruel trick. Kids will think it's an amusement park and then when you get them inside, it's just a grocery store.

The outside of something like this is perfect though, because the parking lot is large and for the most part the outer perimeter is roomy enough that you aren't going to have to endure the surprise of a familiar face. Inside, yes, it's emotionally confusing. There's a mechanical black guy, for instance. Black milk, chocolate milk. He's inside the store with all the other animated electronic life-sized characters that sing and talk and wave. And he sings, kind of a garbled metallic ribbon of Negro spiritual with an indecipherable bluesy sentiment. And the white animated robotic milk cartons just sing; they don't dance at all, so . . . racist, right? They have the dignity of just standing tall and producing a choir's anthem of national pride about America being a land of plenty. The brain and head hear all of this and request that the topic is retired, they tell Matthew that the only thing worse than a racist is a white guy in Westport, Connecticut, acting like he knows what racism is and that he is offended by it.

"Life: All you need is a gun," the mouth says silently without much permission.

And then the eyes realize the first headline of the very first ad they see actually says, "Life: All you need is a plan."

And Matthew thinks barely aloud, "Oh, okay, I see. Yes. Perfect. One should have a gun; it's difficult to argue against having one, isn't it? That's all that's missing for me, I bet. And I bet you anything the rest of the world has one."

He stops reading to think how there must be houses full of them on the outskirts of parking lots like this one; munitions bunkers, basically, where normal folks are armed to the teeth. He should have a firearm too, and never has. And at the very least, it will be a means of preventing further backslide or misfortune or unexpected hardship. Good. Decided. He'll get one. And then the synapses fire slightly out of time like half-assed jazz and the next question that flows from the gently dyslexic tangle inside of Matthew's head is this: *Okay, so how do I go about buying a gun?*

On the cable television documentaries about failed or fallen pop stars, there is always the somebody-who-knows-somebody-who-can-get-you-a-gun method of securing a firearm, but there are some obvious red flags here. The first being that the transaction always seems to take place in a parking lot, so there's the idea that one shouldn't do this kind of business in what is, for the most part these days, one's home. Having said that, buying a gun this way speaks volumes about being properly connected, which is all anybody in Westport ever wanted to be, so there's arguably a certain cachet to it. On the other hand there's an unspoken code of honor in Westport. For instance, parking lot deals that lead to cocaine or low-grade violations of fidelity are largely seen as forgiven—maybe even a somewhat honorable risk to take—but there is the implicit agreement that the lowest one should stoop in securing a sturdy weapon is to steal the firearm from a highly appraised family collection in a self-medicated moment of suicidal panic, marital distress, and/or sudden financial insecurity. With no access to such arsenal, this leaves only one other foreseeable way of buying a gun, which is at the big chain sporting goods stores, and this paints an ugly, premeditated, passive-aggressive portrait of filling out forms, patiently waiting for state approval, and then in thirty or so days' time actually paying a reasonable price on any major credit card for a gun that one is completely allowed to have. And, as one stand-up comedy routine of Matthew's certified social worker pointed out in the past, if you are of mild enough manner that buying a gun this way seems just fine, then you probably don't want a gun the way the rest of us want one from time to time.

Besides, there's risk involved any way you cut it, isn't there? A sidearm is great for the self-esteem, possibly, sure, but it's easy for Matthew to imagine that a gun is the type of thing one might absentmindedly take out in a spirited moment of conversation to impart gesture or flourish and accidentally shoot oneself in the thigh or foot, surviving and carrying on with even lower self-esteem than you had before bolstering the ego with the purchase to begin with. Guns don't kill people, the dangerous potential of suddenly losing the self-confidence that presumably comes with owning a gun kills people. Anyway, the ad that says "One Needs a Life Plan" advertises a meditation class, not a gun. And the eyes have been trying to tell the brain that they've long since noticed the mildly aphasic miscommunication way back before all of this. And word is sent systemwide about the correction, and the mouth whispers a note of retraction.

"Oh, a plan. Right, so, a . . . meditation class is the plan they're talking about."

Matthew supposes he should use meditation to stay level-headed since somehow the plan has become to go forward in this life with a gun under the seat or at his side.

The ad copy under the headline says that classes are Monday, Wednesday, and Friday afternoons at the community center. Participants are asked to pay what they wish. The community center is maybe three parking lots away from where anchor is set at the moment, so commuting to the first class is basically just a matter of moving down a few lots. If there's one thing you can say about spending so much of your time in a car, it is that you are almost always relatively close to anything you want. Realizing this has Matthew feeling just slightly ahead of the curve. It's a small curve, admittedly. It doesn't represent much, this curve, relatively speaking. But it's a curve and he's ahead of the others on it, and this can't be said about many curves currently, so that makes it a pretty decent curve to pay attention to at the moment. The broken gray matter issues more warped marching orders in the name of preparing for today's meditation class; the plan is to drop off and get a few beers.

Choices in miniature merchants are made, since going back to the usual morning convenience store would be out of the question and basically the same as being a week unshaven and asking if there's any chance the clerk has heard of job openings in the area. So, something small and much farther west than the morning stop; this one is not attached to a gas station, and this one has upped the ante of honesty by having a porn magazine that features very portly women, and another title that seems focused on African American women with gigantic stomachs and breasts; almost medically odd in shape and size. This, in a town of mostly upper-middle-class white people striving to stay thin by moderate exercise and robust prescriptions. Both racks are half empty of the issues within them. Beer procured, and even a pack of cigarettes, but only the spiritual ones with the Indian chief on the front of them; cigarettes that are free of big corporate additives and designed to basically prepare one for communion with the Great Spirit and powerful meditation. The plan now is to park far enough away from the community center's large front windows so that one can drink and smoke, but still be close enough to make it into the meditation class under the spell of an intoxicating mix of low-grade Canadian morphine, lethargy, off-brand Heineken-type beer, smokes, and denial. Matthew calls this distance "the sweet spot" of a medium-sized lot.

And in this medium lot in front of the community center, the first beer is opened and the ceremony of pre-meditating begins. It is understood between the brain and heart that drinking does not make situations like the one Matthew is in any better, but for now, let's give alcohol a round of applause;

it has convinced Matthew that he's doing great and that he has some sort of mobile private social club that boasts a roster of one. It's a mobile social club with leather upholstery, an always extremely central location, air-conditioning, reading material, jogging equipment, and a great sound system. The music playing on satellite is of the Adult Contemporary Rock variety, mid tempo, with a mildly fortunate loser vibe disguised as self-appraisal or spiritual honesty. Not Steely Dan, but might as well be. Maybe Fleetwood Mac after all the members had made and lost the money the first time and had slept their way from the left of the band's lineup to the right and all ended up back with the drummer in the middle again. So that plays and says something about going your own way, or finding your own way, or giving it all away; there are still three bottles of beer left, and all Matthew is certain of is that he's in the zone. And he sits there thinking, *Oh, I'll go my own way, sister. No problem. As a matter of fact, it will probably be the best way to go considering it's twenty minutes before class and I already feel like I am meditating. If you ask me, everybody should go my way.*

It is not a meditation instructor's nature to worry, obviously. And it is not Matthew's intention to worry a meditation instructor. That being said, this guy is looking out the window occasionally and one would have to think he's noticing the only car in the lot and the fact that it's only about twenty yards from the huge window where he's setting up some sort of yoga mats for class. More accurately, one would have to think he's noticing the guy in the car. He's putting the mats down, evenly spaced, giving his students the room they'll need to meditate once they show up. Room enough to think about not being fenced in. One cannot be fenced in. The brain pushes through the budget beer and Tylenol 3 warm pre-meditative haze and lays this little gem from the ether: *One cannot be fenced in if the goal is total personal freedom and endless horizons.* Matthew tries to catch it, tries saying it to himself, tries to type it up on his little apple or berry or whatever this phone thing is. He's typing it up completely wrong, the keys microscopic now instead of tiny or small, and adding to the thumbs stumbling is the fact that Matthew is genuinely excited about his new class. *"Don't fence when . . ."* Wait. *"When you fence . . ."* No. *"If you think you're fenced in . . ."* It's not coming back, that one. But the brain is being compassionate today, telling Matthew that it's fine to lose a maxim or slogan occasionally, telling him that it doesn't matter, that it's fine even if it's wrong, and that the universal truth is that if it is wrong, then it was supposed to be wrong. He whispers quietly to himself, "Holy shit. I love meditating already." And as long as we're talking about maxims and slogans, this is the mantra that the instructor is repeating in his head right about now:

> *Who's the man with the dead eyes*
> *Sitting in that car*
> *Drinking in that car*

Singing in that car
Staring at me.

Matthew sees him looking and this sets him in motion, like a curious grizzly spotting a tourist's campsite, he falls over himself to push his body from his den in the kind of cautious curiosity. He slowly puts the last empty bottle under the passenger seat, turns off the satellite radio so that all the love songs in space will have to find another place on earth to go. Waits for the car's antenna to retract, opens the door, and makes his way toward the front door that will allow him to pay what he wishes to be on the other side of the windows from which he's been drinking and at which he's been staring for forty-five minutes. He wishes to pay nothing today. There is, of course, the sudden panic and intimidation at the prospect of meditating with other people. The head interferes here, already asking the body to turn around and get back to the safety of the car/social club/den; the brain starts a slow drip of rationalizing not trying this. Matthew starts drilling himself to continue forward. This is what Milton has taught him, to move forward, to always choose activity; that when one moves forward, they are able to intuitively handle what used to baffle them; that one has to take a first step, has to move a muscle to change a feeling, as Milton says. So on the remaining twenty yards of the walk up to the windows and door, Matthew drills himself forward with a lack of kindness, in perfect meter. Walking becomes quarter notes in perfect 4/4 time, each step slamming down to stab the planet and punctuate the little refrain he's issuing to himself about not getting this wrong.

"Fucking do this. Do this! At least get this one thing right. Because there is a very limited number of things left for. You. To. Get. Wrong. Fuck. Do. This. Please."

The instructor has been watching Matthew walking in this aggressive locked-tight walk from mid-horizon in the lot. The brain gathers data, sizes the instructor up as seeming afraid, and then issues a correction. The instructor is not afraid, he's amused, this fucker. The gray has found a match on the identity — the instructor is the man that threw a blanket over Matthew when he was hit by the car while jogging. The brain continues updating the feed and the crawl now reads: *The instructor is amused by you because he is the man who has slept with Kristin.* Matthew feels the instant desire for petty vengeance and mistakes this for self-realization, actually believing this: *The instructor has been brought here today to teach me how to relax and not let fear govern my life. I have been brought here today to teach the instructor how to be tense and afraid again.*

Matthew thinks, at least for the moment, that this is how things work in the universe — probably the result of the average American's exposure to a peripheral diet of half-baked self-help culture. The brain drifts into this slogan: *Guns don't kill people, a misguided grasp of one's place in the universe, gleaned from intermittent exposure to bestselling self-help books, kills people. Well, that and guns.* Synaptic cues are sent to the hands to type it into the little screen while walking, which adds a hunch to the stagger that Matthew is walking with, and leaves the cigarette bobbing up and down at the corner of his mouth as he silently mouths what he is typing.

6

Meet Your Classmates

THERE IS THE USUAL smattering of people one might expect showing up to this kind of thing. And they are, for the most part, the people Matthew has spent a lifetime avoiding. Which is to say, perfectly well-adjusted people who seem pleasant enough; the kind of people most folks think they should be involved with. But after one summer lifeguarding when he was nineteen years old, one thing sticks in the brain about the people you think you should reach out to and it is this: They are the people who will drown you. It is their zeal that attracts you, and it is their zeal that will kill you. It is their confidence in seeming to know what is best for them. It is the broad wave, the feigned kisses on the cheeks of friends and acquaintances. In Matthew's memory of his training that summer, he recalls that these attributes — overzealous, excited, a delusional sense of confidence, the frantic waving of arms — are the hallmarks of a person you need to assist but physically distance yourself from. The brain and heart both decided long ago that if Matthew ever has/steals a kid, the kid is going to spend at least one summer lifeguarding at swim club if only to learn this life lesson: The only people saved are the sufficiently tired. There are a few of these people sitting in front of Matthew and to the left and right of him, since he's landed, as usual in the case of any class or gathering, in the very back row. But Matthew doesn't have a kid, so this idea of insisting that the kid will spend at least one summer lifeguarding is moot at the moment. His only children to his knowledge are five empty bottles that have been left out in the car in the parking lot, the Empty Bottle Quintuplets, and when they were emptied into the body, they went about filling the head with a smog of hops and miasma that now hangs between him and these happy-go-lucky overachievers who have what it takes to meditate. Something inside of him (alcohol) issues the challenge to at least try to make contact with one of them. There's a guy to the right who one imagines is named Greg or Chad and is probably not daydreaming of buying guns while killing time in his car and tricking his wife like a tenth-grader cutting classes daily.

The rows are all mimicking some kind of warm-up stretch that someone somewhere in the room started them into mimicking; a trend with a cue and origin that is completely untraceable. The brain suggests in flinches and shudders that this could be a stretch started by the muscle memory of someone who was in this room a hundred years ago, which makes the buzzed and lazy mouth mutter: "Jesus Christ, I'm like a drunk who's read three pages of Stephen Hawking." At this, a couple of stretching classmates take note of Matthew just as he is undoing his stretch enough to attempt a moment of social grace and form to say hello to the man beside him. The heart speeds a little knowing this is about to happen. Matthew undoes half of the pretzel his legs have become, and weirdly turns his upper-body stretch into a broad wave of hello, aimed at the guy sitting right next to him.

"How's it going?" he ventures for probably the first time since grade school.

"Shhh," comes the reply.

"Real fucking polite!" Matthew immediately huffs in a hushed whisper.

The neck pulls upward in the warm-up stretch and the eyes size up the others around the room as Matthew displays a helpless look of Can-you-believe-this-guy-is-such-a-dick? and the class is looking back at him with a What-is-your-problem-have-you-been-drinking-in-your-car-all-afternoon? look on their faces. Inside the head, there is much drive about somehow defeating them.

Oh, I'm going to meditate so well that I make all of you disappear. We will disappear from each other and you'll be free to quietly think about nothing, and when it's all over you can wave to one another in the parking lot, you can do air kisses, you can put your arms around each other and pull each other under.

The instructor is the only man regarding Matthew with a kind look instead of a punishing stare. Although, the brain argues that he's punishing Matthew in other ways, and quite well. The brain has automatically inserted him into the post-coital-breakfast-with-Kristin-at-home scenario. And then the instructor speaks up.

"Okay, relax. We're not thinking about if what we're doing is right or wrong. We're not measuring ourselves and judging ourselves as good or bad, fat or thin."

And Matthew taunts himself by thinking, *Jesus, everything he's said so far is basically what Kristin would consider foreplay. I mean, add two glasses of wine and a hair compliment and it's the exact same routine that* got me laid three nights a week *for the first year of marriage.*

Matthew wants to ask the guy next to him if he thinks this is crazy, this kind of talk from the instructor, but he thinks twice of asking when reflecting on how the first hello went over. How is it that adulthood becomes like walking into a new school and never wanting to meet a soul, and somehow knowing that this time the feeling wouldn't wear off after the first or second week of classes? When did it become a matter of quietly knowing that isolation wouldn't stop being an attractive option until old age? At that point, while shoving oneself along the very middle or southernmost route across this country in a medium-sized motor home with a large second or third wife and small second or third dog, it will be time to reach out again, simply because the choices have become:

A. Make friends with the other aged couple driving a motor home.

Or:

B. Ponder the very real and very urgent shadow of death that seems to come to mind when there's too much silence.

Matthew continues to sit on his little square of foam real estate, listening to the instructor seduce his wife, looking around the room and doing the stretches that everyone is doing, it feels like copying the answers off the other students. And then it's time for everyone to leave. But Matthew stays after, letting the class file out to have alone time with the instructor. On the outside this seems ambitious or a good start, in the cracked gray interior of the head, however, this has become a marching order to get inside the enemy's mind and find out what makes him tick. The first line of thinking is that meditating hasn't done this poor son of a bitch much good; a pear-shaped body under a fatty face bearing mileage, probably mid-thirties but weathered more like forty-something; brown curly hair fighting gray for space or just running away altogether; maybe five-eight running twenty-five pounds heavy; nails bitten to the quick and still deep, meaty red at the side from the last time he bit too far in.

Matthew advances with a residue of middle-aged self-appraisal rock and roll from the car, a head of rotted hops and yeast and pills, and a heart dragged back to every public school or foster home failure at befriending people his own age.

"Hi. How's it going?" he ventures.

"Namaste."

"I don't even . . . what's that mean?"

"Greetings."

"You're . . . so, you're saying 'greetings' or is that what it means?"

"What?"

"You're saying 'greetings'?"

"Namaste just means greetings. Indian. Namaste." And with this he tilts his fattened middle into a slight bow with his burger-patty hands pressed together.

"Native American."

"You lost me, friend."

"Nobody says 'Indian' now."

"Why are you . . ."

"That's dick, you think, fuck?"

Matthew's profanity goes poorly in the wake of adrenal glands realizing they're fighting for the first time since maybe the fourth grade. There is a small flash of confusion between them, a tension to this exchange, and suddenly Matthew lunges forward, issuing a weird embrace. Both are a bit confused by this, and it's lasting too long and starting to sway, and then without warning, the brain feeds the film-strip's tag end in through the projector and there is the footage of this guy and Kristin. The heart races and stammers, the head starts thinking of loss and losers, and the embrace turns weird with wrestling when Matthew's leg comes up and around the instructor's waist and they fall to the ground, the energy of things accelerating. At first the brain and head think the body is about to have sex, and then they exclaim in chorus with the heart and adrenal glands and spirit: It's a fight! But the body is picking up right where it left off with this sort of experience, fourth or fifth grade, a clumsy and dumb exchange between Matthew and a bully in the house he had to live in; a boy who tried to take one of the few toys Matthew had managed to hang on to after he had to when he had to live in other people's houses and everything started changing so fast.

And now, with the body so many years older and the heart pretty much the same age, what we have here is a slow and awkward wrestling match that seems to be only confusing the two men involved, no clear line between aggression and tentative entanglement. The conjoined middle-aged beast of many hairy arms and legs rolls slowly across the floor and into a tall pile of mats; the mats fall silently without commotion, really, and Matthew thinks for a split second that fighting is not nearly as glamorous as it seems in the movies. He starts punching, if you want to call it that. He starts jibbing and jabbing with the one arm that is only partially trapped under the instructor — who in a still photograph right now would look like someone receiving CPR, or a cradled lover. The arm starts kind of flinging into back fat in a sidearm jab that looks like the type of thing one issues somewhat firmly to one's own chest when coughing, a simple gesture more than anything efficiently violent or defensive. The instructor finds something within him, probably the same fourth- or fifth-grade experience, he drops the namaste bullshit, and rolls his bear-shaped body over so that now he's on top of Matthew instead of half underneath him. This position effectively renders Matthew's punching arm another three or four inches shorter in reach since he's pinned on his back. Matthew's weird little flipper jab continues now at a faster speed since it is no longer connecting softly with back fat, but landing in midair about four inches from the target when fully extended. The instructor grunts something, what would usually be a tough guy line if this were a real fight or a movie, but in this case it is a grunt and heave of some basic kinesiology.

"You're not connecting, you're gonna hyperextend it." The man says this like someone under only minor duress; like, say, a man crammed in behind a boiler in a basement, telling someone how they have to help him hold a wrench so it stays on and tightens the bolt that's nearly impossible to get at.

"Thank you. Sorry about that," Matthew, oddly, grunts back.

"Is . . . is the stress of this . . . worth it?"

"I'll fucking . . . kill you." Matthew tries to flip out from under him.

"Are you drunk?"

"What the fuck, with people asking me that?" Matthew tries to flip out from under him.

"You smell like beer. And vitamins and . . ."

"Okay, fuck, yes." Matthew tries to flip out from under him.

"Say you surrender. Give up."

"What, this is a fucking intervention? You want some of?" Matthew tries to flip out from under him.

"Say you give up this fight, I mean."

Matthew makes a new fight move; he plays dead. He's heard about this trick and how people will use it in a bear attack or when gunmen have stormed a school in America, or a hotel lobby in some faraway country, and one wants to appear already hit so they can be left alone to crawl out later among the actual dead. So Matthew employs it; goes limp; even suspends breathing and when he needs a breath, he figures he'll breathe just barely, not even enough to inflate his chest. And the brain reels at this request, launches a string of logic at the head that says this:

1. Playing dead makes no sense in this situation.
2. How is it even possible that, in this pathetic, soft white, mildly homoerotic gentle wrestling, you would have wound up dead?

The instructor feels Matthew's body go limp, notices no breath, and calls up the same string of logic, but with the zeal of a nine-year-old playing cops and robbers.

"What? You wouldn't be dead from that! You're not dead!"
Matthew lies still saying nothing.

"Don't screw around. You can't be dead from that."
Matthew is still saying nothing.

"How did this even happen? Hey, say something, man."

Matthew, still, saying nothing, and all of a sudden: He opens his eyes wide and fast in a flash, like some bad actor's attempt at delivering a dramatic flourish to the proceedings. He grunt-shouts his reply like this was a secret technique that has succeeded in catching his opponent unaware: "I slowed my breathing and pulse down!"

Matthew rockets over onto his belly into a push-up position and bucks his way almost all the way free from underneath the instructor, landing an actual punch in the process, a punch that connects solidly, with purpose, and it would be like the movies if the punch hadn't landed squarely to the side of the instructor's head. They both yell in pain, Matthew instantly cradling his hand in his crotch and hunching over a bit, his eyes brimming with tears. They square off, these two, face-to-face and totally still in some weird pose that is perfect parts old-fashioned put-up-your-dukes and sumo wrestlers squatting, and bending down to touch one hand of knuckles to the mat while looking up at each other from the tops of their eyes; the anticipatory tension is boyish, dumb, and silent, and neither man moves a muscle. The anticipatory tension of another round peaks in stillness, and then they both exhale in truce, lose their form, and start milling about the room; as if they're cooling down after a sprint or jerking a huge Olympic barbell of weights above their heads. There's an awkward attempt at a sporting handshake that only half-connects in sloppy grips, then a huff or two as they walk little lazy circles trying to catch their breath; trying to grab a little extra oxygen from the empty community center's air.

"You got me on the head pretty good, man. How's your hand?"

"The cartilage hurts."

"I'm pretty sure there's no cartilage in the hand. Not the human hand."

"The tendons, or whatever."

"Was that a Tibetan trick, when you slowed your pulse like that?"

"I don't know any of this shit, I told you that. I don't know namaste, I don't know Tibetan fighting tricks . . ."

"No, it's a Tibetan meditation thing."

"Most of my fighting stuff is just . . . I just make it up right then, basically."

"Well, anyway, help me stack these back up."

They stack the mats together, and Matthew feels the calm and sense of connection that comes with meditation. It's working, though he knows he can't always meditate like this. But for now he enjoys the silence and sense of camaraderie that it came with.

"These things just went flying all ape shit when we rolled

into 'em," the instructor says, and they both start to laugh and then get quiet and calm again. They continue stacking and straightening the mats.

Matthew smiles and thinks to himself: *not too shabby for basically a free class.*

7

The Truth, Knocked Loose

I N THE HALLWAY LEADING out of the community center, one is free to grab a handful of things. To begin with, a schedule of all classes offered. And below the rack of them, there's a cardboard box that has the phrase TAKE ME! written in felt pen on the side of it. Inside of the box is a book called *Shifting Parameters in Nonlinear Models Optimized for Repeated Measurement Data*. Matthew bends slowly down and picks it up. He reads the back cover summary of this thing, then stands wondering why something like this even gets published, why it isn't just spoken between people discreetly in whatever dull beige chamber they're suffering in together. Convinced this sort of thing is part of the problem, he moves it from the Put 'n' Take box into the recycle tub to the left of him. There is also a magazine about hairstyles, a beautician trade magazine of some sort maybe, called *Hype Hair!* He grabs it and after a moment of hesitation, returns it in a gentle drop back down. There is a magazine about yachting, which won't be coming in handy at the moment. There's a small cluster of paperbacks underneath it, though. A shot in the dark, since the yacht rag is covering the stack. Matthew painfully groans one last bend to investigate and takes something yellow and white, medium in size, paperback, and free.

Back in the Bavarian Motor Ward, Matthew reviews the schedule of other classes offered at this ashram of self-improvement. No matter how awkward, soft, and gentle, he cannot afford many more fights, so the choice of what class to investigate next is a weighty one in that regard. Financial planning class is out of the question, this precarious bridge between steady employment and whatever comes next is precarious, and discussing solvency in a classroom environment is fraught with too much potential for tension and discourse and more physical confrontation. Photography seems like torture, to capture these days in pictures flies precisely in the face of whatever comfort denial and beer bring. But crafting! Crafts are the perfect everyone's-a-winner-just-for-trying environment. There can be some more meditating once things finish cooling down, but it won't be this week. And so, crafting it is. On Friday. Two days to kill, but days have been dropping like flies.

The keys go into the ignition and the beeps are issued from the dash, and before music can distract him, before a plan can be laid, it seems the so-called fistfight has knocked something loose — one word, *territorial*. It falls from the brain and right down into the center of the chest where it causes a deep wince of regret. New Time Media was basically in the business of promoting benign pop music, decent cable television programming, and semi-bankrupt magazines that convince people they aren't skinny enough or happy enough. The doors to the place should've been large, thick wooden doors with quotes from Greek myths or early philosophers that might assuage one's guilt for doing this business. The long corridor to Matthew's office was a calcified artery of framed magazine covers and platinum album awards; sixteen million copies of a song about the trials of love sung by a seventeen-year-old girl with fake breasts who has never had a boyfriend; ten million albums sold by a white kid from San Diego who raps like his favorite rappers from the Bronx and South Central. One of the first magazines to convince men that they need to have twenty-eight-inch waists, wax their chests and backs, and buy jeans that cost two weeks' salary of what average Americans make on average. You're welcome, ladies. That's why each morning involved clearing such stiff security, in case every woman in the world decided to come rushing into the building at once with knives and guns to even the score with the people who made men into hairless, skinny little boys who spend more money on clothes than their girlfriends or wives. And on that Friday — the Friday when the doctor told him something was wrong but they weren't sure what, on that Friday when he had to convince a doctor that he hadn't been, unbeknownst to himself, kicked in the nuts a few times, the Friday that has only been referred to as the Incident — Matthew made his way down the artery of trophies and to his office door. There are tests that will come back, there will be scopes and scans and X-rays that will yield clues, but suffice it to say, this is the first day of the rest of his life. At the door to his office, his assistant told him there were no phone calls except one.

"Office Services called and said they had a couple more questions for you about the smell you were complaining about."

"Oh. It's fine now. It kind of took care of itself somehow."

"Are you sure? Because they can just . . ."

"I'm going to take care of it right now. I figured out how. But thanks for the message; thanks for taking it, and no calls or visitors while I take care of this."

"You seem a little . . ."

"You're the one that seems drunk, if you ask me."

" . . . tired."

The door shuts behind him with the little terrier's exit clearing the slam by an inch or so. In Matthew's head, a montage of how he tried to go through the usual channels with a level head. He had gone as far as putting in several calm, passive-aggressive calls to Office Services simply stating that his office seemed to smell like urine for some reason. He never threw any human or dog under the bus, he went about this the way that is supposed to almost guarantee success. When one calls Office Services to tell them that, say, your office is too cold from the air-conditioning, the reply is kind and pleasant, small talk and a course of solution, and the problem is fixed. But when one calls Office Services to say that one's office smells of urine, there is a deafening pause on the other end of the line that seems to suggest you should simply stop pissing in your own office if you aren't fond of the smell. And if you persist, there are only calls back to ask you questions.

Off with his jacket; hung it on the back of the door; unzipped his pants. After the doctor's office, unzipping his pants in an office didn't feel as out of place as it once may have. Matthew was under contract with New Time Media for another five years of employment. More than that though, he was under the implicit social contract that everyone in the world is honor-bound to, the one that implicitly says you won't urinate all over your workplace. He broke that contract by holding himself, aiming himself, staring up at the ceiling to relax himself, and then proceeding to paint a primitive border; a language that the president's dog would understand on its next visit; a circle that started at the closed door and went over to the desk and looped back again, and then sort of mapped the remaining real estate in short intermittent remaining bursts, demi-borders if you will, that claimed the territory to the side of the desk, and then the last of the bladder's reserve dotting and dashing a small square sub-border to mark the area where he would like to be able to set his bag when he comes in. And then one last small stream began that could be spent filling in any dashed borders that didn't seem solid enough. The entire process was wrapping up perfectly, discreetly, effectively, until the office door flew open and his boss poked his head in. This was that most painful of impromptu meetings with a company's president, the sort where one has to quickly stop urinating midstream *and* think of something to say.

"Woops."

"What are you . . ."

"Nothing."

"Clearly, you're doing *something.*"

"Your dog pisses in my office at least once a week."

"That doesn't make it okay for you to do it."

"I'm speaking the only language your dog understands."

"Have you been drinking?"

Matthew considers. "I had a doctor's appointment, yes."

"I think you're done here."

"I am, I know, I just have to . . ." And with this, a nod down at what he's hiding beneath his hands.

"I don't mean done pissing in your office, I mean you're done coming in to the office. You don't need to come in on Monday. You're being fired, that's what's happening here, in case I'm not being clear enough."

"I literally told her no calls, no visitors," says Matthew, looking at his boss shaking his head, hoping for some shift in focus here, but again, no luck.

There was no surprise in the heart or head; he knew that if it ever fell on him, it would be a Friday. But questions rocketed through, Does this mean no severance package? Does this mean no more health insurance? Does this mean not taking long expense-account lunches to drink and see movies? None of the questions had anything to do with a second or third chance. None of the questions had to do with wondering if the job could please stick around or come back, so there's some comfort in that. And if a day like this is going to happen, good that it should happen on a day of the week when everyone in the entire building was being belched out of the revolving doors downstairs, being blown out to a two-day tiny taste of freedom. It would be hard to notice one who has been asked to not come back on the third day. A weekend seemed like the best way to ease into the abyss, if one had to be met with a fate like his, as if every weekend up until this one was rehearsal; the way every night of sleep is rehearsal for one's death; one tiny little termination after another, all of it, really. And here, now, in the car reminiscing as one does, the Steely lyric that comes earthbound from the satellite in space, out of the speakers as a sound, like a tattoo the way it has stuck around, is going around again seductively crooning about how black Friday has got to come eventually and then the lyric accepts this, but simply asks that it not fall on the guy singing. Well, fair enough, but if it fell and missed him, then it certainly nailed somebody.

8
——

The Problem with
Leaving One's Phone On

THE PHONE, THANK GOD, interrupts remembering how all of this happened. The small typing device
nesting between the seat and center console is, one forgets,
first and foremost, a telephone. Matthew regards its ringing
with the cool reserve of any terrified isolationist; on the first
ring he looks down at it, as if there's no chance he would
stop reading about his new craft class and consider answering it; on the second ring his resolve weakens just a bit; on
the third ring he lifts the device out of the dark little fjord
in between the seats where it is wedged in order to at least
investigate what name appears on the screen. He sees TIM.
MOBILE backlit, and he caves in, presses the little green button that will let someone in. He says hello into the little dis-

traction pressed to the side of his head; in the distance the meditation instructor is leaving, rubbing just a bit where the punch struck him above the ear. Matthew puts his free arm out the window and waves while he stays on the call, and the instructor waves, a little hesitant and uncertain, ideally just because of the distance making it difficult for him to recognize Matthew. The instructor ducks into a beat-up Japanese econo-box that limps and sputters to the far exit of the parking lot and Matthew is left with his call from Tim.

Tim, it turns out, is also a little bit down on his luck and embarking on his own personal recession. Which is comforting in the happens-to-the-best-of-us sense, even though Tim Kell is not exactly the best of us. Tim isn't exactly a friend, mostly because he runs in circles about two atmospheres above mid-six-range media cogs like Matthew. The only reason the two of them met is because ten years ago Tim spilled a drink on Matthew at the restaurant downstairs in Black Rock, the building a block north of New Time, and the only place to get a drink during lunch without looking like hard luck ducking into one of those Irish pubs on Fifty-fifth. And when this spill happened, Tim was more than cool about it. Whipped out cash on the spot, eight hundred bucks, and when Matthew looked at him stunned, he added a couple hundred bucks to make it a grand and also added that he was pretty sure Matthew's sweater wasn't 100 percent cashmere. Tim's clients were well fed and gone, but he stuck around, bought himself and Matthew a round, and they sat drinking it.

Tim nailed pay on Wall Street; the kind of thing where bonuses stacked, a couple months earned like a year of whatever anyone else was doing, and the fringe benefits were weighed in grams and girls with names like Destiny, Cheyenne, and Blue. He came from a long line of that type of thing apparently, his dad made a killing, his grandfather made a killing, by the time Tim came of age he was drafted in, automatic bones, a made man. They exchanged cards that day at the restaurant in Black Rock; Matthew considered keeping in touch with someone in finance to be a sort of passive action taken with regard to planning for retirement; but an action taken nonetheless. They killed a bunch of time then stopped hanging out together a year or two before banks and planes and towers and the dollar all crashed. They milled around places like Cipriani and Odeon back then, like two people who had read all the novels about excess a decade and a half too late. Making friends was easy back when friends were made as fast as venture capital and dot-com cash. After that it wasn't about keeping in touch as much as it was about keeping track. Checking in to see who was doing better, and the answer always seemed to be Tim; but now Tim is in some of the same shape Matthew is in, partly because of the recession, and partly, certainly, by way of his own hand.

Deadwood and loose cannons are the first to go when the economy gets slow, but nobody ever tells you that when things are fat; the economy goes south and suddenly taking a leak all over your office is a crime. And in Tim's case, suddenly it's a crime to almost marry a sex worker, start doing tons of her mostly uncut cocaine, stop going to the office, sell short a huge chunk of your fund by doing the churn-and-skim, and hole up in your $12,000-a-month apartment in Tribeca, sucking up the last of the drugs and dodging calls about where the money is going. Actually, come to think of it, at least two of those things are actual crimes. Tim ran out of town, headed to Yellowstone National Park in Ohio or Michigan or Seattle or wherever Yellowstone National Park is.

"I'm not gonna lie; it's kind of ugly, Chief."

"It sounds . . . yeah . . ."

"That shit was pure. Shit that would've killed most men. It probably left a fucking trail of dead tribal elders in the Andes."

"How the hell did Yellowstone become the solution?"

"Oh, I don't know, let's see, maybe we should get you hooked on the shit she had, burn through your cash and then a small fortune that your clients trusted you with, get the SEC on your ass, and shave your head while you're gagged with socks and electrical tape in your own home, in the bed you tried to share with someone you thought you loved, but who turned out to be someone who handcuffed you and padlocked you into a leather hood, then started inviting her dealer friends over to set up shop. Maybe we'll give you some of that and see what solution you come up with, Chief."

"Jesus," Matthew says, now having picked his community center course catalog back up to read the crafting course description.

"Oh, and we'll put you under four or five months of back

rent at twelve grand a pop. Trust me, a plane ticket to Bozeman to slow down and nurse the one credit line you still have starts to seem like a pretty decent way to fucking catch your breath."

"Okay, I didn't, I wasn't, you know . . . I was just talking, just asking."

"Right, okay, well, I was just replying. Anyway, I don't know, listen, I'm kind of running my own program out here, getting my head straight again, and I need somebody to check in with, so keep your phone on."

"Well . . . ," Matthew starts, distracted by noticing that the grid spells out how one could actually take back-to-back crafting and meditation on Fridays at the community center. "You know, I'll leave it on when I can. My schedule's a little crazy." This said from the side of the mouth, while lighting another Native American cigarette.

9

Stop to Go Faster

IT'S A BRAND-NEW DAY again. It's as if Matthew is being taunted with an endless supply of them. Jogging was a bust this morning. The outskirts of the lot were mostly empty early on. But in the time it took to change into jogging clothes, do a little bit of drinking, smoking, and general warming up, the lot had enough metallic predators moving in and out of it to give Matthew pause; this, on a day when he had thought to bring actual shorts along. So, like most middle-aged men who have decided not to jog and remembered their plan to purchase a secondhand gun, Matthew has made his way over to a parking lot called Park and Ride. An amazing invention, it turns out. A parking lot that boasts both the static isolation of a decent-sized small-to-medium lot, and the chance, every hour on the hour, to climb aboard a train and swing into motion and start the day. These lots, he's heard of them — people who are too smart to burn cash driving into Manhattan commute into the city from these lots — but only recently has it hit home what a perfect combination they had been all along.

You may or may not know that there's a guy named Hernan who will meet you on Ludlow Street, between Houston and Stanton, to sell you a gun for a pretty decent price. If you know this, it's because you must know or at least keep in touch with the likes of Tim, as Matthew has. Matthew is still scraped with rash, still aching from the fight in meditation class, still occasionally seeing mostly blood in the urine and experiencing pain in the testicles, but at least one thing is coming together — at least one thing is making him ten feet tall. Matthew thinks for a minute before locking up and leaving to head up to the platform: *It's like God will help you find a secondhand gun, but not until you're grateful and reaching out to friends.* Typed down on the little tiny keys and jammed back down into the athletic socks covering the calves almost to the knees. While money is still in the checking account, a few hundred dollars have been fetched from the machine on the side of the bank in Westport, and the Germanic leisure sedan has been parked here waiting for the train that will rocket into Manhattan so that life's plan can get under way. There's suddenly so much on the horizon of these days; craft class; firearm ownership; Fridays that offer meditation and crafting back-to-back; a book jammed and momentarily lost under the seat, a book that was entirely free and now ready to read. The train is arriving, all aboard! Darting from the car commences, an empty gets kicked out and clinks on the ground before rolling off on its own travels, point the key chain at the car/house/office, press the button, make it chirp back confirmation that home is safe and secure, forget about the empty bottle rolling, there's no time, dart away, and up, and along, and on board!

Once on board, of course, it becomes clear to Matthew that he hasn't bought a ticket. But you can buy one on board, and since the jogging shorts have a little zippered pocket with three hundred dollars in it, this shouldn't be a problem. When the porter comes down the aisle checking tickets and monthly passes, Matthew needs to buy a round-trip.

"Get a round-trip to Grand Central?"

"Twenty-six," and this is said with a raised eyebrow as the conductor sees that Matthew has whipped out a tiny nylon pocket from under the jogging shorts' waistband and just above his penis, unzipping it to reveal a wad of cash barely contained. He pays, and the man sticks to his own business; tucks a bent and hole-punched tab under the seat's leather strap where Matthew is sitting, and then lays out a little matter-of-fact line that makes Matthew want to kiss him: "Bar car, three cars ahead."

Armed with this information, Matthew makes an honorable effort to stay in his seat reading his free book from the community center's Put 'n' Take box. This book, this manifesto that tells one to eat and pray and bone strangers every so often, it's on to something, working into the brain like easy-listening music, it's digging into the body like Lyme, spiraling in through the skin in tiny concentric circles and then setting off little bombs of ideas inside of Matthew. As these ideas hit, Matthew slowly lowers the book into his lap, tilts his head back, closing his eyes for a minute for some reason. A suit-and-tied man about Matthew's age across the aisle looks on in mild disbelief. He keeps looking as Matthew resumes reading the book and nodding as he identifies with words on the page, wearing the large headphones scraped and cracked by pavement, wearing too-short nylon jogging shorts that can't hide scraped and scabbed road-rash legs, wearing a big blue-green bruise that has bloomed on the upper arm where someone had a grip on him in struggle, evidently. Matthew looks up to catch the man staring, realizes that this man is not on a spiritual journey, and is in fact looking and judging. Matthew gets up and heads three cars ahead to the meditation/bar car where spirituality is understood and probably even celebrated.

"Heineken, please."

"I didn't know anyone still drank these things."

Rally to not take this as a slight; strive to reach out to someone and be positive and make small talk. Because, Goddamnit, where did small talk go? When did it disappear? How is it one day you're feeling Steve Timmel's face at a corporate creative retreat, and the next you're longing for someone to say hello to you; to affirm that you're still existing here on this big round dumb hunk of rock and sea?

"I drink them. I'll drink them all." Woops, not nearly as

witty and benign as it seemed in the brain before it was spoken. Especially combined with the scrapes and bruising and
busted-up headphones.

Concerned pause from the barman before issuing the
price, and then: "Four-fifty, sir."

"There's no, kind of, happy hour that happens, right? Like
if I wait till three?"

"If you wait till three, we'll be in the station."

And judging by the self-congratulatory chuckling, apparently the train bartender knows this is the funniest joke anyone has ever made to a passenger who is entering a period of
their life where they can no longer expense things like beer.

"Is there a happy hour on the return trip?"

"Depends when you come back." And now more laughing.

Matthew slips a hand under his waistband into the little
underwear pocket jammed with gun cash. This is maybe
not such a good thing to do when maintaining eye contact
and trying to appear friendly, as there appears to be concern
registering on the barman's face once again. The hand goes
down, crotch bound, roots around deep, comes up with a bill
to hand Bob Hope before he can break into his next bit.

"Out of . . . twenty." And he uses a little napkin to take the
bill!

"It wasn't in my . . . There's a little place to keep it. There's
a pocket."

Matthew walks over to the center of the car, leans up
against the weird little circular table, drinks from the can,
ignoring the looks, reading his free book about praying and

eating, filling himself with ideas of traveling the world on a quest for redemption; the book is filled with beautiful heartfelt ideas that are wonderful for others and terrible for him.

Next stop, Grand Central Station, and from there, go outside and walk west on Forty-second Street over to Sixth Avenue and board the downtown F train. The F stops at West Fourth and, again, one is borne up from the warm underground womb and into the crisp, even cold, late-spring day. Matthew walks eastbound through the weird central part of the Village to cut through Washington Square Park and head diagonally down, eventually to Houston and farther east to Hernan and a gun. The body is underdressed for a day so crisp, so it contracts, it moves along fast with the arms crossed tightly on the chest, shoulders shivering and hunched, pushing forward past the border of Washington Square with a cagey sense of purpose. This, coupled with the wounds of jogging and meditating, evidently mimics a drug addict, because the resident dealers beeline in from a distance, like hungry coyotes sizing up the opportunity; their speed and aim increase when they detect the remnants of the little sideways limp.

"Smoke? Smack? Rock? You doin' okay, baby?"

"Oh . . . yeah, I'm just a little cold so I'm walking like this. I don't do much in the way of heavy drugs. I mean, at parties, some blow maybe. The only reason I look a little under the weather is from taking a jog and then . . ."

"Man, you fuckin' talk too much."

And with that the first coyote is gone; back off to whatever vantage point it advanced from, and the next one comes on.

"He ain't got shit like this, baby. Smack, rock, buds?"

"Nah. I was just telling your friend that . . ."

"Ghost ain't my motherfuckin' friend, bitch." And he peels away like the last one, the next one rushing up alongside, matching pace and stride, seamlessly.

"They ain't got this. You want a taste?"

"I'm good, man. Tough day, that's all."

That one filled the chest and stride with some casual confidence; felt good, felt solid and honest — maybe even enough to make Matthew feel a bit like a sort of Connecticut-tamed badass; no time for drugs, gentlemen, there's the matter of buying a secondhand gun. Matthew actually believes, for a moment, that this is what it must be like to be famous and too busy to talk to everyone approaching. He secretly wishes they would all approach, in a group, all hollering their questions and propositions, jostling as he keeps moving, fighting for position like a pack of paparazzi. One last straggler approaches for a last chance before Matthew is out of the park and on his way.

"I'll take care of you. What you need today?"

"I'm good. I don't need any more of it today."

Matthew doesn't even know if one is supposed to do it more than once a day if one is hooked. He assumes that if you're hooked on something, you must do it a lot more than once a day. The dealer starts laughing for some reason and walks away.

10

—

Girls, Girls, Guns

Hernan has a slightly larger apartment than one might expect for an aging South American and Lower East Side fixture with a few neighborhood hustles left to grind. One would have to imagine the blocks between here and the alphabet streets have surely changed quite a lot since the eighties and nineties heyday. There are tools littering a corner between the tiny living room and kitchen, a couple of buckets of Spackle and paint, tarps folded, tools cluttered up on a belt and spilling from a box. Hernan is probably Matthew's age, or a few years younger with the difference made up by a streetwise life that wears and lines one a little.

"Hey, Matthew, Tim's boy. Come on in," this at the door to his apartment after clearing the buzzer downstairs.

"Doing some remodeling, huh?"

"I'm doing some of that shit, yeah. I'm doing a lot of things, you know what I'm sayin'?"

"Yes. Yeah."

"I'm doing some contracting shit, and I'm doing some of the shit you came here to talk about; these are my blocks. I don't got the jump shot and I don't produce beats or shit like that, so these are gonna be my blocks forever, B."

"Your blocks?"

"My streets."

"I know."

Hernan puts three guns on the table in front of the banged-out sofa. He's excited, kind, and precise in doing this; like a ten-year-old laying out the baseball cards he's hoping to trade today.

"That's fifty-six; two nines and a thirty-eight. I know dudes that roll with that much for rep."

"Oh, okay, so, well, I don't know if . . ."

"I'm kidding, bro!" And here is more of that kind of laughing the bartender on the train was enjoying. Inside of Matthew the brain wonders, again, *What is it lately with people and laughing?*

"I just . . ."

"You should've seen your face, B! Can you imagine some guy walking around with two Tek nines and a thirty-eight? All Grand Theft Auto an' shit?" And, of course, more laughing from Hernan about what Hernan said. When one person is laughing and the other one isn't, it takes an eternity for the laughing to end. The brain gently screws the face up into a frozen and polite smile on Matthew, the eyes pleasant, lonely, confused, and seeming to be standing by for something to latch on to.

"Yeah, no, you got me on that one. I just wouldn't know, really. But, yeah, I think I only need one gun."

"Let me ask you: How much would you like to spend for all intents and purposes for this inquisition?"

"You know, maybe a hundred."

"I'm not sure a sufficing number of currency is . . ."

"That's not really the way those words are . . . just talk normal."

"That ain't enough money; what are you, fucking nine years old?"

"Okay, well, let's see what, um, what I've got in here."

"Whoa, whoa, whoa, what the fuck!"

"Oh! No, I'm . . . There's a pocket in there; like a zipper pocket. For your money and driver's license and stuff, like, while you work out or jog."

And now Hernan is cracking up again. Matthew, by now used to the people having a great time laughing at something he doesn't understand as funny, doesn't even bother with the convention of a polite smile. He just digs down in under the waistband and above the pubic bone, to the left of where the lump of dull pain lives, unzips the pocket, and pulls up a handful of bills; a loose wad and the rest stacked and folded in half, Hernan looking on, none too pleased with what looks like a paperboy's salary. Small wadded bills littering his coffee table. After rummaging through the currency yanked from the crotch pocket, Matthew counts to a final number.

"I actually have to keep some for a cab back up to the train. What can I get for like . . . sixty-nine fifty?"

This just brings a sad silence from Hernan.

"Shit, B. You ain't walking with a nine for that kind of change."

"I'm kind of fucked because I don't have a job anymore. You're the first person I've told that to, oddly enough."

"Well, you better be telling somebody at the front of the line at the state office, because that money under your dick ain't . . ."

"It's a pocket."

"Well, whatever's in it ain't gonna carry you far."

"How much more would I need for that one?" Matthew asks, pointing at the nine millimeter.

"Like three and a half times what you were hiding under your dick."

"Fuck, well . . ."

"If you want, you can run a pack for me tonight and we can work it out."

"No, I can't do remodeling stuff. I'm seriously, like, I can put in a dimmer switch and that's about it. I can take care of any people that need dimmer switches, but you probably don't even . . ."

"I'm talkin' 'bout a pack, B. You roll with one of my backpacks to some people's places and sell them some shit and come back tonight with the cash. People call me; I call your cell and tell you where you're going. This is weekend shit, nothing heavy; 'shrooms, brownies, X, eighths of bud."

"No, I . . ."

"I'm talkin' 'bout mainly dorm room kids and white chicks with offices."

"Women? So, I don't have to stand around in Washington Square or anything, right?"

"I'm not sayin' you're standing around the park in a ski jacket selling fake coke and two-bit green shit."

"It's fake, their cocaine?"

"I'm thinking you're playing dumb-as-shit at this point. This ain't shake, this ain't kitchen sink scrape, this is out-West shit. These people buy from me every weekend. You'll clock maybe a thousand bucks in three calls, and instead of giving you a cut for running, I'm just hooking you up with one of these since you're light."

They both look at the guns, common sense making this all seem less of a risk. Who among us doesn't want to get their life back on track; to get to feeling like one hasn't got less than he had and one has even fortified what is left? The brain reasons that life is supposed to be a journey, and that means you don't turn down selling shit for Hernan to make this gun thing happen. That one was so close to Zen that the hands produce the phone and typing device from the running sock. The typing starts and Hernan is staring.

"I'm just letting my wife know I'll be late."

"Okay, yeah, take care of the home front, B. That shit's important. Nothing without these ladies, butchu know that, I don't need to tell you. Shit . . . Love and God, that's where it at, B. An' you got that little boo all waiting for you."

"I don't really think I . . ."

"Aw, she all at home waitin' for her man to get off the corner. She want some company up in there, B!"

"Right, yes, we'll . . . jam. We'll be . . . jammin' . . ."

Hernan pulls one purple backpack from a small and immaculately inventoried closet where about a dozen others hang from numbered pegs or sit in bins with numbers clipped to them by clothespins. A purple backpack certainly tops off the evening's ensemble of knee-high athletic socks pulled all the way up to where the scrapes and cuts start on the legs, running shorts stuffed with too little cash, and a promotional tee shirt for a weekly news magazine that New Time publishes. To open the pack is to open up a tiny purple canvas sky above an opaque polyurethane field with a tiny horizon; perfect rows of Ziplocked tops of clean, crisp, categorized poly bags with different-colored stickers on them. Matthew lets his fingers amble over them and Hernan gives him directions through the rows of the field; what the colors are; what the prices are; what the contents are; why it's a sign of quality that the mushrooms look blue at certain angles; what to tell people with regard to storing and using whatever they buy; why freezers aren't great for drugs; why the Ecstasy is only half as good if the customer is drinking alcohol instead of sugars and acids like orange juice or lemonade; why Matthew can't take back empty poly bags and how they should be discarded at the customer's apartment if they're going to be discarded. Hernan doesn't tell him that this last bit could mean the difference between being charged with the intent to sell drugs versus the considerably harsher charge of actually selling drugs, because to discuss getting caught and arrested and arraigned is a bit of a buzz-kill to someone finally getting started selling weekend drugs to pretty girls in order to buy a gun. Lastly, Hernan mentions that Matthew should be polite, should be talkative and jocu-lar and keep things light; that it's important not to act like a drug dealer. And also, one shouldn't stay too long. Matthew stifles a yawn; he has reached for the backpack twice during this little seminar, but Hernan had pulled it away from him both times. Most of the details and instructions from Her-nan run through the brain like names in a meeting one can't wait to get out of, or directions to a store past a barn near the filling station past the pond and around the other side of a country diner; all of it gone the second the head's gray has parsed it with precision. Finally, the pack isn't pulled back when Matthew gives it a willing grab.

11

Ecstasy in Apartment 4-B/C

MATTHEW RINGS THE BUZZER and a female voice without timbre grins through in a thin ribbon of static and says hello and tells him to come in; clicks and buzzes the door open. Matthew leans his shoulder into it when opening it because the brain recalls enough about movies and television to know that the door should be gently shoulder-checked in situations like this; weary and urbane and too tired for congenial conversation, that is how the brain informs the posture here. Up the first flight of stairs with a bit of pain and limp jump; and the head reels up one thousand excuses that would get one out of carrying on. The best of the excuses is probably that you have no idea what the hell you're doing; this is followed in close second and third by excuses such as this is probably a felony, and even if there are no jobs in America at the moment, should one at least be applying at other media conglomerates and corporations in the hope that a job would, sooner or later, surface? But the brain recalls sessions with Milton, how he says that we have to move forward even when we're baffled; that by taking physical steps and keeping moving we would intuitively handle what only hours or minutes ago baffled us. So the steps continue, upward, onward to whatever situation awaits, to whatever situation will be intuitively handled. Therapy has helped, although this is maybe not what it was intended for, but who among us is to say, really? This could be exactly what therapy is for.

At the door, Matthew catches his breath before knocking, pulls his jogging shorts straight a bit, tries to affect whatever face a middle-aged upper-management sort from Connecticut turned friendly low-stakes drug dealer should affect; his face doesn't change a bit. Convinced he's perfectly adjusted and presented, he reaches up and knocks. The door is opened and there stands a female customer. Maybe twenty-eight, maybe thirty-eight, maybe immortal, a face completely unacquainted with disappointment, seemingly unaware of the scale of the world and how quickly one can be lifted up gently in halcyon days higher and higher, only to realize the lift was coming from a rogue wave forming and cradling whatever it would, before pummeling one into hard, wet sand after being held aloft like this. *Jesus, lighten up, you're selling drugs that are supposed to make people happy, so don't bring everybody down.*

She stands there with a slight smile. A pause of about two seconds feels like ten minutes; legs that don't call it quits until the neck below the Irish lips; a narrow, fresh, and fair-skinned face that's never been long; cheekbones never fallen disillusioned; black gunpowder brows above eyes blue as sky. She's one long, tall fuse of cordite to gelignite; the last one thousand sweet dreams left on earth, framed by long, straight black hair and bordered below by medium-small breasts defying gravity and time's cruel pull. South of that are hips equally able to create life as destroy yours, and all of her covered by the clothes that have seen a solid tailor the rest of us can't pay, but clothes that nonetheless somehow paint the portrait of an expatriate hippy poetess living in Paris. And the heart instantly deals up the usual corrupt input, telling the head that this is a perfect job; that selling drugs for Hernan is the job people should be looking for if they're laid off. It goes a bit further to suggest that Matthew has wasted years in the confines of straight and narrow America.

"Oh, I was actually waiting for . . ."

"Right, no, it's me. I'm Matthew. I'm, you know." And with this Matthew slings the pack around the front of him in explanation.

"Ah! I thought you were this guy that just moved in upstairs. Come on in. Tatiana."

"Matthew."

"Yes, you . . ."

"Oh, right, okay."

Inside, the apartment sprawls clear from the front of the building to the back, littered with the artifacts of a rich quasi bohemian—high-end audio and video equipment stares across the big main room at a huge teak table littered with stacks of Beat paperbacks and half-smoked packs of Canadian cigarettes, the giant kitchen looks like it was carved out of the workings of an old mill or sweatshop; the wood beams reach a peak at the ceiling—an A-frame ceiling in Manhattan, a top-floor rarity. Names and phone numbers written on a beam that intersects with the thick wooden counter by a phone on the wall; some dug in deep with ballpoint pen, others glided on in felt-tip or thumbtacked up with business cards and corners of notebook paper; a big steel refrigerator with a glass door boasts of nothing rotting and forgotten past expiration. Tatiana surrenders to a big couch, legs spidering out, and arms pulling a chair over for Matthew to sit in. Matthew sits down to open the purple canvas pack and do the business of selling. Somehow here and now, selling hallucinogens to a rich girl feels as innocent as fairy tales.

"I think I'll get two things of mushrooms and one of the brownies from you."

"Okay, so that's two blue and a yellow, I think." And the field of poly bags is flicked through and harvested for two and one.

"Oh, goodie, there's nuts in the brownies again." A smile, all teeth and eyes, girlish still somehow and free of regret. "The last time there wasn't and I told Hernan that he should put them back in."

Some sack or gland on the brain or spine spasms and squeezes out a drip of some potion that weakens Matthew's arms and knees with the palsy of schoolboy crush and optimism. Goddamn, how could the news be so riddled with so many dire stories when there clearly are no sad times left in this country?

Goods are placed on the table; money is dug from a handbag made to look like the unkempt accessory of the marginalized, but surely still carrying this season's staggering price tag on Fifth and Fifty-second. Tatiana says to double the order, Matthew rakes the translucent field again, brings to market a second harvest of blue and yellow, cash is handed over, Matthew is green and minor-league to count it.

"Oh, I see, you don't trust me."

"Oh, no, I'm not, I think I'm just supposed to . . . this is kind of my first time, so I thought . . ." And this is cut short by looking up to see her smiling at him and quietly somehow getting a kick out of this. Inside his head, a foreboding suburban Greek chorus, hollering warning that the girl is probably already high on something dangerous and just moments away from stabbing and hacking her visitor to death.

"Will you have some tea with me? I've been in town three days and it's all been meetings, and tomorrow I'm back to L.A. to work for five weeks."

"I'm not supposed to stay with . . ." But she's already up and off the couch and into the kitchen with the energy Matthew must've had at some point around age eight, the year before he realized the world's spin was really a slow drill boring into him. He is left to roam the living room for a few minutes.

The brain tries again, tells him to run, that he's slid into being felonious, that he's a terrible manager, that he made nothing of the opportunities a good solid job had presented him, that this is what his parents always saw in him. The heart counters the head, says to mill about politely and be aimless and pleasant, to look at the coffee-table books of Helmut Newton and Humphrey Spender and a book of rock photography from some gift shop in some museum. Flipping simultaneously and nervously between the three of them tricks the eyes; Newton's Amazonian blonde women seem to lounge and lord over horizons of infinity pools and glass houses in Hollywood Hills that somehow look out over a skyline of Spender's bleak, broken, sadly beautiful, burned-out East End of London, where Radiohead and Keith Richards labor in small studio control rooms or perform on giant stages.

An acoustic guitar leans against a chair and goads Matthew into making the mistake of picking it up, which is to make the mistake of being a middle-aged man quietly producing half-assed discordant hum and buzz on the instrument while the hand's indecisive fingers tentatively try to peck out a few dumbed-down measures of the intros to old standards like "House of the Rising Sun" or "Stairway to Heaven." The head hears these attempts and immediately issues common sense; demands that the arms thrust the guitar away from the abdomen, quickly and quietly back down to where it leaned before being picked up. This is done with perfect timing during the two and a half seconds before Tatiana is back with cups on saucers and a little cup of sliced lemon.

"How do you take your tea?"

"Oh, I just, you know, drink it. Straight. No, you know . . . spice syrup or . . . cream, or whatever."

Tatiana regards Matthew's answer and demeanor and smiles again, looking at him from over her cup as she sips, and the head is certain she's making sport of him and that none of this is heartfelt fascination or simple hospitality in action. Matthew picks up his cup and raises a dumb little half-toast gesture and takes a sip.

"So, home is New York?"

"Home is New York about half of the time. Work is kind of everywhere, so I have a place in Los Angeles, and a little place in Paris, too. What about you?"

"New York. Connecticut, really. The . . . tristate, you know, area. This general region."

"You're funny."

"I'm not, really. I just kind of, you know, when you set the bar for a small-time drug dealer then, yes, I seem funny. I'm funny for a dope peddler in jogging shorts."

"Well, that's perfect, because I'm charming for a stable capitalist feeling dangerous for buying lightweight drugs."

"I had a job. I'm actually normal, just so you know."

"That is . . . that's great. I mean, I don't know if I'd intro-duce myself that way in every situation, but, good, good to know."

"Right, no, I just meant . . ."

"I'm kidding. Okay, so . . . you had a job. Let me guess. I'm actually super good at this. Okay, you were . . . the tall, semi-handsome works-in-advertising guy, and one day the client was trying to describe the look of the guy they wanted for something, then the client said, 'He should look more like, well, actually, I mean, like you,' and they used you for something, a catalog job, J.Crew-type of thing. So, thirty-five maybe, a little run-down, a little manned up, you quit the ad agency. You kept doing the modeling, but that's not what you called it, you just called it working on a former client's thing. You had three seasons at it, knew you couldn't bounce to a real modeling gig, but you didn't want to go back to the agency, so you bit when they offered you a job on the cli-ent side, casting the catalog, producing the shoots. You did it for a while, got lucky with women in the same boat, women that were that weird sort of mildly mental pretty, like pretty but they almost look like they have a touch of some kind of syndrome. You thought that was fast living, you got sloppy, went all amateur hour on everybody, snorted a house, a small house, a weekend place upstate. You started missing days, then they cut you loose when the numbers started getting thin."

"Wow. First of all, there were so many unintentional compliments in there that I just want to say thank you for the compliments. Close, very close. I basically sold ad space, and I was dismissed for urinating all over my own work area."

This is apparently something that requires Tatiana to laugh so hard that the girl starts to gag, spits tea into her cupped hands, starts choking, then resumes laughing. Which makes Matthew start laughing, mostly just at what a mess Tatiana has made of laughing at him. It's all very fun, disgusting, humane; an oddly sort of erotic combination of tears, snot, smiling teeth, eyes, joy, spit, and hair. Composure is regained and there's a sporting sense of stepping up to the plate from Tatiana's end: "Pleased to meet you, I am something called a super agent. Which means I am young enough to have managed three young men who have portrayed sexy vampires in a movie. And I'm old enough to have had two of them poached from me by a competitor by the time the sequel came out. I've got one left now, and I think he's going to jump ship before I can get paper on him for part three. So, ask me that question about where home is in about a year and you might be getting a way less-glamorous answer."

"How come your deal still sounds sexier than my thing, though?"

"Well, you had the part where you're fired for peeing on your own stuff."

"Right, well, you almost peed on your own stuff just now. There was snot on your hand, I bet."

More laughing and then silence comes on for a few minutes, the kind that comes after heads and stomachs have jerked and heaved too hard in the heat of humor that nobody was expecting from each other.

"Are you scared?" she asks.

"Why? Are you?"

"No, I'm not scared; I'm a super agent, remember? Yes. I am scared. I think you're the first person I've admitted it to."

"Sometimes I feel like if everyone is scared, there's nothing to be afraid of. Like if we're all losing everything, somehow it's even."

"But, you're scared too, right?"

"I don't know," Matthew says with his cards pretty close to his chest.

"Just tell me."

"No. I'm not scared. It's all just stuff. You can replace stuff."

"You're not scared? At all?"

"I don't, I mean, I don't think so."

"It's not a big deal. I would think a man is lying if he said he wasn't scared when times get weird like this and everything feels like it's disappearing."

"I don't know."

"You can . . . I mean, seriously . . . it's okay, you can admit it to me. I mean, you don't even know me, I'm just some woman you met once. You can say you're afraid. A man can be afraid. It doesn't mean you're weak or something. Women like it, we like to know you're human." Tatiana smiles warmly.

"I mean . . . yeah, I guess I am scared."

"Pussy."

And with this comes mutual explosion, snot and tears, spasms, laugh-and-jerk for two. And after the heads are done jerking about and laughing, the silence comes hard, gigantic this time, a roar of comfortable quiet that lulls. Shadows have gone as long as they're going to except a few where dim orange light falls on furniture while twilight dies for night, in ten minutes that could've been a lifetime.

"Here, you should have a bite of lemon, it kind of makes the tea happen."

Matthew takes a moment to absorb this, the idea that tea could happen, and why is Tatiana saying how to make it happen, and what does this have to do with a lemon? There are all kinds of questions to ponder and wonder and all kinds of half-assed answers to deduce, but right now maybe the most important thing on the list is to figure out where someone buys an apartment that vibrates so gently like this. And where does one find a lamp like that; one that breathes, barely noticeable, the little inhales and exhales of a baby sleeping or a big peaceful python in some sort of hibernation? How is it that the rich can build with wooden beams that have tiny patterns of atomic activity buzzing about on them so transparently; a living pattern that looks like ten thousand tiny drops of oil blooming in little water puddles on a slide of acetate that is being projected onto them? These are all good questions. The head quickly whips around 180 degrees and looks for the high-tech gadget responsible for this. Nothing. No light beaming from the walls that could be projecting this. The hands, completely independent of the brain finally, make a lazy journey up the mouth to feel the lips; they're amazing to feel, full and alive, and the hands are vexed as to why they've never made the small trip up to the face to find this organ in Matthew's forty-five born years; this godly and obscene pout and gape is amazing to the touch! Matthew leans back a bit, continues feeling his own face, and through one of the loft apartment's tall windows, sees an airplane high above the city coming or going from JFK or LaGuardia. This brings another revelation, and this one he shares aloud.

"Airplanes are rooms full of people. But in the sky."

He immediately notes that some revelations are far less earth-shattering when spoken aloud instead of left in the head. But Tatiana looks over after another sip and seems to deeply understand Matthew's very brief thesis on commercial aviation. She also seems to understand what Matthew was thinking earlier about his lips and the way the lamp is breathing. Tatiana seems to follow all of it, and mostly telepathically, which is very convenient and makes for a great and silent conversation. She's no longer looking on in odd fascination of Matthew — finally, Jesus, it's almost unbearable when she is. Now she looks at him calmly and kindly as if to say, *I'm so glad someone has finally noticed how our mouths are at once innocent and obscene, and has also noticed the sentient breathing materials I was able to renovate this apartment with.* She pats the couch next to her. Matthew thinks that she must simply be feeling it, because around here everything is wonderful to feel, it really is, in a top-notch apartment like this one can't get enough of the textures against their skin. Matthew replies by patting and feeling the chair he's sitting in, a gesture meant to concur that everything here feels fabulous.

"The chair is as nice as the couch," he says, continuing patting it.

"No, I mean, come sit."

"Oh. I know. Okay."

The brain has no say in this. The body is up and out of the chair, Tatiana is up and back to the kitchen, so maybe it was a cruel joke anyway: Come sit on the couch next to me and when you try to, I will leave and my lamps will inhale you and you'll finally disappear. But she's back in a fast minute with two little bottles of cold, clear, amazingly flavorful, very sensual water. And sip after tiny sip, side by side on the couch, staring straight ahead at the giant rock fireplace that is held together with a fine blue lace of electrical current arcing in tiny storms of acetylene light over the little canyons of mortar between the rocks while a fire crackles inside and burns away any late-spring chill Manhattan has dished up. The mouth can't believe it has never really noticed water. The brain is gone finally and all hands are free to do as they wish apparently, because one of hers has moved over onto one of his.

Music falls like a cocktail of thick, warm honey and Novocain from speakers hidden somewhere in the big wooden beams above them — or maybe the living, breathing beams are actually making the music, it's hard to tell—and it is music that offers no cautionary lyric, no E Minor Seventh Story of Losing. Forget those songs forever while there's still some room in the heart. Her head has moved over near his, all bodies now free to do as they wish, the best situation ever, all brains laid off, made redundant, sacked, canned, cut, and given their gray envelopes from Human Resources. She takes a sip, her mouth now hovering right at his, almost not separated from his, she rests three fingers on his lower front teeth, pulls down so the mouth opens, she spits into it, ignition Matthew has never imagined, instant smash and writhe, and the eighth or sixteenth inch between the mouths disappears in an instant. Lips mash like one more last chance nobody thought of getting, teeth hit like an adolescent bike accident, here it comes all at once like you never thought it ever might again, the rush, shock, luck, and curse of it.

To the heart and head this makes such perfect sense; after all, Matthew's hand had just moments ago been feeling his own lips for three or four consecutive minutes, so there's really nothing strange about the other lips wanting to come over and press and push against the only other set in the room like this. Her kiss tastes like cool, clean water and eventually warms the longer it lasts, she stops to take another sip, stares down, holds it, shoves her mouth back to his for the warm and cool crash, and pushes half her bite down into stubble and chin; feeds him feeling as fast as he can swallow it. She pours water from the bottle into his mouth, rolls off of him and pulls him on top; opens her mouth, says one word, "Spit," and everything is the fast, wet hard mash again. In bad pop songs and movies, kisses are never said to taste of water. In song, people only sing of them tasting like stupid wine or something, so now one suddenly worries and wonders about this languid and leggy bicoastal alchemist, but that's the brain racing back to work again. The brain is reminded that it has been dismissed; it should not be desperate and come around trying to get its job back.

The bodies have pushed for new position, have gone horizontal in their expansion across the land of the couch, hers on top of his, her straight black hair falls on him like the end of these days; the hands discovering everything now; face, tits — real, too, not the sacks of shredded tires or whatever Los Angeles sticks in chests, and behind them and below that, the waist, small of the back, ass. Clothing — from this new station, suddenly simpleton artifice stitched from shame and fear — is gone in a flash, and life has never made so much sense. Every single stupid, aimless day might have been leading to this; two grinding and even laughing sometimes, and then silent, and then accelerating against each other; the blood screams sex and the heart laughs at the blood, the heart having already left the body more than once during this to hover above the city, and edges of continents and oceans and earth and love and death. God, why have the hands never realized that skin, like furniture, can be felt and regarded for hours like this?

There must be a different name for sex somewhere here on the planet, but whatever name one decides on, it is happening right here and right now and all that matters forever is that the beautiful woman who answered the door is no longer someone on the other side of that chasm that separates all of us for most of our days. Her body is no longer admired by proxy; it is on Matthew, it is all over him, it is wrapped around and taking him in. Her body, at once innocent and full of broken rules, virginal and experienced, quiet as an idea and wet, noisy, nasty as sin; at fevered peak until both bodies wilt into each other and lie in a silence so peaceful it doesn't come around again until the August of life comes in slowly and finally, ready to take us all back into the ether we came from. After the peaking and wilting, neither body has the brain to ruin it, so Matthew lies there smoking the cigarettes bearing the icon of American Indians, deathly quiet until the two of them are talking, then laughing about something, then it starts all over again at a different pace, in yet another position, both bodies wired to get as much of this as possible before it ends, because who knows when it will come again. The clock is somewhere around here, vibrating gently or breathing calmly like the ceiling and the lamps; inhaling at six, exhaling at ten, at eleven, at midnight or one, and then the brain starts to wake again and starts to realize that there are only so many hours left in the night; only so many left in this life.

At the end of it, Tatiana is back into long, leggy pants, Matthew's long legs outstretched and hardly covered at all by the weird little running shorts. The afterglow exchanges are not nearly as stiff as daylight convention would have them.

But the brain has indeed been hired back after its layoff. It races to say that too much time has passed; it eventually demands that the arms straighten the running shorts and tie the jogging shoes' laces then quickly gather the backpack, making sure the hands have very discreetly accounted for the cash while Tatiana is out of the room for a minute. And when she comes back, still silent after everything they've had, she speaks only to make one rather sobering transaction.

"Here, I'm going to give you more money, because you can't go back to Hernan's with one sale for six hours."

"Oh, um, okay well, let me give you more . . . of these . . . then."

Matthew takes more blue- and yellow-stickered little baggies from the pack and hands them to her. She hands them back sweetly and says Matthew can have them; that he can take them with him. So Matthew bends down and tucks them into the running sock that hasn't got a small telephone in it. And she's back to looking at him with a smile again — with the detached and bemused observation from earlier in the evening — as if she's never seen a man between jobs who is finally getting back into jogging. The brain insists that none of this is good. She kisses Matthew good-bye, smiling the whole time. The brain is back full steam to ruin a kiss, saying that only bad things can come of this. Her hand finds his and delivers a little bunch of lucre thicker than the last. The brain announces inside the head that this isn't the way one is supposed to work as a grown man between jobs;

the head agrees with the brain, but estimates the cash to be at least five hundred and argues that maybe this is exactly how one should be working. Down the stairs, head and brain half hoping that they never land at a front door out of this building, and then downstairs the shoulder pushes into it, and outside on the streets a New York night is in full swing, probably the way it always is in those stacks of Beat paperbacks she has.

12

—

Honing One's Craft

THE MORNING ROUTINE went along on time and on cue; a precision production that hit all the marks from bed to the front door, to the car to the minimarket, to the expressway to the exit out of sight, to the side roads that double back, to a grocery store, and here again. The leased sliver of Bavaria has come to rest in the medium and fairly decent parking lot of the community center. Coming home last night went fine. Matthew made it in, Kristin was still out, and sleep came fast. And only then was the place alive with Kristin and what she thought of him. High-beam headlights hitting the bedroom window, the front door shoved open then accidentally closed loudly instead of discreetly, and laughter while this was happening. Then glassware rattling from the cupboard, ice hitting the glasses, two drinks

111

poured, company was over. And even in sleep the brain and heart were heavy after deducing that the guest was a man. There might have been some sort of miscommunication earlier that day; Matthew may have accidentally tried to cover his night in the city by saying he was on business to Chicago or Miami — it was hard to tell what story the malted hop fuel and jazz Tylenol 3 might have come up with to account for the time it takes to sell drugs, have sex, and buy a handgun. At any rate, God intervened with tea and leggy out-of-league sex in Apartment 4-B/C and that has left a warm, smooth salve on the heart; a salve that takes the sting out of what one ear heard during sleep.

And now, today will start swimmingly. A night like last night means the heart is free to beam even in the midst of an endless and rudderless journey on rising seas of anxiety and receding tides of currency. There is the faint memory of depositing another stream of red at the toilet before bed and that memory must be tamped down with something now and, eventually, dealt with. The way the doctor left it was that Karl Rove's book is really pretty darn good and that Matthew would need to deliver himself to Alpha Imaging on Thirty-third Street in Manhattan for a CT scan that will spell out the truth. The brain knows the truth, that this life is coming to an end faster than the body imagined, that this is why certain gifts like guns and girls and meditation-fighting have been bestowed on it. But this is not the day to think about it, because shortly Matthew will attend the first craft class and pay what he wishes.

So for now, the satellite radio pulls down whatever steely sentiment is playing up in outer space, and Matthew drinks the tea he bought at the gas station minimarket this morning in lieu of the usual coffee. But for some reason the tea isn't doing it like Tatiana's tea did it. The minimarket tea refuses to happen. There was even a side trip made to Stan Leland's to enter the massive land of mechanical Negro dancing milk, if that's the acceptable way to say it, to purchase a single lemon. This drew a few looks from the woman at the cash register, and then a few more when Matthew asked her for some sort of complimentary plastic knife; maybe from the deli section of prepared meals, certainly something like this existed. Anyway, now with the tea not happening, Matthew is trying to cut slices of the lemon with the individually wrapped plastic spoon he was given by the disdainful checkout woman. A hole has been crudely gouged into the spot he was able to peel and now pulp bleeds out of it and all over and even into the tea a little bit. But nothing is changing with the tea's act, so the brain reasons that either a: Tatiana actually does live in a loft made of beams that are alive and it is furnished with lamps that breathe and have feelings and that the tea had nothing to do with it, or b: Perhaps she added something more than simple lemon to the tea.

There are a couple of beers still rolling around on the back floorboards after their migrating south when the car accelerated to the park-and-ride lot yesterday. So Matthew opens one and adds some to his tea. The taste is terrible and the effect is nothing. So he crushes up an old Vicodin and stirs that in. Somewhere in a sock or in his bed or in the Bavarian Motor Works here, or almost anywhere, are the blue and yellow parting gifts purchased by Tatiana, and the head deduces that these would be the active ingredients that made Tatiana's apartment into essentially a large land mammal. The heart is not pleased with all of this figuring and begs the head to leave last night filed away in the gray as a much-needed mysterious and magical respite that doesn't need to be explained and duplicated; and the heart wins in this. Mr. Fagen's Steely lyrics beam in from light-years above the parked black beast and seem newly relevant and much less cautionary. Lines that stroll along with an arguable optimism, talking about drugs that are kitchen clean instead of laced and junked up with stuff like kerosene. And A-frames! And lines about going to L.A. alone on a dare! It's as if this guy could see everything last night from way up there on the radio satellite.

These words are certainly about her and last night, the heart posits. The head argues that almost any aged pop lyric seems highly relevant when one is sitting in a car wrestling the cruel and delusional haze that comes the morning after an inexplicably lucky bout of sex and psychotropic leisure time spent with a beautiful woman, and without a job, and with a handgun under the front seat. The hands lift the non-happening tea to the lips and the mouth is left wondering why it was awakened to drink hot beer with bitter pills mashed into it. The ears have no sympathy for either lips or mouth, as they and the brain are once again left to listen to, scour, and file lyrics and try to assemble them as maps, legends, and topography of a downward spiral. But none of this legendary topogammawhatever downer shit matters much, to be blunt, because a real buzz is coming on fast, and it is courtesy of a stiff little substance called Craft Class.

Someone has already shown up to unlock the place and prepare for it. The whole lot was empty except for Matthew's car, and now this person has parked one space away. She's aiming her eyes right for the Bavarian land yacht, looking on and peering in past what she doesn't know is dried spit from fits ago, apparently possibly mistaking Matthew for someone else. Jumped up on the junky tea, a freshly lit cigarette, and the optimism still left in him from last night, the brain sends word down the left arm to depress the button that will roll down the window so that the mouth can smile and roll into some small talk and convince the craft woman that Matthew is normal. Signal goes down the arm and into hand then down through the button, the car's electronic brain just some manifest of the synapses and cells and switches inside us. The window hums and glides down into the door panel and Steely Dan floats out into the morning air in loud, fair warning to the craft woman. Upon the spat-up window's reveal of Matthew, he raises up a little toast gesture with his plain white paper cup, smoke from a Native American cigarette swirls out the window to complete the portrait, he exhales the initial drag, and the mouth screws into a weird, soft, suburban nice-guy grin that stands in stark contrast to the glassy eyes above it.

"Good morning." And the simple gesture of declaring this makes Matthew start coughing in a fit, and he raises his eyebrows in bashful acknowledgment of this.

"Oh, I thought you were someone else."

"Someone else, yep, I know, it's like I'm someone else. Like we're not . . . like everyone thinks they're the person they thought was . . . oh, what am I saying anyway, right? Okaaay." Fucking Christ on a stolen bike, the worst part about drugs — even the relatively harmless ones that come in tea and brownies — is the way they leave one in a state like this; a piece of biological litter along a shortcut road that is supposed to parallel the highway to awareness or spirituality; bloodshot and babbling for days afterward, with no clue if it will go away or keep you locked like this, like a happy San Francisco hobo acid casualty. It is not a small price paid.

"I mean, you know, I just mean that I thought you had, yeah, obviously maybe mistaken me for someone you knew."

A rare moment of lucidity — thanks to the junked tea — seems to have put both Matthew and the craft teacher at ease.

"Well, anyway, I've got a class to run, so I should . . ."

"Right, well, see you in there."

"No, it's . . ."

"Basic Creative Crafting."

"Right."

"Yeah, I'm taking that." This while holding another drag of the spirited cigarette a little too long; like it's pot or something.

This seems to elicit nothing but expressionless silence. What the hell is it lately with people not being able to figure out the most basic shit in conversation? Matthew presses on, takes the last hit of his cigarette, and pours some of the pilled-up tea on it to make sure it's extinguished before tossing the butt over his shoulder and onto the floorboard behind him. The tea, while not happening, is certainly working at the edge of everything.

"And on Fridays, I'm doing back-to-back Meditation and Crafts."

"Okay, well," she says, and just pauses trying to figure a way out of this conversation she only accidentally started.

"That's cool, I wouldn't know what to say either. Shit's weird with me right now, I get it."

Oh, good, a smile. Matthew presses on a bit, the blood semi-fortified and jacked up with this half-assed tea that jigs and jags him.

"I am going to craft so hard it blows your fucking mind," but the mouth says this only quietly as the woman is already walking away.

Matthew lights another smoke, slams the tea circumstance and squints, tries to kill the taste with a drag, and drums on the steering wheel to the pout and grind coming from the speakers, as he stares out the windshield up toward the community center. Pre-crafting has officially commenced. Once in the zone, Matthew leaves the car the same way a snake leaves a den in chilled suspended animation upon realizing that spring is here to warm its skin; slowly at first, a little bit sleepy and stiff, and then with gradual fluid movement at a decent pace.

Inside, one finds a completely different set of people than the type taking meditation class. Here are maybe eight or ten women, twenty and thirty years older than Matthew, and they all seem to know one another. These women have had kids; not had kids; outlived kids; had husbands come back from war; had husbands not come back from war; watched what was left of Kennedy, a hole in his head, laying it one last peaceful time on Jackie's lap while getting whisked away in that motorcade in Texas then back to the place we must've all come from; they've envied Diana's wedding, pitied her funeral; had hysterectomies, mastectomies; survived economies; had jobs; had careers, you name it. These women have kicked ass and they've done it without Cadillac SUVs and collagen. They're kind to Matthew and perfectly pleasant, crafting people are decent people, turns out. The meditation snobs were small clusters of impenetrable cliques containing three to five insufferable narcissists each. And meditation brought in the worst kind of narcissists; the kind who were convinced they were enlightened or on the verge of it. But crafters are a sturdy, good-natured bunch. Walk in as an unfamiliar face and within a few minutes of milling around getting a Styrofoam cup of coffee one gets three "Hi, hons," and a "It's nice to see a man who appreciates this type of art," as well as one "You're gonna love this group. We're not a bunch of old duffs sitting around pissing and moaning. We keep it pretty funky in here. It's a neat bunch in here." There is a whirlwind of hellos and welcomes. A cloud of names drift by fast with the introductions that have been extended: Ruthie, Jan, Suzanne, Lori, Lynn, and two more of them that disappear from the brain almost the instant they hit.

"Okay, so are you married or gay? What's the catch?" This comes from one of the sort of saltier members of the group; Jan, maybe.

"Oh, stop, listen to you! You're terrible! Don't listen to her, Matthew. She's a sad state of affairs; you're looking at the effects of paint thinner in a non-ventilated workspace," says a Bonnie or Lori as the laughs rise again.

"Hey, if you had my last twenty years, you'd work with thinner and enamels in a non-ventilated space, too." And they're off to laughing again.

And now Matthew is, too, even speaking up to answer what was probably a rhetorical question. "The answer is that I'm not gay, I'm basically not married, and I don't have kids. The catch is that I've become highly unemployable recently and I don't seem to care, and cocktail hour starts at noon, in my car, alone. Also, I am not licensed to carry my second-hand firearm."

This gets a gigantic swell of laughter from the group and a Bonnie or Anne chimes in, "Wait a minute: Was I married to you briefly in 1967?" With this, the group is in *whoops* and titters again.

Jesus, Basic Crafting is awesome. The heart scolds the blood for spending pre-crafting time in such isolation; should've brought the smokes and junk tea in here to get things rolling in the system. The instructor — the younger woman that Matthew met briefly out in the parking lot — is numb to this bunch and busy putting boxes of supplies on two eight-foot folding tables that are in the middle of the room. She must be getting something out of this, but it's not really clear what it is. Matthew surmises that she must own a small ceramics shop in town or something and she's running the class as a way of gathering up some cheap advertising and grabbing a few craft fiends who will need to come in for supplies or something. She issues the score about how things are rolling in class today; that if one has a project in progress from the last class, one is free to work on it, or to prep anything they want from the boxes on the second table apart from a lesson or instruction. Which is all basically a way of saying, take some of the ceramic shit out of one of these boxes, do something to it with paint, leave it here in class, then pick it up after the instructor has fired it at night or over the weekend or whenever the semi-polite, distant woman from the parking lot has time to cook shit in the kiln for you.

So Matthew takes a step up to the second table, takes a look in these boxes the way men his age approach tables of appetizers at dinner parties, looking in like, *Oh, hey, hmm, what's this stuff here? Okay, well, maybe I'll try one,* when really you know they can't wait to dig in. It's all rather random plaster stuff. A couple of coffee mugs, a small deer and bear, a log cabin, a seascape with a pelican on a pier, all white, chalky, unfinished. Matthew grabs one of the coffee mugs and investigates the paints and charcoal pencils in the other boxes. All the ladies have projects already going from prior classes; real pros, but Matthew is finally someplace on the planet where he is undaunted.

He finds a place at one of the desks and starts to work. There is some attempt at making a little something appear on the mug; an illustration of some kind that is so far looking like a defeated stick figure, and the brain panics for a second that crafting may be too revealing; like doing group therapy or something. So far, within minutes, a bowed, broken, and disheveled stick figure, clearly male, is starting to manifest on the chalky white mug in black painted lines. What else is going to pop up on the dumb thing, a woman with a man in a bed laughing at the hunched little stick man? A boss pointing at the stick man while it urinates in an office? But therapy has been on hold for a bit now, the same way the trip to Alpha Imaging has been on hold, the same way everything has been on hold in this time of financial uncertainty, so maybe pay-what-you-wish crafting is a way to work a few things out on the cheap. So in hopes of holding his cards a bit closer to the chest, he starts making the man possibly a woman; the stick figure starts becoming more non-gender specific.

In trying to paint some color onto the little human, a crude blotch of blue is laid on at the middle of the abdomen, which is maybe a shirt or possibly a hiked-up skirt the way it's fallen on in a triangular splat. A weird little red triangle is added in midway on the face, which is looking like a lipstick mouth if indeed the figure is a woman, or easily a bloody nose if the figure is a long- and narrow-faced man. The hour passes in the kind of calm that students were promised in the meditation class but didn't find until physically confronting the instructor; Basic Crafting is obviously delivering on its promise right from the get-go. As the hour winds up, Matthew realizes that the little square-inch stick figure's crudely rendered little left claw looks like it could be a gun. And so with the smallest, thinnest brush of black, Matthew paints on one of his maxims that has been typed into his emailing phone thing, and under the little asexual, cross-gender stick person, he starts to letter the realization that came to him at the park-and-ride lot yesterday, *God will help you find a secondhand gun, but not until you're grateful and reaching out to friends.* But there's the small problem of fitting the entire phrase, and he ends up with GOD WILL HELP YOU FIND A GUN IF YOU'RE GRATEFUL, which still has a nice ring to it, for a mug.

The instructor woman issues another smiling and distant order to the class as it is winding up: that they should start thinking of little labels or logos to mark their projects with, just for fun. This is really nothing more than a way for her to mention — and certainly not for the first time over the course of weeks, one would imagine — that her store is called Aurora Design and Supply. Then she talks about putting an address on there as well in case someone sees a piece you've made and would like to know how to order more. This is basically a way for her to remind students where her shop is located. "So my logo is a star above a mountain, and it says Aurora

Designs and then it has the phone number right there." And it seems stupid, but between last night and today, the heart has tricked the brain into thinking that Matthew is a can-do kind of guy who likes to try. So he paints on a name that will also function as a loose legal disclaimer or warning on the bottom of the mug: NOT ZEN, INC. And the address is simply MADE IN MY CAR. A Lori or Lynn or Bea or somebody, the same woman who asked Matthew if he's gay or married, comes over and looks at the mug; an instant *whoop* seems to call the others over like hens and the whole place is clucking and laughing and then, from one of them, "Okay, how much for that one once you get it back from being fired?" and Matthew still shudders a bit when hearing the words *being* and *fired* so close together.

"Oh, it's not, you know . . . I can't charge for this. Right?"

But the instructor just sort of looks over at him now more confused than she was in the parking lot first trying to figure Matthew's situation. Then she answers the question; gets all high-road crafting philosophy on him. "Well, it's your work. It's something you're connected to after creating it, so whether or not to sell a piece is always a bittersweet question and no simple price seems equitable when we consider what we put into a piece."

Matthew seems to really consider this for a moment — sleepy, stoned, and confused about what the instructor woman said — and turns to the interested Lynn or Jan and says, "I could do fifteen on this . . . piece."

"Sold. I've got a son in California who loves *Pulp Fiction,* the John Travolta movie, and he'll get a kick out of this. His wife will hate it, but you shouldn't take that as a reflection on your work, the woman is predisposed to hating anything I send him."

The head reels to imagine what forty-year-old man with a wife, and probably a family, is simply known for loving a movie that came out about twenty years ago. That's apparently the way it runs in actual families, people kind of remember one thing you said you liked, latch on to it, and that's your thing. Weirdly enough, this is also kind of the way it works in the kind of fast, temporary families Matthew grew up in; you're the guy who likes jeans because you wore jeans a lot this week so you are now forever The Guy Who Likes Jeans when clothes are donated or a character like Fonzie comes on television. Hey, Fonzie is like you, he loves wearing jeans! And this actually fills the gap in the heart some nights; it actually works. It sounds like it's not enough, but if the heart has been cracked hard and fast enough, and the head is still trying to insist that things will be normal sometime soon, it is more than enough for some guardian to see Fonzie on the TV and say that he is like you and that you are like him.

So the deal is struck, fifteen bucks. Matthew stares at his hands, thinking: fifteen, thirty, forty-five, sixty, seventy-five, ninety, one oh five, one hundred and five times fifty is five thousand two hundred and fifty; all from something thought up in a fit, from the hands doing their bit, from some oven or something. The mug will be back in time for the next class, when Matthew and the gals are back here to craft and gab. The head is abuzz at all of this industrious hustling of late. Within just about eighteen hours, cash has been generated, controlled substances have been procured, and even a sturdy firearm to fortify the freelance life has been bartered for. The brain feels the confidence and happiness coming on and quickly cues the little vacuum, sponge, and turkey baster machines to suck and soak up the last drop of serotonin buzz; tries to keep the neurochemistry of good fortune under control.

The body soldiers on in a light shuffle, feeling aglow, thrilled that so much good came of the last day or so. Out of the class as the covey sends a flutter of "See ya-soons." Down the hall, a peek into the Put 'n' Take: That issue of *Hype Hair!* is gone, should've grabbed it when it wasn't, the paperbacks are gone and off to better homes, *Shifting Parameters in Nonlinear Models* lies at the bottom of the box. The fact that some janitor rescued it from the recycling bin steadies Matthew's faith in people, but the fact that nobody has inflicted it on themselves or another is what bolsters Matthew's real faith in the human condition. Hey, look, next to that, in the corner there, an issue of *American Craft,* and with a spring in his stoop, with some jaunt in his bend, it's gone in a flash.

13

Telecom and Going Down

THE TELEPHONE HAS BEEN on lately, which is just a way of half-hoping Tatiana is calling any minute for any reason. Matthew knows the phone is on and thinks thoughts in its direction, like *Dream about me*, or, *Hear something ticking inside of you*, or, *Feel tired of disappearing.* But all the telephone is saying at the moment is TIM. MOBILE. *Hello* isn't out of Matthew's mouth and Tim is already talking about how he's going to make a comeback after losing everyone's money. This, evidently, starting by mailing out a form letter to everyone whose money he has skimmed and fucked and snorted, and it is apparently a form letter that starts with the line, "I am sorry I failed to make you millions as we had planned. But if you can stop thinking about yourself for a moment, I'd like to tell you about my new plan."

And there's a line, not long after that gem, that says, "Let's, just for a minute, quit worrying about how I was supposed to make you millions. Stop and think what it's like for me at this impasse." There are other accusatory lines even worse than those that can only serve to strengthen any prosecution's case, and Tim sees fit to read the whole letter to Matthew, stopping only to occasionally say, in a broken, maybe drunk, certainly speedy voice, "I mean, right? Fuck, give me a fucking break, right?" And then the letter of apology that Tim wants to send along to all of his clients ends with the line, "I'm going to be up front with you: I'm in need of a short-term loan." That's it. That is essentially the way he signs off.

"Are you still doing tons of coke?"

"Fuck you."

"That's a yes."

"I'm living in a van . . ."

"It's an RV. And it's a rental. And seriously, what has gone wrong for you? Not much when you think about it. You have everything you need. You always have. Yes, fine, some woman shaved your legs and fucked you with a bat and tied your balls up with . . ."

"My fiancée, thank you very much. And wait, she what? What are you saying happened? Because that's not what happened."

"You were going to marry her?"

From across the lot, the instructor from class is making her way toward her car.

"Yes."

Matthew waves to her as she gets into her car.

"You were going to marry the woman who dressed you up like a schoolboy or a maid or whatever, made you wear some kind of dildo helmet and . . ."

"What the fuck, where do you get this? It was just a hood; just like a leather hood thing."

The instructor smiles in reply to Matthew's wave; this sort of suburban, perfunctory, and pleasant smile without any eyes to it.

"Just?"

"Fucking relatively speaking. Why would I be a schoolboy?"

She loads the box of class projects into the trunk of her medium-jumbo somewhat-luxury sedan. Matthew brightens. In one week the mug will be finished and back and then fifteen dollars, then thirty, forty-five, sixty, seventy-five, ninety.

"Your letter thing sounds sad. And vengeful — as if you're the victim. I think that's why I figured you were made to wear one of those helmets; because you sounded like a victim. A victim doing tons of blow."

"I was."

"You were what? Wearing the dildo helmet thing?" Matthew waves politely at her once more. No matter how many times he waves, she doesn't turn into Tatiana.

"There was no helmet; who's saying that? Why would you buy that shit?"

"That's the question I should be asking you."

"So, yes, I was doing coke. While I wrote it. The client letter."

"That's what I asked to begin with."

"I know, and that's what I just said once you gave me one fifth of a second to talk, okay? Jesus."

"Well, you said you're running some kind of program on yourself out there and that I need to be some hard-ass that you check in with."

"I never said to be a hard-ass, I just said I needed someone to check in with."

And then Tim talks for minutes on end again. Throwing around all of these tough-guy lines about kicking the savage drugs she kept him embalmed with; about Montana, Wyoming, or Idaho and wishing he had a better idea of which state he was a six-wheeled resident of while anchored in Yellowstone National Park for this federally inspired but supposedly totally self-imposed reevaluation and detoxification program of his. Tim keeps talking and talking and talking to Matthew, which might be part of this program he's made up to get this life straight again; the whole thing might hinge on sitting in a rented RV talking to Matthew and other friends when he can get a signal to dial them. While Tim keeps talking, Matthew keeps beaming thoughts at the phone, trying to make call-waiting interrupt the moment. Feel something ticking in you, get tired of disappearing, and: "Dream about me."

"What?"

"I didn't say anything."

After the phone, the book about food and praying and flying comes out again and gets the heart all jumped up about traveling the world. There's also the new issue of *American Craft,* and Native American cigarettes, dire dispatches from Steely Dan, and a montage of about nine different driver's seat positions found by reaching down to the little electric buttons while the eyes take pages in. Finally the sun gets old and fades to deep orange and barely warm. The last of the light looks filtered through high clouds and smoke and all it wants to talk about is the past and it plays sucker ballad chords like that thing where a G major falls a half step to the F sharp root, then down again to E minor with the seventh or ninth added in to make that weird happy-and-sad sound that feels like a thousand Sundays or summer ending or a girlfriend leaving.

Soon enough the Bavarian sedan is aimed out of the lot and toward the homestead. Once at home there is every excuse in Matthew's head to leave again and head out for a night alone somewhere: Kristin hovering on stairs and whisking past quickly in the darker periphery of the place, for instance. And the pain that feels like being kicked between the legs comes around with the stream of red urine that Matthew's trying to forget. He tries to convince himself it's just vitamins in the urine, that it's some sign of the body already doing some sort of self-healing; that he will not be required to call Alpha Imaging to pay cash to be slid into some giant tube that photographs sixteen slices of the abdomen to find out what he already knows in his heart and head.

There are bills, some sorted through, some falling between cracks again. There are some that won't be opened until the voice mail about the email about the unopened mail forces his hand. There are a million questions, and maybe the best one to start with is: Who on earth would want to stay inside tonight with all of this bouncing around in here?

At night it isn't hard to slip out, for either of them. It's probably easier for Kristin to slide through a crack in the wall and out of the house. After all, she's able to vaporize into a room with complete silence, like a deadly government assassin letting you know she could have used lethal precision to remove you from the planet but decided to just observe you and not go through with it. So who knows how many times she comes and goes from the house in the evening. Matthew, on the other hand, bothers to at least devise a decent premise in his head. He will usually go through the trouble of convincing Kristin that he's meeting Tim for dinner or to go see some band, but really, he's trying to convince himself and he's the last to know. But this premise feels good to hold inside, because Kristin has never met Tim, and so would know nothing about how he's getting his life together by sucking up the last of his tribal quality drugs alone in national parks.

14
—

Yes, About Last Night . . .

WAKING UP, TRYING TO add it up, and there are some significant dots one must connect. The temptation to get out of the house last night proved to be too much, the brain recalls this, but that's really all that the faculties of Matthew can recollect at the moment, which is where connecting the dots comes in. The first dot, the biggest dot, is a dot called The Gun. Matthew recalls drinking, and this was after walking past on the sidewalk in front of Tatiana's apartment on Bond Street more than a few times; on the first pass he walked a crisp pace with purpose; then after regrouping around the corner on Lafayette, he walked by again, this time slowly, trying hard to appear poetic and pensive; on other passes Matthew was walking by at any pace that might have looked great on the off chance that Tatiana was in from Los Angeles. And on the off chance that she just happened to be entering or leaving her building. And on the off chance that she would even recognize him. But she wasn't, and she didn't, and she probably wouldn't, so then there was drinking.

The Bavarian mobile office and den was parked on East Third or Great Jones or somewhere near enough to Bond but not too sadly and desperately close to it. Wherever it was that the land barge was anchored, there were evidently bars all around it, practically closing in on it and slowly surrounding it, actually. Chances are that the car would be slept in, especially with Tatiana being a safe three thousand miles west of it. So the first bar was Jones and the booze there made the migration from the back bar, to the drink mat, to the bar's top side, and finally down the hatch. Mardi Gras beads, and a menu that never changes because it's painted on the wall, a bust of Elvis on a shelf, a blue bulb in the bathroom, a bartender splitting his attention between making solid stiff drinks and serving bowls of crayfish and jambalaya to people who wanted to waste their buzz with food. The whiskey did its seductive dance right up to the handshake with the lips, which led straight to a little romp upstairs with the brain. The jukebox was tons of old stuff you never get to hear; it was lit and loud like everyone, it did the tighten up, and there wasn't a steely cautionary downbeat parable to be had in any of it; there was Cash, there were Raconteurs going into the real nitty-gritty of Southern Culture on the Skids. Each drink took Matthew a hundred miles south of

New York City until he was, well, about nine hundred miles south. The jukebox went on until it sounded like every song in the world featured Katy Rose Cox on the fiddle; it went on until Matthew was feeling guided by voices.

This leads to spirited conversation with anyone who will listen, and surprisingly three young people did. Two guys and a girl, maybe sixty-five collective years between them, they kept listening to him, stayed the long haul of Blenheim's and Maker's, and Buckhorn and Maker's, and Maker's and Maker's. And as the long haul went on, all four of them, all one hundred and ten collective years of them, went outside for a smoke together, once or three or five times. And then they even set forth on an expedition to the car when Matthew enlisted them to search for the little bags marked blue and yellow or green and blue or whatever the hell Tatiana had left him with. And that's where the gun comes in. But one has to understand that the gun wasn't brought out in any sort of menacing way. There was a certain amount of edge to Matthew's inspired street sermon, sure, probably only the effect of not finding the drugs and finally being fresh out of cigarettes. Matthew was simply trying to emphasize some of the points he was making while talking to these kids. So as a means of underlining certain points, if you will, the gun, yes, fine, was taken out and waved around a bit. It's important for the head to make a level argument while waking up this morning that the gun was waved around only as a flourish, really — and only during the underlined words that Matthew felt needed emphasis.

"I've torn my car apart for twenty minutes and I don't know where that stuff is. I probably sound like some nutcase dipshit, but basically I was this, like, superhot millionaire woman's dealer. Just for one day. She's, I don't know what she is, but she has houses all over the world and she just, you know, she's rich. She's beautiful. And we hooked up. And then she basically buys a bunch of shit from me and hands it right back to me and is like, 'This is for you because you're connected to something so, like, huge in the universe right now,' or something like that. I can't remember everything she said."

The three young people were kind of laughing about this, and that might've been what started Matthew feeling the need to employ gun flourishes in the conversation. But it wasn't unkind laughter on their part, though; it was spirited; these kids saw Matthew as another random measure of jazz after years spent living in a world where dinner had always been served at six and every adult who loved them or taught them was hoping they'd end up squares with sensible hair-cuts and dental insurance. Here were two long, tall young men whose eyes, only four or five years ago, were staring at the ceilings of suburban bedrooms on sleepless nights with parents just down the hall. And her, she was a stick figure of a girl, skinny jeans barely letting her ankles out, thin lips on a narrow, pale slivered moon of a face waiting for a kiss from someone who wasn't a best friend or a steady bore betting on a future going according to plan.

"I don't even know what you guys do now. I mean I think

I've got a basic grasp of what growing up in America is like for you guys these days. When you're fifteen you use the Internet to tease kids from school until they commit suicide. Then you live with your parents until you're thirty because there's no shame in it now or something. You skip college to invent Internet stuff, you stage weird homoerotic gang fights in basements, and you sell your companies for billions and have bonfires and orgies in the desert. You buy old vinyl records from the seventies, which actually kind of appeals to me, but it's also kind of condescending. The three of you probably have enough cash liquid at any given moment to have me killed on a dare. You know what? I feel awesome. I feel awesome tonight. Right now. Now. We're all here now and this is the best night of my life. Tonight is our time. Time is finite. We can't stand still; we can't die. We cannot die!"

And on that last note, that last emphatic wave of the gun, that's when they started looking a little skittish and concerned about the situation. In retrospect, Matthew gets it: Basically you can't use a gun as a conversational prop when you're screaming into the night about how the four of you will never die; the nuanced subtext becomes too easy to misunderstand when you introduce the gun. But all Matthew meant is that time is finite and you have to live each day while you have it if you want to live a full life. It was something that Milton had told him in almost every session. He would say that we have only so many days. He would say that we have to choose action and live the days we have; that staying sedate and not moving a muscle and not choosing action over being static, that was what killed us. But before Matthew could explain it, they all scattered in a blitz, running off and yelling shit over their shoulders back at him.

At the time, Matthew rationalized their behavior. Stood there by the car quietly watching them disappear, convincing himself he understood yet another thing about their generation. He told himself that it was nothing to do with him, that the mind and body simply do funny things at their age when an entire young adrenal gland is emptied in spasm with too much speed to handle, flooding blood already thin with booze. But then Matthew felt his own chemicals change and administer a surge of disbelief and sadness. And this is probably just the buyer's remorse that comes with owning a weapon; but still, it wasn't long ago, in the office, that anyone their age would display a workplace reverence if even thinking about asking his permission to leave before him.

He stood next to the car, looking around sheepishly in case there were police the way there always are in movies when things end up like this. He puts the gun back under the seat way too gingerly; he gives drunken gravitas a shot and comes up this flat: "I basically have seniority. Over all of them."

And now, here, this morning, waking up in the car, there isn't much point in doing the math about how he and the Bavarian motor situation navigated this blind path back; no sense trying to figure what the brain had in mind when it parked them here in front of houses clear on the other side of Westport, nowhere near the one Matthew is supposed to sleep in. The gray light outside puts this at about six; maybe seven. Waking up in a car was more fun at seventeen and even twenty-seven.

Your heart won't hang on much longer.

"Shut up," the brain says.

Find someone to fall in love with before everything in you stops working forever.

"Be quiet."

Water, water, water.

"Yes, water!"

The mouth is all Mojave and cracked dash, and every move it makes feels like razor blades on new skin. Water, water, water, water, there's no other way to say it emphatically. It can't be stated plainly enough, this level of thirst. You'd have to wave the gun a dozen times and fire it twice to even underline the word *water* enough. Matthew opens the door and rolls from the car in slow motion and crawls a few paces, pulling his pants up to cover the crack of his ass, he walks a straight path hunched over a bit so that ideally nobody sees him making his way from the street and up into the lawn. Who knows whose house this is, but it's a house with a hose on the side of it and hoses are full of cool, clean water and hoses pump it into you faster than you can drink it. A drive to someplace where a bottle of water is sold would be a drop in the bucket; it would be like waiting thirty days and wading through paperwork to buy a gun with the credit card in your name and in your pocket; no, the body requires a flood aimed into the neck and unleashed in almost homoerotic folly;

brought on like a flood that rages in, biblical in scale. Up the little walk, and the reflection on the window makes it hard to see in, so Matthew's crouch gets lower and he attempts precision; tired and hungover but locked into this low-profile recon posture like a man sneaking in to the enemy camp. Up to the hose and turn it on, and here it comes, here it comes, here it comes. If there were a fire hydrant next to this house, he would get his mouth around it somehow.

The body is filling up now, cold and clear, and all the brain can think is: *Drain this home of its bounty; suck this thing like you owe it money.* The eyes close, the cool, clear flood pumps in faster than the throat can find a place to route it; the mouth is a reservoir too full in the first millisecond, the stomach is like the town below it sandbagged and nervous. The throat is quenched and chilled too fast, the stomach stretches to get more in, and then, Jesus, what, yes, vomiting. But the water is hosing it from the face as fast as it can splatter out. Violent heaves yield mostly booze and a few soaked-soft and waterlogged tails of crayfish, the hose fills the stomach cool and clear and anew at almost the same second it is evacuated. The eyes wince closed with every hard heave of this cleansing; this system is instant and insane, and for a flash Matthew is thinking that this is the cleanest anybody has ever been from outside in. Slaked and free of the cracked dehydrated longing, Matthew is clearly not unbowed from the last night's damage, but he's also oddly brand-new again. A man finds out what he's made of when essentially fellating another man's real estate; doing that to another man's home is the moment when one tends to take that fearless inventory of the shape things are in, really. He's hungover, for eyes he still has chipped blue and red marbles lost in dark ocular caves, he's still lonely and aimless, but he's also reset and all better. If one is not careful in a moment like this, it's easy to think every morning should start this way.

Open the eyes now, open them and look at the man standing in the house's living room staring out at you, silent and calm, in awe of this stranger's depraved morning constitutional. He was hidden, for who knows how long, by the sheen of early morning gray light putting a haze and tint on the living room window. Matthew finishes, shuts the hose off, and tosses it back to where it was hanging coiled. The face feels a thin, warm southbound migration toward the mouth and realizes the nose is bleeding generously. The brain's simple directives are to walk back to the car, walk like an athlete off the field; long and languid, head down a bit, walk across the grass and oh, what the hell, turn around and wave at the guy after what you just did to his house. So Matthew turns and gives him a humble wave like the man is a fan who's been waiting for acknowledgment. The quiet man stands in his robe; there in his living room window taking it all in, probably figuring Matthew is evidence of exactly what waits out there away from the comfortable confines and routines of marriage and employment. This strange man on the front lawn; who slept in a car in front of the house; who snuck up on the garden hose like a drowsy, half-assed sniper; who vomited and gagged when he pumped his stomach with delicious water; who waved casually like an exhausted hero while his nose bled a warm crimson river — the man in the living room looks out at him, probably thinking: It's so hard to tell if that's what freedom is.

15

How to Ace Therapy's Stupid Trick Questions

MATTHEW TAKES THE ELEVATOR up to Milton's apartment and this is where this stuff happens. And one pays in cash from the bank machine for this. Every twenty that comes out these days is starting to look like food or electricity or gasoline; Jackson's face concerned and grave about the shape things are in. But one doesn't have to pay for therapy until the end of it; and maybe Matthew can talk fast and do a half session.

Into the elevator, the smell of food from every floor means the air is one huge, terrible soup. Out of the elevator, down the hall, and the door to the apartment is left ajar in welcome. One walks in through the door, fresh from the elevator and hallway of bad soup, and into the smell of yesteryear's tonics wafting from the apartment's bathroom. Moving farther still, down toward the living room, and here is the best painting in the city as far as Matthew can tell — a pumped-up and saturated pallet of hyper green and red against gray-and-white resignation. This painting, this photo-realist thing, depicts his therapist mowing a perfectly square lawn in front of a perfectly pleasant house in the suburbs, in his trademark suit, in this case linen, eyes miserable and sunken, face ashen. The routine most weeks is that Matthew stands in front of it, courting Stendhal syndrome, until Milton pokes his head from the small office next to the kitchen to say they can get started. One time there was an exchange, and this was years ago, and it went something like this.

"That's you? Mowing?"

"It was a gift from a client. At one point I left the city for the suburbs, when I was married."

"How was it?"

"A very pleasant picture for a long time, and then a lot like this one." And on this line Milton stands for a beat to let it land, turns his head slightly to try to see Matthew and whether or not the joke sticks. In the old days he wouldn't have done any of that, but this is what signing up for improv and stand-up comedy classes at age sixty-five has done to Matthew's therapist.

Matthew is sitting on the sofa in the little room now. The last few sessions have been canceled and allowed to go unpaid, completely against the usual policy and custom of paying whether or not one shows up, and whether or not your life felt any different after the session. Maybe being back here again is good, but maybe it's still too soon after black Friday at the office — maybe one should wait a year, because the session is already rooted mostly in Matthew issuing personal spin with regard to how things are going; he sounds like an athlete doing locker room press. And the stuff that comes out of the mouth, it's almost actually believed in the heart and head: Matthew wasn't fired so much as he saw an exciting opportunity to take advantage of; his marriage didn't explode in his face so much as he's questioned monogamy like some kind of sporting intellectual cad; money is fine, things are good financially, and besides, money isn't everything. There is no talk of frightening young people with guns, drinking and doing drugs in parking lots all day long, meditating/fistfighting, being a freelance drug dealer for a night, sex on hallucinogens, or crafting. Matthew talks to his therapist the way most people talk in job interviews or when being pulled over for driving while intoxicated. He issues what he guesses must be the right answers, hoping something he says triggers one of the jokes at his expense and is laced with advice for better living. Before the stand-up comedy classes, Milton tended to just land straightforward maxims; homespun turns of phrase that brought cold comfort; that rolled off the tongue and into Matthew's head, arguably never sinking in.

Slow down to go faster.
Learn to stand still long enough for
  something to happen.
If you feel guilty, you're probably being had.
If you haven't cried since you were nine,
  maybe you haven't tried.

And while we're on the topic of crying, Milton is aware that Matthew hasn't cried since he was nine. Years ago, when therapy started, Milton made it a habit of making sure to draw attention to the box of tissues on the table in front of Matthew; nothing overt, subtle stuff, but as the two of them were settling in to begin, he might have moved them forward on the table while acting like he was simply rearranging things after the last session. One time he asked Matthew to please check and see if there were still plenty left in the decorative box that dispensed them. And Matthew made note of it, and also note of the fact that his reserve needed to be fortified and steeled in this environment where crying was being encouraged like this.

And so if the topic were to turn to the parents and what happened, or the homestead and the heartbreak, he would answer questions like a soldier taught to handle questions without getting too wound up in them. He would use any number of tricks to keep it together in his head. Probably the most common of which was simply thinking of work stuff or wildlife or sex — of anything to distract himself emotionally. So Milton would ask him how he felt about death or divorce or his parents and let him know that it was okay to feel sad, even as an adult. And Matthew would stare back and reply with an unwavering voice, and in his head he would be thinking: *blow job, blow job, blow job*. Once he almost said the word aloud while the brain juggled the tasks of answering and thinking. And when you're talking about your parents to a trained mental health professional, and you blurt out *blow job*, you may as well just go ahead and book three years' worth of sessions, because it would open a can of worms, to say the least. But in today's session, after issuing the hand- ful of levelheaded responses about how things are going and generally creating the impression that nothing has changed without Matthew's permission or even his insistence, the brain administers a twitch and a squeeze of serotonin that lies on its surface and is spared uptake. It seems that the stiff upper lip has earned him his walking papers for the day.

"Okay, so, in closing, everything is going well, is what I'm hearing."

"I mean, yeah, you know. I mean, yeah, I'm interested in some other opportunities possibly. I don't know if I love, per se, what I'm doing for a living. So I might investigate some pretty interesting offers and ideas and things that are coming my way. And I'm reevaluating some things. Personal things."

"And how does it make you feel when you consider this?"

"Just the way a person, you know, feels when thinking. The normal feelings, really. It makes me feel like a man think- ing about other opportunities. You know that feeling, you've thought about other opportunities, I'm sure. I mean, no, everything's good. There have been some tough breaks, there have been some lucky breaks and good times, really the basic mix that everybody has. Really pretty normal; pretty average."

"I noticed you were limping on the way in; just a little."

Matthew pauses here trying to size up whether or not it's a trick question, or trick statement, or trick observation; whatever it is, is it a trick? It is. Right? Yes. Has to be.

"I . . . was hit. By a car."

"You really had to think about that for a minute."

"I was just, yeah, I had almost forgotten to be honest with you. It just. I was shopping. Got hit shopping." This is such a good lie that it's basically the truth.

And then Matthew just stares, waiting for the next question, wondering if he's nailing them, wondering if he's passing the test, wondering if his parents' battered and bruised ghosts, soaked in fuel, are stuck to him; wondering if every single stupid thing he's pinned with these days is written all over his face in a rash of tells and ticks. Kristin doesn't know what she's not supposed to know, Milton doesn't know what he's not supposed to know, the guy at the gas station in the morning is sewn up fine and doesn't suspect a thing has changed. Matthew isn't fooling anyone and Matthew is the last to know. Hey, the bell on the timer made the *ding!* And here's the part when Milton says he's afraid their time is up.

And then he might add that he'd love to show Matthew a video of his recent stand-up comedy or the most recent student film he's acted in, but only if Matthew feels okay with that; only if Matthew has the few extra minutes. If Matthew says yes, then he'll see his therapist in a host of roles. He'll see him act like an elderly man propositioning hookers in what is supposed to be a comedy; he'll see him walk out into a field in a white suit and die of a heart attack in what is supposed to play as poignant drama or something. Or maybe today it will be a video of him holding down a ten-minute slot at The Comedy Cellar with rough-hewn impressions of rednecks largely informed by old American television like *Hee Haw* and *Laugh-In*. And these awkward five minutes will start once the bell rings; once Milton speaks up to say time has had its way with the session. But first maybe just reaffirm that things are going fine.

"So, yeah, no complaints, really. I don't know. Things are fine. I'm fine." Here lies a last, long pause, born the moment one wonders how well they've gotten over, and dead once the next words are finally spoken.

"Would a little loan come in handy? A couple hundred dollars for a few weeks?"

"Yes."

16

Gut Feeling

THE DAYS STANDING between Matthew and the next craft class pass about as slowly as they can, just for spite it seems. There are a handful of things that don't help; a day spent going to have a machine take sixteen X-rays that deliver a sliced-up cross-sectional picture of the abdomen, for instance. The head is screaming inside, offering up this sturdy piece of medical advice: *Why confirm what you already know is bad news and more than a suspicion?*

The way this goes down when the insurance is gone is that one goes to a place called Alpha Imaging and waits in a waiting room that boasts Home Depot tile, leatherette sofas, and a Mediterranean mural that work in concert to try and make you feel like you're not in an X-ray imaging facility at all, but rather burning your vacation days on a rustic seaside plaza in Barcelona. Matthew waits until one of the stout, tough, tired Puerto Rican women gossiping at the front counter call the correct name. But first they bitch about the Bronx number 4 train and how it's running late every day. Then they show each other their long nails somehow painted like a cross between a floral print in a hotel bar and a custom van from the eighties. Then one of them picks at a lunch in a container from home; heated up in a microwave. Any organic smell heated in this room somehow instantly smells like something gone wrong; like stale blood and hair; it floats by duly noticed and steadfastly ignored by the waiting room full of long faces resigned to distracting their worst thoughts with celebrity gossip magazines. After signing in and filling everything out, Matthew steps back up to the counter to discreetly say that his plan today is to pay with a credit card. And then the receptionist or admissions woman or whatever she is announces this at stage volume to the rest of the people relaxing in the clean Spanish courtyard by the sea.

"So dares no insurance? Den you nee to pay today."

And Matthew feels like he may as well turn around to the room behind him filled with a dozen everyday people waiting to find out if they're ghosts, and announce plainly: *I went to the bathroom all over my office, so I got fired and now I don't have insurance. I drink and take pills to forget that I'm going bankrupt quickly and bleeding inside slowly; everything's fine, though, I'm fine.* Even the gun wouldn't fix it today, this esteem that hangs in shreds, like a flag faded by the sun of a hundred hot days, only to be left out in a hurricane. Matthew remembers to clarify one other thing.

"My doctor said to tell you I need to walk with films, not with a disc. I have to bring films to my doctor's appointment next week."

"I know, *Papi*, butchu steel got to wait until we call you name. Everyone else, they waiting too."

"I know, I wasn't saying I . . ."

And on his way back to the leatherette sofa in front of the big aquarium, Matthew tries to give the other people waiting a kind of look like, *Of course I have to wait to be called, I wasn't asking for some kind of break, I just needed to tell them I have to get film and not a disc . . . isn't she ridiculous?* But they've got themselves and their situations on their mind, like anyone here in a right mind would, so nobody catches his look.

When it's all over, after Matthew has been dressed in gowns and slippers that are about three pieces of bad news away from being something one's body gets wheeled off wearing, after he's taken dumb big breaths and held them for the technician, and been slid into a metal tube smaller and tighter than the one his parents stepped into and fell from the sky in, after the machines circle and cut their slices of view, Matthew leaves with a big square envelope of X-rays, jammed under his arm like one of those oversized checks they give contest winners, but what a stupid contest to win.

Then Matthew is at home in the kitchen, holding each giant black-and-white snapshot up to the light above the stove, trying his best to make heads or tails of sixteen sequential peeks at everything inside the body. The emulsion around the edges is black but his name and date of birth are clear, and so is today's date, and so are the heart, intestines, liver, and pancreas. And when a person looks at something like this, frame after frame of guts and a birth date, one thinks about how long they've been living, how long they've got left to live. And at the edge of each little snapshot is your doctor's name, and on the edge of each giant page of little snapshots is the word *emotion* with a little ® next to it.

Matthew would be better qualified to read a fortune in tea leaves, but he holds these things up, scans them, and tries to see what he can see. Sees his heart, sees everything one only hears and believes on good faith to be inside of them. There are the ribs forming the cage for the delicate vital stuff. There's the breath being held, keeping inflated these lungs to which one has done whatever they've done. There's the liver, there's the rest of it, a bunch of stuff that requires eight years of school to identify and get a read on. But then there's the one thing there that keeps showing up: a solid mass; the light is bouncing it back; the film is screaming out how this foreign matter doesn't fit — you don't need to be a genius to see it. Matthew stands in the kitchen, pulling each sheet out of the large envelope, holding the big squares of emulsion up to the light above the stove, then up to the light in the ceiling, and there it is, again and again. He double-checks the name, and yes, it is his name. And he double-checks the doctor's name, and yes, it is his doctor. Film after film, the same solid matter, the same two names in the corners, and one date of birth, then a hyphen, then a blank with no end-date yet. Film after film, emotion 4, emotion 5, emotion 6, emotion 7.

There are a few beers to be fetched from the floorboard of the car. And there are a few shots of stiffer stuff in the kitchen to erase the pictures from the head. The drinks flow like drinks and then the arms flail in terrible tantrum. Smash this all now, fuck it all, the brain knows there's something wrong with the biological container that houses it. Everything's cracking inside, everything's packing up and ready to hit the road to leave this earthly stint behind, the head knows it, the films show it. There is more beer in the car even after these, there is more of the stiff and strong in the cabinet above the stove, the one with the door torn off and thrown into the dining room like kindling for this place's final disappearing act. A plastic bottle shaped like a bear and filled with honey smashed into the counter in a fit of tics and sobs, all the sticky golden insides of the bear now going wrong just like Matthew's guts. Bags of shit that was bought on larks, things that they were supposed to eat in front of fires in the fireplace or in front of love stories on the television screen, stupid bags of sweet, hard comfort that never came, all torn and smashed and thrown.

The head wonders for a minute why it is that every big,

dramatic, violent fit or fight in this body's life has been so silent; gummy candy thrown, honey punched and smashed, yoga mats in giant stacks tumbling silently while soft hands pummel the soft pillow of fat on a man's kind, warm back. The head fires up harder trying to think of better things to destroy, things that would make loud manly sounds, but no luck. And the gray stumbles into remembering that there is a gun around here now. One that presumably has bullets in it, one would assume based on the price and connection. So the tantrum of medium-grade destruction of honey bear and cabinet door could end in a loud smack, flash, and powder burn. A tight metal *click*-and-*bang* economy ticket to heaven, a quick end to this situation inside of him.

But the heart is having none of this, the chest is reminding the entire system that the gals in craft class are expecting Matthew; there is the matter of the mug for Jan, the matter of her middle-aged son, who likes *Pulp Fiction,* getting it and loving it regardless of Jan's prediction that his wife will not. There is also the matter of a slip left on the door that says United Parcel Service is dropping by in the morning with two large parcels. And there is a lyric, rocketing in, in the quiet calm that comes after the, well, equally quiet destruction, a Steely Dan song that has not come up in the cerebral satellite shuffle before. It bears double-checking, but tonight — in the middle of this sticky mess of smashed bears and snacks that have been ripped from cupboards after the cupboards' doors were quietly bent down and back and forth on hinges that eventually broke — the little stanza sounds all about carrying on; about how minor worlds break apart but also fall together again; about how the demons won't be at the door once morning comes repeated over and over in the head, from every angle, it seems there is not a downbeat loss to be found in it.

17

In the Morning, at the Door

MATTHEW'S DAYS ARE ADVANCING without certain things happening, the scheduling of a follow-up appointment with the doctor who touches him and has terrible taste in political biographies, for instance. The denial has been thick enough to keep the delusion of reprieve alive and kicking, and then there was last night, which has landed squarely at this morning. Rocket from the bed and into the kitchen, and he keeps walking without looking behind him to see that he hasn't made the bed and that the room is wrecked just like the kitchen. He has hidden the CT scan films, mostly from himself, between the wall and the stove in the kitchen. On the counter next to the stove, the white stone horizon is littered with tiny bear bodies; the contents of the honey bear's head have thickened right where they spilled out after his head exploded from the pounding. A crowd of gummy bears looks on, rubbernecking and milling about, staring down at their feet and feeling the weight of just how wrong things went for the honey bear, and if it happened to someone so much bigger, couldn't it happen to them at any second?

Matthew steps over cabinet and cupboard doors, walks to the living room, and peeks from behind the curtain to make sure the UPS guy has jumped back into the truck and driven off before he creeps out on the porch quickly and recedes back into shadowy safety carrying the parcels left by UPS. Parcels that rested directly beneath a door slip signed and hanging there trying too hard to say something; to say that during the weekday hours between nine and seven, of course nobody would be here to sign for a package; why would they; why would someone be here when normal people are at work during that time; of course the recipient of the parcel of product ordered from a tiny classified ad in *American Crafting* wouldn't be home — what, do you think he was fired or something? Well, he wasn't.

Inside the house, Matthew opens the boxes and double-checks the order against the invoice with some scrutiny. After all, a business owner unaware of his inventory is not a business owner for very long. Two dozen (24 count) unfinished plaster mugs without graphics (Mug, LG16, nonfin/nonGFX) with no chips or damage, shipped UPS 2nd Day Air, paid in full by credit card. The mugs are each inspected, each repacked with their respective ball of corrugated-card-board packing wad, and the box is humped out to the Bavar-ian Motor Warehouse. The sleek, black, long, overpowered, aimless cockpit of denial and optimism is pointed toward the community center again. The brain keeps sending word down through the blood that something is wrong; that this is the wrong time of day to be leaving the house; that the dot on the film is winning whatever war it has waged; that a grown man is not supposed to be looking forward to an afternoon craft class with the craft ladies. But Matthew turns into the lot at the community center, suspending disbelief, at least for the moment — a rare gift for the semi-afflicted.

To the trunk to fetch the inventory; across the lot and in through the glass doors and down the hall; past the Take me! Take me! Take me! box where the book about data measur-ing continues to lie alone, filled with creased heartbreak and hopes of being taken home by some maligned and crushed soul in the kind of dire spiritual debt that drug and drink haven't learned to solve yet; and finally, through the class-room door. Matthew cuts a direct line straight up to the box on the instructor's desk, barely affecting the periphery of the chirpy, cooing craft covey. There it is. There's the finished product. The words are as clear and as clean as Matthew re-calls them having been: *God will help you find a gun if you're grateful*. The illustration never really looked like a hand, and time and fire have not remedied this, but the gun is very plain to see in the illustration. It's a gun held by a hand moving so quickly it appears to have seven blurry fingers; a gun held in the hand of a burn victim — you can make fun of the hand portion of the illustration on the mug all day long, but one thing's for sure: For fifteen bucks Jan's son gets a sweet-ass mug with a gun on it, and a saying to buttress his faith.

18

The Business of This

FIFTEEN DOLLARS FROM Jan wadded and rolled and stuck into the pocket and the second it happened, adrenal corticoids raced fifteen thousand ideas right through the head. That was the moment all this sprung into consideration, this little production line that preps and glazes and fires under state supervision, then packs the mugs into the little white boxes. After the fifteen dollars created the explosion—the idea of making more mugs, and more little wads of dollars—there was a search online. It's called The Norwalk Developmental Work Training Center, it turns out. There's a video to click on. Matthew had heard about this place from Tim, of all people, years ago. Tim had said there was a place where people with physical limitations and so-called disorders enroll in a work-training program and are supervised and authorized and certified; they do piecework assembly for your business. You drop stuff off, you pick it up assembled or gift-wrapped, or whatever. Tim didn't explain as objectively as the Web site does, of course. Over drinks one time, Tim said something like, "There's a huge factory full of retards up by where you live. People hire the place out for contract work. Just simple shit, though. When I worked at Solomon, we used them to stuff prospectus envelopes, but they eventually fucked a bunch up so we had to stop. They'd put keys and gum wrappers and shit like that in the envelopes — one had a nacho in it; just whatever the fuck catches their eye. They don't know; you can't get mad. But can you imagine that? You're a client, we mail you a prospectus on a new fund and there's a fucking nacho jammed in there?"

Anyway, Matthew went online, Matthew found the site, he clicked on the video, he got a stupid lump in his throat watching it, then he made a phone call and spoke with a guy named Jim, the executive director of the place, and the conversation went like this:

"So they're coffee mugs basically?"

"Basically, yeah," Matthew says.

"And you need some spot art, firing, then some packing. Okay, are we doing any fulfillment; any drop shipping to fulfill retail orders or anything?"

"I'm . . . Okay, there's one thing. I'm not sure if the stuff I need put on them — the art I've come up with that I need replicated on the mugs — is too controversial for your . . . special, you know . . . for the people that . . ."

"For the twenty-eight- to fifty-year-old grown adults who work in our program?"

"Never mind, I know, I don't think they're . . . you know, I just . . ."

"So, we've reviewed your project and I've assigned Chris as your team leader." Which is Jim's way of saying, *Let's move this along, shall we, you condescending idiot.*

Chris has Down syndrome or a mild palsy or maybe both. He can turn around a case of mugs in a few days, in time for Matthew to try and sell them over a weekend. Since he's a team leader, he decides how many staffers will help and everything. Today is maybe the third or fourth or seventh Friday that Matthew has made a pickup. It's hard to tell what time is doing these days; days grind by in near halt like winter sap, and weeks fly by fast. But there are moments like this, Chris shaking, twisting, smiling, and trying hard to stay straight in his chair and not show a thing; to play it cool when Matthew comes around, to keep it all in, but it doesn't work. Another batch of mugs, another Friday, another visit from Matthew — these are all things to twist and smile and make sounds about. And when his happiness peaks, you see it cross his mind to settle down, you see him admonish himself.

It's hard on any heart watching; seeing him get mad at his body in a flash; seeing him trying to hide excitement the way the whole stupid, average world has mastered hiding excitement when life is trying to make them glad to be living.

And when Matthew sees him try to reel it all in and tear

the heart off the sleeve, Matthew waits until the executive director of The Norwalk Developmental Work Training Center isn't looking, at which point Matthew catches Chris's eye and acts like he's humping a case of mugs as he puts them into the car's trunk. And the twisting and laughing and smiling are all back! Full bore! Full tilt! Who can hide it! Who would want to! Matthew is cracking up, too! For some completely predictable and wholly unseemly reason called the human condition, nobody really jokes with people like Chris, so acting like you're fornicating with a boxful of coffee cups — a chestnut to begin with — gets an even bigger laugh than one might expect while standing behind the car and loading another case in. Another case into the trunk — mugs, once blank, now fired and glazed and burned and brave. Maxims clear, beautiful illustrations blurry. Crude paintings of heads and phones, and hands holding guns, and tall girls that are Tatiana, all drawn by way of shaking hands, and heads that bob like those of jazz musicians feeling phantom time signatures and meter that we can't keep no matter how hard we listen, a curse on days, a ballet of this earthbound urgency.

There's a little picnic table on a concrete slab next to the place and Matthew sits with Chris while Chris has lunch. Matthew smokes, which is probably another in a series of the bad hunches like guns and jogging. Chris points at the cigarette, shakes his head, makes a *tsk-tsk-tsk* sound, and starts smiling. Matthew smiles bashfully back, shrugs his shoulders like he's busted, rolls his eyes like he knows Chris is right, and Chris starts laughing and claps his hands.

"Oh, no, I'm busted now, right?"

"No! Hey, don't!"

"No, I was just kidding. I'm not leaving, I was just saying you busted me for smoking, get it?"

"Yeah. But if, you know when people go? I miss them. It doesn't, but it doesn't, make me sad. Some people get a baby inside of them and then they're gone; it's boring. Boring baby, boring baby. I don't have a baby inside. I can't have a baby inside, since I'm a man."

Chris starts cracking up and he won't stop. It is pretty funny, actually, and Matthew is laughing, too, mostly because Chris points to his crotch a superlong time when he says it, which, again, is kind of one of those classic hits no matter how you play it. When he's had enough of it for a laugh, he gets back on track and talking.

"I keep working. I get haircuts with it. I get pizza with it. One day you can stop, one day you are dead again. But not now because we're lucky and sad, like wizards. There's other ones that didn't come with you; they couldn't find a belly to come out from. So you forget you knew them. Until you meet them alive. That's why people fall in love. Because from when they were dead together. But then they came to life and got lost unless they meet again."

"You're a smart guy, you know that? I'm not fucking being cute, you're smart and I mean it."

"I'm joking! We are not sad wizards!"

Fucker. How'd he do that?

"Mmmusic is. Good!" Chris says like he's glad to finally get it out in the open.

"Not all of it, Chris, I'm afraid I have to draw the line here. I'm tired of some of it. Like the sad kind. It gets boring."

"Music is litter. I have so much money, so I keep working."

"Why?" asks Matthew.

"To help you. Then you're gone. To help me, then I'm gone, too."

"I hope you and I don't go away for a long time. I get sad when people go away, too."

"If you get sad, just have fun. First have fun, THEN close your eyes, THEN die."

"Yeah, no duh, I already know that."

"You need a belly to get here, but you don't need a belly to die. So the mom goes away. She has fun, then she closes her eyes, too."

And then there's a little bit of silence while Matthew and Chris just sit in the afternoon sun, just two men thinking for a minute.

Matthew is thinking: *I love you.*

Then Chris quietly says, "Work, pizza, haircuts."

This conversation with Chris, it's the only talk lately that makes this much sense. And the heart and head are together for once, working in concert, agreeing with each other. It's one of those times when a man thinks to himself: *It's that same old thing all guys deal with, where you're in love with the thirty-six-year-old man with Down syndrome who makes coffee mugs, but for some reason it's always a woman you want.*

The lull stays there between them the way lulls will when any two men on earth sit at a table sizing up their own lots during lunch. Chris gets up, starts to walk back inside to work, thinking about something, almost not noticing Matthew, but then he stops and turns and waves good-bye, making a hilarious stupid-guy face and saying bye-bye-bye instead of bye-bye. The head says to make something sad and beautiful of times like this one, but it's too late for following the head, and maybe it's always been. Two hearts know it's a good laugh, this super hilarious, weird face Chris makes, this bye-bye-bye riff.

The woman at the craft class, the teacher or whatever, she couldn't handle the volume and pace, not even with a cut of the eventual profits that Matthew promised. One case of mugs to fire (not even to do the art on!) was too much apparently, unthinkable, evidently. So never mind talking to her once the UPS man was showing up at the doorstep with two cases. Fuck anyone who doesn't feel how fast life is ending; fuck anyone who hasn't got the heart of Chris and his helpers and friends. These people are excited and determined — they soldier right into coffee-mug production; and news flash: They know, they know, they know. They know they forget to tell someone about the burr in their sock that's wearing a bloody spot into their ankle. And they know they'll be lucky if you ever figure this out from the way they stop walking for a minute and start to cry at the sting of frustration that comes with knowing something simple is probably causing their pain. They know that you won't know why they suddenly decided to try and punch the sky instead of continuing to cry. Punch it. Punch the Goddamned heaven that spat down the genes and bad codes that brought these physical limitations; these cruel and permanent grifts and gyps that play out in the wombs of people never expecting them. Fuck average people; fuck everybody who can't be bothered to race death and beat its perverse pace to win any argument for sticking around another year or decade; fuck everyone who can't handle any number of mugs waiting to be turned into ones, fives, and tens rubber-banded.

So when the normal people look at you like you're crazy, there's one place to go, go to where the definition of normal means nothing — to the place where you can infer that one who is normal is sadly average. Go to The Norwalk Developmental Work Training Center where people with so-called behavioral and physical challenges will prepare 144 mugs; where they will shake and twist and smile when they're excited. It starts to feel like common decency when they do it, it starts to be a relief compared to so-called normal people; with normal people, you have to stand there second-guessing how they're feeling. After a month or two of coming around picking up mugs for selling, one starts to believe that everyone should shake and twist when they're excited — when so-called normal people are excited about something all they do is drink, or say something like, *New Time Media couldn't be more excited about the opportunity to be a part of Fashion Week.*

19
___

Pottery Fair: A Blind Mongrel Bitch Bent on Bloodlust and Degenerate Hunger

HERE'S THE THING about the pottery fair situation in the little gazeboed block of grass and walking paths centered downtown: It is a cruel and vicious little labyrinth of bureaucracy, greed, and craft. Matthew tried, you know. He tried to procure a space. But there were forms to fill out, there were EIN numbers to submit, there was money to be paid up front, there were only certain half-assed spaces available to newcomers like Matthew. If you've never done it before, they stick you next to the obese Christian who makes these super tiny, basically dollhouse-scale plates and jugs, and who won't stop yammering about faith and kingdoms and shit. Forms to fill out, lines to wait in, money to pay out of thin air; all the same things that made Matthew skip college and hurry his way to making low six in a high-rise.

He tries to lament the oppression of this system with the other pottery men and women, but for what's left of a sixties counterculture, they seemed quite content with fees and rules and an application process. Yes, these tamed social insurgents, virile and possessed decades ago, seem to be just fine with the shit crockery scene; mugs that don't even say anything! Little teakettles that make only one cup of tea! For $180! Matthew smiled politely when noting prices and thought: *What, did you make it from your fucking jawbone and mortar from Versailles?* He walked the grounds; he tried to figure out where he fit in with these artisans, as they were referred to mostly by themselves. He carried one of his mugs around, he tried to catch on to talking the talk of craft and glazing and firing.

"So, are you gas-firing those, or wood?" This from a stout and gray man that looked like folk singing had beaten him badly enough to saunter to his plan B or C or D.

"It's . . . I do UPS for these. From a Web site," Matthew said, and he said it cheerfully, in his good-neighbor voice, and it was still met with traces of snide derision.

"When you get serious about seizing the clay, you're gonna have to figure out what your kiln situation is."

"Oh. Okay, well . . ."

"See," the stout guy says, looking at the mug in Matthew's claw, "technically you're a graphic designer, not a ceramics artisan."

"Fucking, seriously? That's how you're going to come at this, that's how you're going to talk with me, your little fucking spoon holders or whatever they are put you in league with, what, da Vinci or somebody?"

This kind of elbow rubbing is the kind that seems to happen when one crushes some fat lines of decongestant to get going, to get in the mood for reaching out and being a little less isolated. And Matthew is as surprised as anyone that the conversation goes like this, given that a fair amount of morning beer was taken on to balance the speedy kick; one would think the combo would land one in the zone a little more dependably. Walking away to try again, Matthew thinks: *Maybe it's the speed and beer, and maybe it's the world that has a problem.* But in the spirit of trying to make this work, Matthew walks down to the end of the pottery fair, to the Siberia where they put new exhibitors, just to see what he's missing by not coughing up a ransom for rent, plus a deposit, plus a one-time administrative fee.

"Hey, how's it going, nice work." Matthew reaches out with the standard craft-culture greeting to a very large man spilling over a pair of paint-stained trousers, his hair having run back to the halfway point on the skull, presumably corresponding to the point on the front of the skull where Matthew sees a slobbered-up baby-pink bud of a mouth.

"It's not my work, actually."

"Oh, well, tell whoever did it, I guess. Tell them I like it."

"I will."

A long pause grows between them, time that Matthew uses to consider suicide as a solution to all of it.

And then the giant man-baby continues. "I'll tell him when I talk to him tonight. I talk to him every morning and every night."

"Okay. Well, tell him someone likes this stuff. I guess."

"I'll tell him you like all of his work."

But suicide is messy, ultimately. And sad in that it's so hostile and cruel to the body, which is a nice body and had nothing to do with this morning going like this.

"Fair enough. Even though I haven't seen all of it. I've seen these, the miniature, what are these, you would call them jugs, maybe?"

"You've seen everything he's created. Look around . . . the sky, the trees, the grass, everyone you've met, you yourself, even me, even my work that you're appreciating. Do you want to tell him yourself?"

If not suicide, then maybe compulsive travel. Just fucking going places, like the lady who wrote the book about eating and sleeping and praying, maybe. But it's time to reply, time to talk again, each lip so leaden now, and so much work to make more than a slit with. And what do you say to this, because you can't break people's spirit. American spirit is all these people have, and you can't roll it up and beat them with it, even though abuse is arguably precisely the thing that would make them interesting eventually. There must be a way out of this. Matthew says the only thing left in him for this.

And with that, walks away with a tepid wave good-bye, thinking: *That is fast becoming my favorite prayer.*

"Oh . . . fuck, I don't know, ya know?"

So what? So what to all of this; so what that Matthew is a man who orders his mugs premade in boxes of a dozen; where is the crime in that? *Where,* thinks Matthew, *is the crime in not wanting to sit in the mountains of Upstate New York staying up all night to stoke a wood fire in the barely maternal belly of a kiln while listening to a formerly fecund and virile folk singer coo about serenity through a little set of portable speakers?* Matthew tried to be a part of the pottery fair, but the pottery fair is a mongrel bitch bent on degenerate hunger and nourished by fistfuls of a bloody mulch of purism and exclusion. Well, the pottery fair is about to be tamed.

And another thing, it's not lost on Matthew that not one of his classmates from the community center craft class has staked claim here. Look around and not one Jan, Ruthie, Suzanne, Lori, or Lynn. There's the only moral and social compass one need follow in navigating this pottery fair; the real deals on the scene aren't even showing up here. The thing is fueled, instead, by a coed knot of Nathans, Melissas, Skylers, and Rebeccas. For every ten resigned gray ponytails, there's one fuckable, loveable thing just barely having talked herself into spending her nights with ovens and glaze-clogged sinks to save her heart from another dead-end man doing the kind of math that tells his heart to run if prospective kids would be ten when she's passing forty fast. Matthew tries with a couple of them, but no stare gives chase. Matthew, chipped and cracked goods to them, really — long legs, eyes at half-mast, thin and too hungry for something, hair approaching longish, disheveled, a speedy tense jaw on a long face braced with the cologne of failure and optimism — just another mouth and moan, daring and alone.

Evidently, the cardinal sin of the pottery fair culture here in Westport is pulling your car/office up to the edge of the curb bordering the official green, grassy, ordained, and sanctioned park and treating this parking arrangement as your pottery fair space. Yep, selling the shit right out of the car trunk, with a nicely tightened 11:00 AM buzz, to anyone with a twenty looking for five bucks change and a mug that says, *God will help you procure secondhand firearms* when you're in a fucking bind, folks. And over the course of the day, guess how many people will come up to get serious about finally drinking from a coffee mug that actually means something? Well, not that many of them, really, but at least enough to start adding some cash to the situation under the car seat.

That's where the last third of the severance package is, taken from the bank where it felt like it could be taken at any moment by any number of phantom agencies seeking to force Matthew to make financial amends for any number of missteps over the years. So there may not be a lot of cash coming in from the mugs, but there's enough to be adding to the tight and filthy little rolls of severance cash rubber-banded and jammed under the seat like a gun or porno; these days, that's where the money goes. The days race by in between the usual indiscretions and derelictions, and as these days are wont to do, and the brain races right along, killing the downtime with spasms of basic math: fifteen, thirty, sometimes even forty-five or sixty, godly and full of possibilities these little torpedoes of lucre, stuffed into a dirty little heaven, under the driver's seat, next to spent and bent Sudafed foils, Heineken empties, and the gun; just imagine it; it's probably possible to make more; it might even be possible to somehow make forty-five times forty-five. Maybe get some press somehow, maybe rush at the president if he's in New York, push past the security detail of secret service and CIA and thrust a gift mug at his chest, the papers all pick it up, everyone wants a mug. Finally, life feels a little bit like options, and a little bit like it's actually happening.

But there are other matters. The spot on the film — are you ready for this shit? — is an eleven-millimeter kidney stone. No small stone, a giant by kidney stone standards, has to come out; the body won't do the job on something that big. Still . . . hardly a life sentence; hardly worth pissing all over your office because you think your life is certainly ending sooner than you had anticipated, hardly death. However, having a Republican jam an eighth-inch-wide scope into your urethra while he tells you a story about his dead grandmother, rest her soul — this may as well be one's death. It is, maybe, what the French call "the small death." And there's the matter of Tatiana and where is she now? How can the heart do these things and then just stop working, and why are people so custom-made to disappear one way or the other, time and distance, or faulty jet engines, sticking them in the ground too soon?

Matthew kills his days trying to sell a few mugs while sitting in the car, reading the book about eating and praying and loving. At first selling was easy. It was a matter of parking on the border of the pottery fair, crafting a perfect over-the-counter jazzed blaze on the brain that made the speakers in the door sound like canyons of truth; that made customers feel like beautiful discoveries, each and every individual. But then the pottery cops crack down. This is success in America; start making a couple of bucks, and everybody comes sniffing around for a little look-the-other-way dough. So then it becomes a matter of principle, and Matthew will do anything but pay for a space. He parks at a lot just down the street and trolls the weekend fairgoers, shows them the mug he's carrying, looking around nervously, explaining he can sell them some if they'd like to follow him back to his car, or he can bring some back if they know how many they'd like. But one would be surprised by the wariness of pottery fans; it takes a sturdy pottery fan to follow a man like Matthew just a few short blocks away to a car where a deal can be done; all very on the up and up, these people, so it's pretty tough going.

It takes only a week or two to find other corners and lots to clock; he should've thought of it ages ago. The community center parking lot where people take the free classes, that's a go, especially on weekends. And then one starts considering the effectiveness of hopping around on the scene — one does a rush over on the far border of the pottery fair until hemmed and hawed, bitched and barked, and shooed off. One moves it to a parking lot across town and gets slammed there for a bit, trading these things for small bills in fits and starts; long on downtime and then inexplicable speed and urgency of moving a mug or two, usually pity sales where folks need to feel like they're supporting someone doing their thing. It bears mentioning that the one about God helping you get a gun has found an unlikely but potentially broad and lucrative audience; conservative people who seem to embrace the sentiment as some sort of right-leaning maxim to bear arms in America. There were a few of them over the last couple of weekends. They don't seem to understand that it's a mug about the moment fortune smiles and allows you to procure a gun because you have a hunch that petty crime or suicide may be the next logical step in how things are going to progress.

They smile kindly and buy the mug like Americans standing up for something, but this is a mug that is all about God finally throwing you a bone by letting you sell Ecstasy to pay for a weapon from a cool Mexican guy or South American or whatever, and then God lets you get an unbelievable piece of ass in the process. Being embraced by a mainstream audience is at once disheartening and stirring, finding this polite conservative following bodes well for eating, but it feels fraudulent to let them drink so proudly from a coffee cup painted with memories of a drunk, unemployed Democrat being grateful for having sex on psychotropic vegetables.

And they always act like the art is a mistake — a mistake! Like, Oh it's blurry, I think something happened to the drawing on this one, oh do you have another one maybe since something is wrong with this one? That's the fucking art part of it, you guys! And they're like children; once you explain that's the way it is because it's kind of cool, they pause a minute, look at the art again, and suddenly it is art — and they're fine with it. Anyway, move the hustle often, then on to yet another location, and so forth. One actually ends up doing more business than just catering to the pottery fair spillover. You can double your take some days if you move enough. It's not a lot but it will keep you in cigarettes and those little foil packs of Sudafed.

So far the numbers are small, but the big hits are, yes, the one about God helping you buy a gun, but also a new one with a man urinating in his own office. This mug says nothing, just has a drawing of a stick figure peeing next to a desk while some other stick figures at desks point, proving that art still sells. There's another one that has sold three copies, so not a hit, but certainly doing decent sales; the one with a leggy blotch of a woman confidently sprawling on a smear of a couch that says, *Selling hallucinogens to a rich girl feels as innocent as fairy tales.* The trick now is probably to combine the mainstream attraction to God with the excitement of sex and drugs. It might be as simple as *God loves sex and drugs.* This is true. So Matthew starts typing it out.

There are matters to deal with, the matter of crafty cops to outfox, but mostly, at the moment, there is the matter that

Westport is like four walls closing in; even the parking lots of Westport are places to feel tracked and watched. And whatever brief comforts were once found in this house, it has become a tomb of good intentions quickly staled; a hallowed haunt that feels like breaking and entering. This town is just parks and parking lots dogged by phantom pottery cops; this house, a field of decent carpet and expensive tile, roamed by a ghostly housemate with a fouled heart. But there is cash under the driver's seat! There are cups turned into cigarettes and gasoline, and under the driver's seat, those little wads plus the rolls of severance cash scream that it's time to start living like the woman in the book about eating and praying; that it's time to get out and start traveling this world never seen.

20

Two Counties, Separated by a Common Gene

WHEN MATTHEW TURNS OFF the steep, narrow dirt road, the cabin owner is standing on the porch, saying good-bye to the cleaning lady. Matthew pulls into the gravel driveway, gives the car a bit too much push, and the tires make a stony racket tearing up the grade and scratching a wake of gravel and dust to the flat landing patch at the top. Seeing that the cleaning lady's good-bye is under way, seeing no need to rush a hello and handshake, he is now in the driveway, on his knees. The midsection twisted, the head askew, the shoulder anchored down and trying to get the most reach out of the arm, now crammed up under the driver's seat. The way this sort of thing usually takes place is that there are checks exchanged weeks in advance—that's what the vacation rental Web site prefers, but plans were made in haste, the mission was launched last night, late. And so it was agreed that payment could happen on arrival, there was probably the presumption that this would also mean a check changing hands, but that isn't the way things are rolling these days, is it?

There's not much in the way of a balance in the checking account and there's simply no way for a man to appear employed when toting all the tight bundles and bindles of jacked and stowed cash. And if the coffee-mug business ever blows up enough to pay real and delinquent bills, there will be the matter of figuring how to choke the tight steel, prudish slit of an ATM with a mouthful of mug cash, and then hoping that the green makes it past human hands and posts to the account is plain unnerving. But for now it's not a problem; for now the bills don't get paid and the bank is in the car; the whole system is very self-contained. If the crafty hobby ever turns into bestselling wares, the obvious solution will be to head into Manhattan for deposits every so often; into the city where tellers probably see this kind of binge cash banking routinely from serial blood hawkers, low-stakes deviant pornographers, and misdemeanor tramps. It will be a hassle, putting the grift on the books, but it will be better than these little rolls and wads jackknifing the adjustment mechanisms under the seat like this, caught up in everything.

If the arm can just fish this wayward roll from behind a jam of empties and a dirty magazine, some deli napkins and a wrapper from a Reese's, an empty water bottle with a tiny nicotine-stained swamp of butts settled into it, then, well, won't the cabin owner be happy to have solid payment in cash in these times of recession and instability? The mountains up here are so quiet they scream, the only sound at the moment is Matthew grunting, determined to reach up under the seat to get the roll of cash he needs. He yanks the glossy, torn, and wrecked pornography free and sets it out absentmindedly behind him on the gravel without looking; same with the candy wrappers, and the smokes that are empty.

The owner may be happy to get some cash, if it's coming, but he's currently just staring from the porch at the wrappers and torn pages of glossy porn shifting a bit in the breeze like leaves; at the dead cigarette packages — it's like a hurricane picked up a hard-luck convenience store and slammed it down right here in his driveway. Matthew is grunting and yanking and finally: The roll of cash comes free — just a little more than he needs to pay for a two-night stay in a two-story cabin here in the beautiful Catskill Mountains of New York. Call it rehearsal for travel — Big Indian, New York, is a far cry from Italy and taking lovers for spiritually fit boning like that woman in the book did, but it's good practice. One can't just go from one's car and out into the world so large without a dry run or two. Better to be working out bugs like all this shit jamming the cash flow here than in the parking lot of La-Guardia or JFK. A half-spent prescription bottle of Vicodin hits the gravel and Matthew immediately reaches back and down without looking and snatches it right back up with urgency. Yes, cabin owner, this is your distinguished guest, the man on his knees under the American flag waving over your American white-gravel driveway, surrounded by the filthy litter of broken-down days; the one you're about to let pace and weep and masturbate all over the beautiful cabin where your beautiful American family spent its summers and holidays.

Inside, the place is amazing, a time capsule, stained pine plaques with pictures of Indian chiefs varnished onto them and prayers to the great spirit wood-burned into them, a big fat radio on the desk — from an age when radios had FM, AM, and weather-frequency bands; a thick, silver telescoping antenna stretching to the corner up by the window, stretching and aching for a signal. There's a shotgun in a rack on the wall, the heads of deer who haven't had to worry about life's undignified folly for maybe forty or fifty years. There's a huge fireplace, big, split tree trunks and logs making a staircase up to bedrooms, there are bear pot holders, bear kitchen towels. On shelves, there are small framed snapshots of bears being cute and almost human — standing on hindquarters to outfox the lid on a garbage can, probably only after figuring there was no chance of snatching a kid or an elder from the porch and dragging them to the tree line to crack a rib cage open for the sweet marrow.

Cash is handed over, agreements are signed and initialed — something about not smoking, something about trash and bears — and at last the owner departs and Matthew is free to feel that the heart is almost instantly heavy here. Where is Tatiana? How can one go about missing so deeply someone they don't even know, really? To that point, who is Tatiana? What year was it that we became a nation of lonely people able to do such intimate and gorgeous and obscene things and then disappear completely? Never mind, out to the BMW, the Bavarian Moan Wagon, get the groceries in, because in a couple of hours the sun will be down and it will be time to sneak up on the barbecue when it isn't looking and figure out how to light the Goddamn thing.

A steak is cut from its shrink-wrapped Styrofoam grave, and rushed out onto the grill, with the urgency of a waffle house slammed and trying to get out of the weeds. That is the mountain feeling summed up, really; hurrying among a quiet hush that feels like death, and the knowledge that things both big and small can kill you here; gigantic teeth and claws; little fangs and hemotoxins; tiny stings you didn't know you were allergic to. A place where one always wonders a bit: *lying down to sleep? Or simply waiting to be quietly dispatched by the black widow or brown recluse?* After cooking fast under the primal urge of not wanting to share a kill, one eats like a convict, standing in front of a fireplace with no fire in it, and that's when the paranoia kicks in.

What exactly can bears do? Can bears shoulder open a door and pluck Matthew from the cabin to make ground chuck of him? Or do they sit out there on the mountain silent until they decide they'd like to come in and have a nice tall meal? Do they sit in the dark, in pairs maybe, just out of reach of the porch light, waiting for Matthew to step out for a smoke so they can then advance, ready to violently mount and mate him up against a damp, rotted stump full of slugs and grubs? There are the rumors of bears smelling women who are menstruating; blood! In the urine! Remember? From this kidney stone tearing its way around up there! Matthew puts his plate down, walks very quickly and efficiently to the desk with the radio on it, starts rifling through the binder of guest resources next to it, tearing through it fast, right past brochures of thin-soup tourist attractions and historical pamphlets, right past the menus of restaurants in the town thirty minutes from here, a fast, desperate leafing, slapping, pawing, until the big drawing of a black bear stares him down on top of an informational card from the State Department of Fish and Game called "You Should Know About Black Bears." And the head thinks this: *Fuck yes, I should know, thank you very much!*

There's not a lot of good news in the pamphlet, that's the first thing one takes note of. They can outfox mechanisms and get into things, it turns out, but the snapshot on the bookshelf already proved that. They're smart, it says, but apparently not smart enough to know they shouldn't rip a human being from ass to eyes then open him up and scoop out the warm tripe in dumb, bloody frolic. But there is even worse news about them: They can smell like a motherfucker. Admittedly, not exactly the way the brochure words it, but the bear's reliance on olfactory glands is supposed to be amazing, paramount in their foraging. There are tips, how to play dead and let the virile beasts toss you about like a rag doll in a filthy orgy of appetite and good old-fashioned curiosity; very specific procedures for how to throw away and secure your trash properly. Matthew bolts over to what is left of his steak, tears a few last panicked bites of it, then wraps what's left in plastic wrap, in foil, in a paper bag, then a plastic bag, and into the freezer it goes. Utensils cleaned with dish soap, grill burned clean and wiped down, the wrapper from the steak — this bloody plastic cling, it has to get sealed and wrapped and frozen, too.

Matthew rushes to finish this kitchen trash, rushes to brush his teeth, because they can smell meat on your breath! So one might step outside exhaling a warm waft of bloody mouth and one of these bears could decide it's a little bent out of shape that you ate and he didn't; could reach inside your face to grab the smell, tear your identity off like it was zippered on to your skull, one must suppose! The mouth and breath situation are all locked down, everything's brush, rinse, spit, brush, rinse, spit again, spit until Tatiana's voice is in the head, on a loop, a whisper with a lilt; the one phrase burnished on the brain from that chance smashing into each other; maybe the most exciting thing a woman has ever said to Matthew in bed in his earthly years so far spent: "Spit." The thought of it in his head a thousand times, the idea of it blooms and dies and does it over again, but backward from death to bloom, the brain's perverse and innocent little stop-motion animation called longing.

So now what? Now go into the living room and relax under huge, pitched log ceilings and paintings of Indian chiefs, have some sort of epiphany, which is evidently why the mountains exist. A twenty-minute, absolutely epiphany-free pause spent staring at a fireplace made of stones, wondering exactly when and how death by bears would come, is interrupted by a sudden little beep and chime of confirmation that there is suddenly cell phone service where there was none earlier. Maybe the night skies do something to usher in waves or bars or signals to anyone out here and hopeless. Maybe it was always nighttime when the family that owns this place gathered in here and stretched that radio's antenna heavenward into the corner, reaching out to grab stations that would fade by sunrise. The phone rings — Tim. Mobile — and the ring of it makes Matthew jump up into some kind of half-assed fighting position. He answers on the first ring, as the desperate often will. "Hello."

"Reporting in, Chief."

"Tell me how you handle bears."

"I had one around the rig last week. I handled it. I did what you're supposed to do, I think."

"The play-dead thing?"

"Fuck that. I played dead for three months and when I got up my head was shaved, I was bankrupt, evicted, and the SEC was witch-hunting me; not a huge fan of playing dead, Chief."

"What did you do, then?"

"It was one of the last times I had to use the drugs. It was a life-and-death situation as far as I could tell, so I don't need a high-road speech on using the drugs for a minute again."

"Just tell me. I could be in a situation with them at any moment. I've rented out a cabin. I'm alone up here."

"It's not like that, they aren't looking to get you like everyone thinks."

"Well, one came looking for you apparently. What happened?"

"Fucking weekender in a little Four Winds Majestic had the space next to me and started cooking up bacon on a grill welded to the bumper of the thing, then he poured the grease on the ground, and later that night, I was sitting in here and, sure enough, a bear came around. So I had to slam up a couple of lines of that shit, the stuff she left me hooked with, you know . . . just waited for it to hit, and when the big rush came, I grew a pair, unclamped the tabletop here, and flew out the door screaming and swinging it around."

"The tabletop comes off?"

"Yeah, it can slide down to become a bed. But you can take it off though, if you need, like, legroom in the lounge area. For watching movies or whatever. This thing's nice, it's a good setup, and it has a little area for . . ."

"I thought you were out of drugs, or done with drugs; all of that talk about reporting in with someone, staying off everything, sobriety in God's country and all that."

"Well, I saved a little, obviously. Just basically in case something like this happened."

"Did the table thing work on it?"

"Fuck yes, it worked; he didn't want any of what I was

selling, trust me. Prison rules, Chief — you have to come at them unhinged, and when they see you're fucking crazier than they are, they walk away. Back into the woods. They're like: 'I don't know what the fuck is wrong with that creature, but I want nothing to do with it.' "

"You got really lucky, Tim. You did all the wrong things," Matthew says, while retracing the What to Do If . . . bullet points of the brochure from the binder.

"Well, it wasn't all good. There was some bad luck, too. The guy from the space next to me comes out of his rig when he hears me on the warpath; comes running up behind me and I spin around, real basic primal instinct, and fucking clock him with my dinner table, basically. Just, *THWACK* — four-foot slab of pine and Formica to the back of his head, courtesy of yours truly in space two-twenty-seven."

"What's with this word *rig*? Everything's a rig now?"

"Not everything, just the RV, that's what we call them in the campgrounds. But I can't stay in most of the campgrounds now in Yellowstone, that's what I'm saying. I'm banned from Canyon Falls, obviously, where it happened. I'm banned from a bunch of them. Well, I'm banned from all of them, technically, but I know a few that are too big for them to ever notice me in if I just stay a couple days and move."

"You're banned because of hitting that guy, or, you know, your . . . other stuff?"

"Fuck you, other stuff. Dude: I am down on the ground, in

case you haven't noticed. In case you haven't noticed, I'm up against the ropes, you know? Have a little decency."

"No, I didn't mean other things, like drug things . . . I literally, just, I don't know; I thought, like, maybe they ask people to take a break from the campgrounds if they had a close call with a bear or something. Like maybe the bear recognizes the truck or the scent or something."

"Yes, banned because of hitting the guy. Which only happened because he literally fucking came up on my blind spot when I was already in a defensive state with large game, Matthew; with fucking wildlife that would have me if I didn't come out swinging something."

"Well, in a state from fighting off big game, and also from really clean cocaine, though."

"Okay, here comes the high-road scared-straight shit. Go ahead and judge me, and keep pushing me away when I'm trying to help you. And when you get eaten like wet trash, I'll explain that I tried my best to teach you how to live around wildlife and be safe, but you pushed me away with judgmental bullshit."

"Tim, I'm just trying to do whatever it is you want me to do. You said you needed someone to check in with, and be accountable to while you're trying to get shit straight; your words."

"Fair enough, fine, okay, well I've checked in with you, and I thank you for that." A huff and a dead connection.

Sleep, which comes first by lying on top of a bed built for

a boy, the bed upstairs, because bears can't climb stairs, is hard-won but amniotic in its calm. The boy-sized bed means Matthew's arms and legs and head hang over, but wadded up in a prenatal curled hunch and policed by gravity, a man will fit on here. And the first half hour or so it's just about lying there and wondering what you heard. Everything out there sounds like a bear or coyote tearing someone limbless and being super quiet about it, but is probably just gentle breezes ruffling leaves, which is something one is supposed to be enjoying and cooing over. And what of the tiny things waiting to descend on you from the corners and gutters and screens? Or the reptiles delighted to flick tongues at new, warm blood in prostrate repose, delighted to be able to warm and regulate their own blood then find purchase on a vein so that their warm carbon-based boarder can be converted into a meal? After the paranoia passes, sleep comes like something that should require a prescription; there is something about the air or the stars or the body being convinced it will be devoured or poisoned while prone, something about it brings a sleep like honeyed Novocain.

Morning is black coffee and trying to remember why someone comes to the mountains. There is a less-honorable reason than convenience for coming here instead of going and praying in Italy like the woman in the book did. Everybody at New Time Media used to talk about how David Bowie had a place somewhere up here. And you get to thinking that all it takes is a drive up the highway a couple of hours, and that there must be such limited mountainous terrain in New York that any vacation rental here would mean being neighbors with David Bowie for the week. So when one is a little confused about how to be modern in areas of the heart, when one finds themselves untethered and floating away from the mother ship of functional marriage and employment, maybe one gravitates to the only place they've heard David Bowie might live for months at a time. Sitting here now, drinking black coffee from a cruel electric stove and metal pan defiled by the parade of a thousand summers' strangers, it's easy for one to feel a little foolish.

One afternoon while pacing in front of the Indian prayer plaque, trying to ignore a neighbor whining a small engine at peak, Matthew whispers to himself: "Christ. Bowie and that fucking leaf blower he got for his birthday . . ."

One morning when Matthew tries once again to meditate in front of a fireplace that has still not seen a fire by his hand, a gasoline rev down the road gets: "Bowie and his Goddamned log splitter blaring away out there again . . ."

And then on another aimless afternoon, while Matthew was busy giving up on spirituality and spirit in favor of trying to read a copy of the airport novelette another vacationer had left, a motorcycle tearing its way up the small trail to the other cabins gets an offhanded: "Fucking Bowie. Treating this place like a motocross track with that Goddamn dirt bike of his."

But the motorcycle turns a hard right, comes right up the

secondary trail and into Matthew's white-gravel drive. And the head has caught on to the game, silently issuing a stern *Jesus, Bowie. Call first.*

Heading off a knock at the door, Matthew walks out onto the small concrete porch from where he was once the one being watched and judged, and stands there sizing up the man taking off a helmet. The man who spills over the medium-sized motorcycle's seat and frame is far from Bowie. North of fifty certainly, but a hard north, a tough piece of road to get there. A body fueled by nachos, by Fridays, by reduced-calorie beer consumed in such volume as to render the calorie reduction moot. A crew cut, they love these, men of a certain blocky frame and fashion and head. A sweatshirt and shorts, both making certain you understand that Steve attended a prestigious-for-the-left-coast university. The font that boasted this choice he made to continue his education thirty-plus years ago is just as blocky and stout and collegiate. It's a font that's supposed to bring to mind hallowed corridors of passionate endeavoring in the name of culture and knowledge; a font meant to call to mind Ivy League schools on the eastern seaboard. In fairness, it's a font that demands a little respect when it's spelling out the name of a university, but the baggy and prefaded indigo-colored XL sweatshirt undermines this solicitation of respect. And whatever respect the shirt has managed to hang on to has been thrown under the bus by the shorts also pasted with the name of the learning institution.

But you never know. Some of the smartest people decided

not to drop out; not as rare as you think, the schooled winding up interesting raconteurs of life's rich pageant; this college stuff works on some. So, let Steve open his mouth, open
your mind a little, be open to meeting new people, that's the
sporting attitude required of even temporary neighbors. This
is the moment; Matthew knows it, this is the moment when
he learns just how wrong he was in his shallow and base as-
sumptions that reek of class insecurity. This is the moment,
Matthew is certain now, where this dirt bike interloper in
lazy logo-covered clothing soars into the conversation, el-
evates small talk with ease and admirable aplomb!

"Holy shit, this thing's fast! Did you see me out there, hau-
lin' ass up that trail?"

After the opening salvo, the man walks right up across the
porch. And Matthew thinks about how Buddha said: *A man
walks across the room and he comes back different.* The still-
unnamed neighbor advances, meaty hand outstretched and
claiming the name Steve, as if it were up for grabs just seconds before that. Matthew grabs the hand in reach and says
hello, forgetting to say his own name, probably forgetting his
own name altogether in the haze of disappointment.

"Been meaning to come over and say hi all week, but I've
been fucking around with firewood and getting this thing
running again for when my son comes up."

"Oh, okay, well. That's all right, stranger," this comes from
Matthew's mouth in surprise even to Matthew.

Stranger? But that's how people talk in the mountains,
right?

"I don't know who you've met, but you've got great neighbors here on both sides."

"Who is it? Who's the neighbor?" Matthew asks with the urgency of a man still half hoping he's landed next door to a holed-up rural Bowie.

"Well, you've got Hank just down the trail on the left; that next big cabin you can probably see the roof of when you're on your back deck."

"Oh. Okay."

"And if you drop in around five or six, we've usually got a good fire going out back there and the cocktails are flowing," he says this with a flourish of the hand that's a cross between a drink being raised to his lips and a mimed dove or pigeon fluttering its way into his mouth for some reason, or a trumpet that has a thumb for a mouthpiece and four human fingers waving about frantically. So far, judging from this small-talk exchange, Steve's two main passions seem to be dirt bike motorcycles, a size or two smaller than his frame requires, and booze. Which, oddly, make him a much more inviting social prospect than the college souvenirs he dresses himself in would lead you to believe.

"Oh, okay, maybe I'll come over and say hi. It's nice . . . you know, having a drink with friends, getting out of my head . . . I usually drink alone; in my car or whatever."

Woopsie, bad form, indeed. But Steve plows through, not leaving any time for the conversational D Minor 7th note to hang in the air and create suspicion or sadness. Viva Steve, then!

"We had the big bear over there last night; you seen that big male around your back deck yet?"

"No, what?"

"Yeah, he's been coming around. Big male."

"I've been really good about trash and stuff."

"Hank throws sweet corn all over the back for the deer, so we'll sit out there making margaritas and throwing corn all over the hill, and last night that big fucker comes down and, of course, I'm a little buzzed, so I start goofing around with him, trying to get him to come down to the deck and stuff, we were laughing our asses off."

Holy Christ! Matthew is disposing of dinner trash like it's medical waste and biohazard and all the while there's a neighbor whose idea of happy hour is chumming up savage mammals! And now they've got a taste for corn! So now, thanks to Hank, no matter how careful one is with dinner trash, all it would take is making some popcorn or stepping outside for a cigarette after some tortilla chips and *wham!*

"Oh, okay, well . . ."

"I got him to come right down from the back hill there. I tried to get him to stand up on his hind legs, but he just stood there staring at us!" And with this, Steve's laughter explodes like a hearty cough and takes an eternity of minutes to fade off.

"Yeah, okay, he was probably . . . yeah . . . ," Matthew tries to say.

Jesus, can you imagine? This bear staring down at Steve standing there with his arms stretched heavenward, refusing to put down his margarita for the sake of the charade, probably pumping a boyish growl through the plump frame, hearing the basso as tenor in his heart. The bear must've been thinking: *The prey is volunteering himself, he is presumably slow in stride, being so thick in the middle and all wrapped in ill-fitting, aged college-bookstore souvenir sweatpants. What's the fucking catch? Where's the trap? Fuck it, I'm walking back up into the tree line, I didn't get this big by falling for shit like this.*

"You here all week?"

"I rented it for a couple nights, so, but maybe, you know, the owner said it's not booked till the fifteenth, so I can just leave money if I want to stay the weekend, too."

"Burning some sick days, huh?"

"Uh, well, more or less. They're kind of all sick days now, Steve."

"I hear that, brother. I've been on disability, so I moved up here in, what, ninety-nine. I still do consulting, but I'm up here full-time. I don't know, you know, you spend the first half of your life trying to live up to something, trying to prove everything to everybody and yourself, and then you realize every single person you were living your life for is gonna be gone someday, just like you're gonna be gone someday, and that's when things get interesting."

The head cheers: If only everything Steve just said could be typed up fast by Matthew and sent off to himself on the small email thing; if only everything Steve just said could fit on a mug! The heart reels: If Steve had breasts — well, he does — but the point is, if he were an attractive woman, Matthew would be face-to-face with the woman he's been waiting to hear something like this from for a lifetime.

"I agree! Okay, yeah! Yes! This . . . finally . . . somebody, yeah, when we die there's . . ."

Matthew's stammering fanfare and poor paraphrasing leaves Steve staring and confused, and he's looking at Matthew probably exactly the same way the bear was looking at him last night.

21
—

Station to Station

N IGHT FALLS AS IT DOES up here, at the pace of the bankruptcy in that book by Hemingway, first gradually and then very suddenly. The sky is black and smacked with more stars than one thinks there are, and you can almost feel the signals coming through like ghosts spotting a crack in the door. Over on the desk of another era, the old radio's thick telescoping antenna seems to silently bristle and stretch an extra inch into the corner of the cabin in hopes of picking up something; the dusty little nineteen eighties Sony television aches to let a night of phantom stations from Tokyo and Taipei come rushing through. At night in these mountains, it's hard not to feel like a receiver — hard not to long for whispering or typing the heart's every secret to satellites and servers. The sky has opened, the signals have strengthened, and Matthew's phone chimes to indicate that a message has come in; chimes to indicate that the giant night sky has allowed it to awaken from another daylong silence.

Matthew walks over and grabs the phone from its lifeline, from its charger cable anchored into yesteryear's wall socket. A text. From Tatiana! And the heart thinks: *Under these skies, something beautiful and strange is able to happen!* And the head rolls the kind of weary eyes that come from having too much experience, screaming: *There is nothing good that can come from this. I can list twenty reasons in a flash why you should not get near someone.* And Tatiana's message falls somewhere dead center between the two sentiments offered up by the guts and ticking gears of Matthew's biological container:

> hope it's ok that I got yr # from Hernan. still in LA. known you a nite, missed you for weeks on end. Sound a tad desperate, desn't it? :)

With the abbreviations, arrhythmia, and misspellings of the way people are communicating, it's a wonder some days that anyone on earth is still falling in love; hard to believe anyone is still taken aback by somebody. How, in this century, does one maintain the memory of a dashing and dangerous night of magic unexplained? Suddenly in the head, the graceful and gorgeous woman from an evening hurled down from heaven without explanation is reduced by tiny keyboards to a bumpkin; standing in Los Angeles, wearing a barrel and suspenders, chewing a sprig of dried grass, and bleating through tobacco-browned lips: *Sound a tad desperate, desn't it?* Matthew says a prayer to God or The Great Spirit.

In front to the plaque of the Indian or Native American, Matthew asks the sky that life stay fast like this, and that his heart learn to come up to speed with it. In the next breath he's asking anyone or anything up there bored enough to be listening that it all goes back to the way it was for him. There are moments in days like these, they come rushing in when one least expects it and they remind a person, in what one thought was one's strongest hour, that it wasn't always like this. The thoughts cry out like a kid in silent tantrum, a sudden reminder that there were years and years of order; of living right, of living like they say one should at this age. Sure the marriage thing had become a ghost, but it was a ghost here on earth somewhere at every moment, one could take comfort that it wasn't someone gone to heaven. Sure the job was probably sitting there just waiting to feel the crush of these times; waiting to make yesterday's news of deadwood like Matthew; of jobs and offices and salaries that made sense only years ago when things were fat—so who cares that Matthew beat these times to the punch by urinating all over his office?

The point is, for a decade and a year there was work until six, there was a commute until north of seven. And for years there were dinners to cook up and make the house smell like chicken and spices and smell like a home that had people in it instead of a house making boarders out of the hearts of lost kids. There was an annual ski trip, there was watching romantic comedies on the couch with pillows clutched to chests for comfort in making heads or tails of the feelings from it, there were photo albums of the new house and vacations, and even the nights spent on the living room floor making them. There was staying home together on New Year's Eve because it felt better than being out there in the fray of mania of love being thrown around like party favors or cheap sentiment. There was the silly, dumb old-fashioned thrill of a fun thing for dessert that one of the two had brought home. There were simple little things like deciding together to splurge on a pay-per-view movie and of sitting on the couch for it, having showered early and gotten into clothes that were comfortable and dumb, clothes that neither of you would ever be seen in; sitting there showered and pj'd with a special dessert treat and feeling like one was circling back and getting some of the fun of being a kid again; of being a kid for the first time, really. There were simple little things like two feet touching in bed after a long day in the city working; the top of one pressing into the arch of the other, and it always felt like there must be no better feeling on earth. There was simple, sweet excitement about deciding Friday night to sleep late together on Saturday morning and then do something good for breakfast.

It wasn't always parking lot longing and better living through chemicals; it wasn't always guns and unscheduled sex that came on like a summer storm that nobody predicted. Then again, there's something just fine with days like that, too. But they leave one reeling, don't they, these days, they're nothing that can be sustained, or are they? To wonder what the answer is, and live one's life as if only half alive, is torture. How many years can one spend sitting still waiting for the world outside to come wandering in? At a certain point it becomes important to seek it out, to go wherever one might find the truth — it seems like the woman in the book about eating and praying and loving knew this. But is this smart thinking? Haven't people made a pretty compelling argument for succeeding through routine living, sensible actions, and levelheaded thinking?

These are all great questions to address. But not now, not while texting back and forth feverishly with a relative stranger and using a phone's tiny Web browser to cash in frequent-flier miles for plane tickets while night skies permit the connection. Not while packing up at a vacation rental cabin and rushing to aim a long, dark, lonely car three hours south toward an airport's long-term parking. No, these are probably not the times one questions whether or not one should be living like this. The heart shoves this line up from the chest and it comes right out of the mouth in a whisper for nobody in particular: "Jesus, enough, just go see her."

22

The City of Angels Bleeding and Peeing

S O, THIS IS WHAT THEY mean by flying economy. But who is blowing ninety thousand miles to sit up front, certainly not Matthew, not even with half a million miles amassed during gainful employ, all waiting to be spent. Traveling is quite different when it's not on the dime of a media conglomerate, that much is certain. Still, the routine is comforting, like prison. Sit down, belt up, shut up, here comes your cup of hydration, we'll tell you when you can use your electronic gadgets and when you can't, and it's for your own good, damnit. Make your little cup of water or coffee last, make a pillow out of your sweatshirt, make perfect order of your trash to be collected, make a dream about driving down dirt roads from the way the window rattles you back here when you lean your big dumb head against it. Save your tiny bag of peanuts like it's something you can trade for a cigarette or protection once the beautiful screws aren't looking; a general sense of surrender and you-can-make-this-easy-or-you-can-make-this-difficult logic wafts through the cabin.

And it turns out, way back here behind the wings, the plane rocks and bounces like mother swaying child. God, if only someone would key the intercom during the maternal sway of it and say that everything was going to be all right forever; remind one that even if things don't go well with the woman in Los Angeles that they're rocketing toward at 549 miles an hour, one could visit their failed Wall Street friend who is living in a park in Wyoming or Montana or something.

In the amniotic calm of discount commercial aviation comes the moment when one understands why career criminals get a taste of freedom and then violate parole to rush their way right back into the penal system. The authority figures sitting in the very front of this thing have flung the steel tube up over Long Island and banked it hard right to head west where more temporary living awaits. With the cabin lights dimmed, one gets to feeling like part of a silhouetted troupe dedicated to the mission of going to any length to find another one of life's magic moments that make all the other days worth it.

In Los Angeles, Matthew checks in at The Standard downtown, far away from the Four Seasons on Doheny and even farther from the Mondrian and Chateau Marmont. The lobby is a late-night gaggle of twenty-somethings dressed poorly in a way that only youth permits. If you're young and beautiful enough, you can wear something terrible and ridiculous as if to say, *See, even in this ridiculous shit that looks like it was stolen from retarded teen runaways and even with my hair like this, cut in chunks so randomly it looks like I was the victim of a perverse crime, I am beautiful and most likely living longer than you.* They undulate under lights like half-blind bioluminescent sea life; they gush over a DJ for subjecting them to one endless dirge of house music. This is one of the rare moments when Matthew realizes there are dear prices to pay for youth and its vitality; comforting to think that it's better to be carving one's way through their forties than to be standing around hearing this so-called house music, ears trying to find one measure that sounds like it might be leading to the bridge or a big finish.

Upstairs, the room is physically modern and sparse and emotionally very similar to the lonely pornography that comes from this side of the nation; which is to say that after one walks past the glass wall to the room's shower and imagines the ghosts of travelers past, after the small baggage hits the bed, one simply sits in a hard, plastic urbane chair in front of a long, skinny bureau staring out at downtown Los Angeles, feeling equal parts aroused and ready to be drained and instantly done with the experience. And so Matthew sits; a lonely man in a sparsely furnished temporary den, wondering if this is really all there is to travel and leisure. He walks to the little refrigerator in the corner and silently hovers over a small wicker tray of snack items and scans the prices on the laminated card that accompanies them. The clock radio is playing a thin ribbon of community radio jazz that the maids must be instructed to tune in after they clean and abandon the room for a new check-in.

He switches on the television and stares at a handful of channels; flicks through them with a remote even though he sits within arm's reach of the television. All reality shows; one about sixteen-year-olds with wealthy parents, and the kids are dealing with the rigors of being rich in America and trying to have a better birthday party than their friends. One about a pawnshop where desperados sell what little they have left for a fraction of what they paid for it — wasn't there a time when television was an escape from reality, not a lonely hotel room overdose of it? It's easy to start thinking that this is not what one is supposed to be doing as a tourist in sunny Southern California. It's hard for Matthew to imagine a brochure about the region that boasts a big color photograph of a man sitting in a sleek plastic chair a few feet from a television, with a lump in the throat and eyes brimful with salty tears waiting for surface tension to break and permit their ocular exit. But there's hope for the wayward man here in the lonely little room, there is the hotel restaurant that's open all night and mostly empty at an hour when the jam-packed lobby has no interest in food.

Tatiana shows up at the restaurant like she texted she would. There are hugs, kisses, that way people kiss on each cheek, but not with actual kissing. Matthew is dragged through this choreography like a grandmother unsure of what to do; or an undercover cop trying to participate in the secret handshake of a gang member and figuring it out as he goes. Tatiana ducks and weaves gracefully through this intercontinental ritual and Matthew follows the cues like a fourth-grader learning to square dance, or like a forty-five-year-old man from Connecticut in over his head again. But the thing about modern love and modern living is this: You can be slow and old-fashioned, but if you look the part — if your hair is going long in unemployment, if you're prone to wearing the kind of clothes you learned about and were given for free at the magazines you created marketing plans for, if your legs and trunk are long and skinny from a diet of heartache and financial uncertainty — the initiated will drag you into modern love and fast living, no matter how square and slow you are on the inside. This is a dangerous situation for all parties, really. If you don't look the part, count yourself among the lucky, take comfort in loving someone, and take comfort in your home and watching movies and living correctly; go to sleep next to each other assured that you are missing nothing.

After the ballet of hello, and kisses that land four inches shy of skin, Matthew starts his version of hello, which is basically staring at Tatiana for seemingly one solid minute, unable to say anything during it. This welcoming homeostasis ends with Matthew jerking into action and presenting Tatiana with a coffee mug that has a blurry picture of an androgynous, long, thin person sitting on the floor and beneath it, text that says: *I'm going to meditate so well that I make all of you disappear.* Tatiana reads this and squeals with delight.

"Is this for me?"

"Yeah, yes. This is this thing I'm doing now; I'm making these coffee mug things now. Well, I come up with them. I have people making them, some friends, this place in Westport makes them for me after I give them one as an example."

"You're selling them?"

"I have been, yeah, but it's hard."

"No, I'm sure, you have to glaze stuff and put it in kilns and all that. My mom used to make tons of pottery stuff."

"Guys do it, too."

"Oh, I know, no, I'm just saying I know it's hard to do."

"Making them is pretty easy, really. Since I basically don't do it. I just meant selling them is hard. It's hard trying to figure out how to make it a real business. And there's the cops and all of that."

This last part about police brings silence and more staring. And so Matthew and Tatiana quickly move into the business of menus, ordering, eating, and the luxury of using eyes and millions of muscles in the face to telegraph late-night sentiment instead of having to text or dream it.

One can drink rum with an order of French toast, but it isn't recommended. It takes three or five of them to do the proper work of corrosives and soak through a gut of doughy night breakfast and find some blood to thin. And the road to the brain and heart seems laced with speed bumps of eggy bread soaked in syrup; the buzz comes, but the whole commute for the booze is roughshod and gimped; gummed up and sullen. After the bloodstream's traffic jams, Matthew pays the tab by stretching and breaking a rubber band, hacking, and unfurling a roll of wad. Tatiana stares at this form of financial management, so Matthew offers up a breezy explanation.

"I'm kind of not using the bank and ATMs."

They get up and head out of the hotel restaurant into the lobby, Matthew rummed up like a mail-order bride who just landed. Once through the sea of American youth plankton still balled up under the lights and beats, one assumes there will appear a bank of elevators waiting to whisk them up to the roof for drinks or something. Instead, after a series of gentle pushes through the clouds of youthful brine shrimp, in which Matthew follows Tatiana the way a shark is followed by pilot fish, they are at the side door leading outside to a gas fire pit surrounded by chairs and chaise lounges.

Tatiana doesn't break no stride; walks past the fire, pulling a piece of cash and ticket from a tiny pocket up near the top of her twenty-one-foot-long leg. She hands it to a handsome young man with hair styled to the day's fashion and a red jacket with narrow lapels that feels like it was stolen from a Las Vegas bellhop in 1967. The kid smiles and says hello to her, disappears in a flash, comes back around in a car best described as a long, dark blue piece of sculpture stolen from a museum; a form of transportation boasting hood- and trunk-logo medallions from the other side of the Atlantic Ocean. Tatiana jumps in smiling, Matthew approaches the passenger side; pulls the door handles about an inch, at which time the door handle starts pulling itself open with a tiny hydraulic hiss. His ass hits the passenger seat, he yanks the door shut, but the door won't slam, it rushes pretty quickly closed over 95 percent of the space and then just whispers a *hush* and very slowly completes those last few inches of closing. Real money will not let you slam doors behind you, it bears considering as French toast sponges continue to time-release half of Jamaica into the blood and brain at the moment.

Tatiana takes them on a drive up Wilshire then a right or a left, or an upside-down clover or corkscrew to Hollywood via La Cienega to Sunset. Her car's speakers ooze truth from young people playing bluegrass, lyrics asking musical questions like whether or not a gigantic crush can tend to a young man's dog for one week because he's about to be gone for three. And another song that says we don't know what lies in the days before we die, since we never know when we're going to die. Somehow none of it is sad; somehow banjos and fiddles and half-assed washboards and drums played with heart make the sights of Los Angeles whizzing past the passenger window feel beautiful and quaint. Melrose turns to Mayberry, a sign for Rodeo Drive reads like it's alerting motorists to a rodeo that's in town tonight, and Sunset Boulevard, one is reminded, was named for the fact that you can see a beautiful day's end by driving westbound on it.

"I need to get to a store at some point. I have a friend I'm visiting while I'm out here. I'm driving up to his, um, house.

So, long drive, need some water and snacks, and stuff like that."

The head likes the idea of having a backup plan, and taking the pressure off the visit. Tatiana is smiling for some reason, as if she's never heard of putting good snacks in a rented Ford Taurus so that there's stuff to munch on for a road trip. She whips left with the long, slender, and slightly oval foreign art piece she's driving and starts up Laurel Canyon and pulls in at the tiny parking lot next to the Country Store. They get out, the two of them, walk across the little lot and up onto the wooden deck in front of the place, the smell of jasmine making strong synaptic connection between the landscape and the sight of Tatiana, triggering some spastic switch of dopamine and cueing the pursuit of her heart and sex. She moves with arch and sway, looking back over her shoulder to compensate for Matthew's lag, saying things about Jim Morrison, pointing to the building that borders the tiny parking lot, talking about how he used to live right there.

Inside the store, mug money is stripped from a roll maintained only by the tender's muscle memory, then pulled through the fingers and flattened for spending on granola, trail mix, three big bottles of spring water, hippy muffins and bars, some organic mints, some Native American cigarettes, and a disposable lighter since the land of the free has stripped Matthew of his during airport security clearance. A good bag of fuel, to be sure, enough get-some-go-again in case the idea is to make it to Yellowstone tomorrow or the next day to catch up with Tim. Once back in the car, at the end of the little parking lot, pause and decision seem required. Making a right will take them up into Laurel Canyon, and certainly to some gigantic house in these Hollywood Hills where the Tatiana creature lives. But she points the car left instead and coaxes a silent growl from it as gravity does its thing and pushes one back into the seat.

"Let's go to your place," she says, as if this is a good idea.

"I just have . . . the one in Connecticut, really."

"I mean, your room."

"It's a basic queen. With sitting area."

"Oh, fun! Don't you think it'll be fun?"

"It's, you know, yeah . . . it was pretty fun when I was in there earlier, I guess."

The drive back downtown brings scenery of the aged haunts of Hollywood's ghosts of everyone who tried it here. Motels like The Lamplighter and the hard-boiled noir voices of also-rans still echoing off the neon sign: *Why, I've hung around gin mills long enough to sign up the next hothouse flower and now I'm in town, ready to make a picture — dial me at The Lamplighter!* Los Angeles whisks by like opening credits and Tatiana sits there in the driver's seat, a perfect portrait of temptation. *Say something, say something, say anything.* And so Matthew tries; just says what's on his mind.

"In Swedish folklore, right, there's this girl; more of a wood nymph, really, if that's the term I'm looking for. You know, this sort of sexy . . . forest ghost. She roams around in the woods, and she's beautiful, here's the thing though:

She has seven faces. No, wait, two faces. Two faces? Wait, you know what, she has one face, actually; so, she's normal in that regard. But the point is, she wanders around in the woods, she is unbelievably sexy, and any man, like, lost in the forest and unable to find his way out is defenseless against her, basically. And these are men who — not that the legend stipulates this, I'm taking the liberty of assuming this next part — these are men who are terrified because they're lost in the woods, so they're not even remotely aroused; sex, court-ship, flirting, all of that stuff is the furthest thing from the mind of a man lost in the trees with nightfall coming on. And that's precisely when this chick appears. At the most hope-less point, basically. And so, a lost man in the woods sees her just before he basically gives up on ever finding his way out. And he's thinking: *Fucking, no way, this might be my only hope of living.* And she basically whispers something like, 'Don't sweat this, I got it. Follow me, I've been in here tons of times.' And so a lost man will follow her to get out of the woods, and when she gets you out of the woods, all of a sud-den, she turns around, and she's a withered old hag; she's the devil, basically."

"Who cares if she's the devil? She gets you out of the for-est so you don't stay lost in there and die, that's all that mat-ters."

"Oh, I know, I agree. But some people will say, Oh, you shouldn't follow the devil in that situation."

"But you don't know she's the devil, you only see her from behind, is what you were saying."

"Oh, wait, no: She *gets* you lost. That's the thing. You weren't lost to start with, you were fine, but she lures you into the woods because she's so beautiful and you think you kind of have a chance with her or whatever, and *then* you're lost. And you die. So . . ." Matthew holds what he hopes is an intense and worldly look on his face, ideally making the fable still scary, even the way he messed it up.

A left into the parking lot. Back at the hotel. Up the elevator. Key the door. And then, upon stepping into the room, Matthew is shut down. Cock-blocked by coffee mugs, if one can be so forward. Prior to departure, back at JFK, there was the last-minute thought when leaving the car to put a few mugs into the carry-on bag. This thinking was along the lines of: One can't pack the gun, one can't pack the leftover beers from the cabin, one can't pack the mix of crushed-up antihistamines and Valium — so almost for lazy spite, one may as well pack a few of the coffee mugs. And now Tatiana is gushing over them instead of gushing over the idea of hotel sex.

"Wait, there are more of them?"

"That's one of each. Well, of the most popular ones. There's a few others."

She picks up and unboxes each one. The one about God helping you buy a gun. The one that has a blurry, disheveled, androgynous person and a long, stacked, unruly caption wrapping around it that says, *Fuck it, I'm not old. Unless you're nineteen, sober, and looking right at me, from a few inches away in natural light.* The one with a terrible drawing of Matthew with giant teeth, in a smudged black car, and text that delivers the good news: *When the angry jerking about and spitting stops, the serenity starts.*

"I love these! I love the little random stuff you put inside some of them!" And with this, she pulls out a dime and a piece of gum that was in one of the boxed mugs.

"Shit, that's . . . see, they're kind of made and boxed up by people with Down syndrome and stuff. Chris or somebody must've put that in there."

"That's sweet that you reach out to people like that. It's kind of cool in a weird way, having something random in them; it's kind of collectible. It totally suits the tone of the product."

"Well, the thing is, they'll start putting nachos and shit in there if I don't talk to them. I'm going to have to go through the batches I pick up from them when I get back. Goddamnit."

"I love these so much."

"You can take those so you have one of each. You'll have the whole set."

And with that, thank the sky and dead Indians, the mood turns silent. Matthew sees to it that the alarm clock thing next to the bed finds a way to play something slow and not too sad, something rhythmic and blue that isn't wasting lyrics on bad news. The two of them lie on the bed, staring up at the ceiling of the room, the floor of the room above them. Matthew's rum hasn't let him down, but it's hard to tell if anything is working inside of Tatiana in the way of substance. But she did, after all, have to talk to Hernan in order to get a phone number for Matthew so she could text him, so she could've lined herself up with something. But she seems all business. She called Matthew's crafts products. She used words like *collectible* and *tone*. Frankly, the room feels a bit like two pleasant conventioneers on a bed after a vigorous bout of networking a Novelty Card and Gift Show. But then, progress! Tatiana starts a westward expansion from the bed, standing at the side of it and slipping out of her pants.

"I'm going to take a shower."

"Oh, okay. There's clean towels in there."

Jesus, the heart lurches; *there's clean towels in there?* It feels like going from a drugged-up fling to a quarter century of marriage in one six-hour flight. But then, halfway to a whisper Tatiana says, "Wanna watch?" Even with boozy bread in his stomach, Matthew feels himself practically blush at the idea. This prospect of watching, inviting to be sure, is also sort of embarrassingly pragmatic with that wall of the shower being glass and bordering the bed; the glass shower wall is really kind of the centerpiece of the basic queen.

"I think, you know, I'd have to watch. Unless I sit over at the . . ."

"No, watch."

Her eyes snap to half-mast and dreamy in an instant, her mouth suddenly languid, gorgeous, candy, sin, and she makes a joke of begging Matthew to stick four of his fingers in it. Tatiana can do this. She can be just another person rocketed here to earth, halfway through her thirties or forties, then instantly an otherworldly sweet and potent mash of adolescent funny, depraved and high-spirited. It feels equal parts deadly and harmless, and one is instantly lost in it without life's usual chart or compass. The only two times that Matthew has looked up at her to witness the shift, it has felt like being brave enough to stare at the sun for a minute; or like boyhood has finally come around to make him a rare and lucky witness of lycanthropy or aliens, chosen for this moment by something bigger than him.

The room goes dark a little; fades in his peripheral vision, like standing up too fast, or a fighter staying down listening to the count of ten tick past; giving in to it. Tatiana is all legs and inward belly button, and a brain that's doing who knows what at any moment; ankles, California feet; tits and ass, and gravity be damned. She moves, shower bound, westward in heather gray favorite underwear, around the corner, and in through the bathroom door, gone for a flash, and then reappearing behind water and glass, barely lit, but brighter than a silhouette. She moves around under the deluge falling from the ceiling, and there's nothing canned or soft-core stupid about what she's doing. She stands bored for a second, then she presses her tits, face, eyes, nose, and lips against the wall of glass; hair smashed and smeared against all the wet skin, a cross between a half-assed, gross-out prank and some kind of hot, deranged thing drowned or crashed. She pulls back and grins, she gets all business and actually showers, actually washes, really goes about the pedestrian rigors of soaping up and rinsing armpits, neck, ass. She turns sideways and gets lost in thinking for a minute, she snaps out of it, reaches out to the sink for the tiny bottles of expensive shampoo and conditioner, pulls her body back into the shower, turns to the glass, and gestures for Matthew to come in.

Matthew silently bemoans being coaxed; isn't he still married, technically? Isn't he even uncertain of Tatiana's last name? The head has a million little questions like this. But the body is up, appendage hanging half hard, thick and primate; the body is ready to round the same corner into the bathroom, through the steam, and the gray's sugar-and-rum fog is making this okay just one more time, one more time, one more time and that's it. Matthew recalls songs and movies that made this sort of thing okay; he recalls a character in a Southern poet's novel saying, "Grace of God!" three times fast when tried and tempted; he recalls how quickly all of our lives will end and leave us in the palsy of inventories that ask what risks one really took while down here; what limits one pushed to be certain they were living in this physical plane. Banged up by a gray noodle's kettle of chemicals, fueled by good old-fashioned dopamine's desire, sold out by synaptic ruse and pull, lulled by adrenaline's peak and fade, it's easy to take one's clothes off in moments like this; it makes more sense to be as naked as the day you got to the planet.

And so good-bye pants, hello shower with Tatiana. Warm water washes over Matthew's head without having the heart to make him awake and sober, and both of their brains must be thinking this, upon the mashing of lips: *There's that mouth again, the one not quite familiar yet.* And something warm jets against Matthew's leg with decent force, it hits just above his knee, warms it down to the shin, and almost cools by the time it's at his feet then on its way down the drain.

"Woops, peeing," she says, the side of her wiseass smile cracking.

After the announcement of this strange and delightful breach of shower etiquette, the mouths are pressed together again, teeth clipping hard up against each other when Tatiana and Matthew start laughing in the middle of it. The warm still hasn't stopped and Matthew moves his arm, straight and skinny-stiff, down between the two of them, turns up his palm to intercept it. The laughing stops and there are those eyes again, eyes that could stare for the rest of their mortal years and then some. Tatiana breaks from the stare they're lost in, looks down, at first curious and serene, then instantly slack-jawed, aghast, terrified, and Matthew's head races with its refrain: *No Damn it. No damn it. No damn it. No. Fuck. No.*

Matthew is a fountain of blood; a nightmare stream of red gushes from about midway on the biological container, his body having succumbed to the warm shower and following Tatiana's lead of peeing, but with a big, jagged stone somewhere inside of him, moving ever so slowly a fraction of an inch across the kidney, tearing whatever red-gouged path it needs, and taking months to move two or three inches to the renal pelvis, in what the doctor said would eventually be an impossible migration without surgical intervention. Nothing will put a damper on a highly charged shower with someone the way becoming a human blood sprinkler will; a scarlet fountain of twenty-first-century potential biohazard; plasma spattering everything red, like red-soaked pay-per-view horror flicks.

Tatiana is mildly hysterical, weird breaths, tiny tornadoes fluttering into her and coming out in little hushed screams with the inflections of questions. She jumps out of the shower, onto the white shower mat, leaving reddish pink wet footprints of blood and water over to the towels, one of which she yanks off the rack and clutches up under her nose, her eyes wide open in shock and peeking over it. There is no song in the world that will repair the evening's misstep and restore the mood.

Back on the bed, each of the bodies rinsed and dried and a bit shaken, Matthew offers up a hurried and sobering explanation. His voice as kind, benign, and pedestrian as those filmstrips about puberty, sexual intercourse, menstruation, and erections—the ones that they used to show in public schools when he was a boy not yet stained with any of this mortality bullshit. With every word he uses—*urethra, diameter, deposit, calcium, penis, renal pelvis*—the mood runs screaming out through any crack in the door and windows; runs any way it can find out of the Basic Queen with Sitting Area. After all of the reasonable addressing and explaining and absolute humiliation, Matthew and Tatiana lie on the bed like a fruitless Bonnie and Clyde; a bathroom choked with balled-up bloody hotel towels and no getaway car or sacks of cash to show for it. The silence seems endless until nerve returns to Matthew, if not grace.

Television to the rescue, and the thumb stops pressing forward through the channels at the first note of the calming voice-over on a PBS documentary about mathematician John Nash. The voice speaks calmly about game theory and Nash going mad and getting strapped into state beds and roughed up by state employees trying to tame him with needles and pills; numbers and theorems and failing out of Princeton and MIT until he's falling asleep alone in wards manned by the state, then rising again when Stockholm gives him the prize. And the silent conversation between Matthew and Tatiana might be the one everyone has in front of a television with someone they love. Imagined silent reassurances and pledges to believe in each other no matter where it leads the two of them, all spoken without a word or glance, all requited with a mute and implicit contract, one quietly hopes.

And then something comes out, is actually said, Tatiana breaks the silence to say it. "You have a touch of what he has, you know; that brilliance."

Seems unlikely to Matthew, based on any number of proofs — getting hit by a car while jogging around a grocery store, for instance. Or, say, selling psychotropic brownies in order to afford a used handgun after being fired at work. But it's easy to lie there letting Tatiana be wrong, entertaining for a fleeting rush that genius comes in many forms, and that too many people on earth have been too quick to let the tiny failures of navigating day-to-day life in the suburbs be faulty barometers of a brain's potential.

And she speaks again during a pause between the documentary voice-over man and interview footage with Nash. "What's your favorite prime number?" she asks.

A long, thoughtful stare to middle distance, the way geniuses pause, and then finally: "I'd say fifty."

Tatiana is silent long enough to make one think the brief conversation is over, and then she whispers: "Fifty isn't a prime number."

A beat in the timing, and then Matthew and Tatiana erupt, laughing, and it gets to sounding like crying for all the snot and tears and coughing. And then another half hour passes in silence, and a decade of John Nash's life goes by, and the eyes are slits lit by flickering blue.

"Can I smell your stomach?" This from Matthew, and brave considering the way things went in the shower earlier. Matthew falls asleep there, on a gorgeous and soft belly, Tatiana's warm skin cooled on top by air-conditioning, and smelling of summer already happening; of jasmine and Laurel Canyon somehow, he's certain. He drifts off listening to what everyone did to John Nash, convinced the story is about what the world did to Nash's heart, not his head.

23
—

The Lonely Stretch

BEFORE MATTHEW'S EYES are open he knows she's gone; the feet have roamed the edges and felt nothing there for seemingly an hour or two. Hard to tell what time is doing at the end of sleeping, so maybe the feet have been searching for two hours, maybe ten minutes. The last part of sleep was all dreams of plane crashes; of the dumb black caskets going into a hole at the feet of the guy from the church acting like he knew them; into the hole underneath the frowns of neighbors and friends that Matthew hasn't seen since. Waking up and the head is racing: *She's gone, people go, that's what happens, don't get too close, keep it light, get on the road, go see Tim.* And then the numbers tick by: 9, 331, 269 plus 12 percent, 301.28, and then the head offers one last bit: *You're like* A Beautiful Mind, *but all you can figure out are hotel bills and heartbreak, both of which prove you're not a genius.* There are morning people, evidently. One is probably not a morning person if one wakes up at 9:00 AM in a hotel room saying, as the day's first words spoken aloud, "Fucking early." But the bag is packed, even easier without three mugs to cram into it. And checkout happens in the phonetic laziness of the region coupled with the fast rhythm of wasting no words at this hour:

"Three thirty-one, checking out."

"Okay, total is three twenty-one twenty-eight."

"K."

"Need a receipt?"

"Mmm, no."

"Leave it on the card?"

"Um, yeah, thanks."

The morning valet kid is thirty-eight or forty. He doesn't whip the car around the corner as much as he lurches the rented Taurus into the driveway like an apology that's difficult to get out at this hour. Matthew gives the guy a couple of dollars as if it's going to make a difference, crams his legs and knees into the cockpit, closes the door without any foreign hydraulic pageantry, and instantly winces and wonders if two dollars was enough. If fifty people check out before the guy gets off work, that's a hundred bucks. If they tip him four instead of two, dude walks with two hundred. If he works four days a week, he's making thirty-two hundred a month. But forget fifty times two, and forget the generous raise from two bucks to four multiplied by a four-day schedule — if you're parking cars downtown at forty, math hasn't worked like that for you, ever.

If Tatiana's British car situation was sculpture stolen from the Tate Modern, then Matthew's ride for the next week is a Dumpster taken from behind a Walmart; feels like riding on a cinder block that somebody tied to a bad soft mattress. But it has snacks, it has satellite radio, it has a full tank of gas that can be filled again and again.

South Flower leads to Eighth Avenue, which takes you to the 110, then 101, 5, 580, 280, and they all unfurl in front of the teal or moss or wintergreen chariot; the midsize Ford Taurus or similar. Leaving Los Angeles the long way, the scenic route, the way that avoids the trap of Las Vegas. It's like going four hundred miles out of your way to avoid driving by the bar that you know will mean bumping into your dealer and your ex; sometimes the long way is the shortcut in the long run. Hollywood fades to Pasadena's streets of little houses still strong in the stucco of dreams from a couple or few generations ago; the freeway on-ramps, bordered with immaculate ice plant, and below them the residential streets lined with little squares of old green grass and yucca trees. Everything across the seat and out the passenger window feels sturdy and perennial; everything is little white houses of two or four good people with good intentions, and prickly side-yard agaves that creep up these houses.

The day-by-day chariot pushes on past it and eventually on the left stands Magic Mountain, one last stab at reminding departing motorists that life can still be a theme park dream, and if not Disneyland then it's not too late to pull off Interstate 5 before the pass to chase the dream at Magic Mountain; but, hey, seriously, last chance. Up the big, long uphill stretch of 5, up the grapevine, where the big diesel trucks modestly admit they're beat, pull to the right, downshift, and refresh the rev and whir, like that part in every song that huffs a tired wheeze under its own weight before getting the idea to change keys and feel new again for a minute. Eventually families in cars pull into the big rest-stop parking lot in front of Pea Soup Andersen's; safe wagons from Sweden or Norway or something, piloted by modern dads who never scream about how they're gonna turn this thing around and take everybody home; moms that talk to kids like they're already at Stanford.

Keep pushing up Interstate 5 and the sensible Scandinavian cars start turning into well-worn economy boxes from Japan and worn-out pickup trucks in small and medium sizes; Bakersfield, already sending word this far south, letting one know the dream hasn't made it up this far from Los Angeles, and whatever fortune is up in San Francisco sure as hell won't be coming down this far south. The heat is starting to do a decent job of making waves and ripples over strip malls, cinder-block taverns, and old Taco Bells or Kentucky Fried Chickens turned into half-assed local Chinese joints. Someplace between Bakersfield and north of it, Matthew pulls off at a combination gas station/produce stand/ Mexican grocery market/Laundromat/diner and seller of area rugs with dramatic portraits of saints and virgins on them. The woman working the counter is where luck stops; honky-tonk hair beehived above a face that makes it clear there's nothing around here that would pay the likes of Matthew middle six to come up with marketing plans. The only marketing plan in the works of any place or person around here is: Live through this as long as you can, then try again. The aged beehive soaks up mentholated smoke as the mouth below exhales it heavenward, her eyes framed by reading glasses hung on a lanyard of fake gold chain and emeralds. To her immediate left, pieces of greasy chicken sweat under lights behind a case of thick nicotine-yellow-and-brown glass. Matthew peels off a run of paper from a medium-sized wad and puts the bills on the counter. Says he wants to put it all on pump five, unleaded.

"*Jojos?*"

"What's that?"

"*Jojos.*"

Long pause.

"But what is it? What's that mean?"

And with that, Lady Hard Luck stubs out her long, skinny menthol into a cat food can of ashes from the last ten, and gestures with half her heart over to the glass case where the chicken is. Chicken must be *iojos,* or maybe they belonged to someone named Jojo, or maybe the tanned-dead, damp potato wedges or whatever the fuck is in there with them are *jojos.*

"Just the gas, I think."

So legal tender is tended. Matthew moves outside back

235

to the ride, pump side, putting the get-there juice into the tank, staring at a beautiful Hispanic woman painted or dyed or woven right onto one of the area rug mural things hanging outside the *jojo* cash hut. The woman on the rug is gorgeous after enough time spent lonely behind a windshield and on a plane, she's heartbreak and gasoline, she's cigarettes and caffeine, she's the vision that gets a man driving another eight hundred miles on black coffee adrenaline. She's the patron saint of a thousand bad decisions waiting to happen; just the idea of trolling roadside fruit stands and taverns for someone who looks like her is the siren tempting the SS Taurus to wreck on rocks. So onward, onward, onward!

The drive continues, the brain makes a game of checking and rechecking in the side mirror to make sure the gas cap has been put back on, so every five minutes there's the refrain of: *Oh, shit, is it on? Oh, right, it's on. It looks like the little door thing's closed. Okay, good. Should I pull over and check? No. I'd know if it was off. I'd know; I'd see it going empty on the gauge too fast.* The drive's decent pace eventually carries Matthew right into San Francisco's workday traffic, office people getting out of the cage, cars creeping up off Market and Third and Embarcadero onto 80 to crawl across the Bay Bridge. Across the bridge, Matthew's trek continues over the land between the city and Berkeley where everything feels like a nineteen seventies movie, over Davis and the Yolo Causeway and Sacramento, onward east past places with names like Truckee. Up around Donner Pass, the eyes feel shot, and everything inside Matthew is slowing down as the

Taurus continues locked into a stiff shot of cruise-controlled speed. Pushing on, there must be caffeine and Taurine on the horizon. The rental ride is free of the BMW's vices that are locked up back in JFK's long-term parking; but on the drive to find Tim in God's country, it feels good knowing that one can't reach up and crush a line of an over-the-counter cocktail of pep to keep driving. This is real American living; this is pulling off when you're feeling sleepy. Well, not pulling off and sleeping, but pulling over in Reno, anyway.

There are probably a thousand or two interesting places to buy fat little vials of vitamin-pumped energy potion and tall skinny cans of energy drink in this tiny city. Reno probably has myriad dicey and effective opportunities to duck into a parking garage or alley and get jumped up on something. But the pull of this little place scares someone like Matthew enough to stay on the freeway; its pallor, every sad lyric and disease in top shape waiting for someone like him to get off the interstate. The nerves light up with synaptic warning, Matthew is a deer bristling at the danger of eating grass next to a highway. Even just driving past the place one feels this way; just driving by, okay and, yes, pulling off the interstate for one quick roll down that tiny strip that has the sign boasting of being America's biggest small town, or smallest bad situation, or biggest little lie you've ever told a loved one, or whatever the Reno motto is.

Through the windows of the tiny Harrah's the eyes catch a flash of strippers dealing cards and a casino Starbucks in a food court, yes, but what are the chances of getting past the traps and into that Starbucks? Certainly there are good people here, maybe the girls in underwear and tuxedo collars are good eggs at heart — there are probably honorable situations to be found here, but Matthew would be detoured for three years if he stays here more than about a minute. A left and another left on the street heading back to the eastbound interstate, then the chain drugstore is probably the least exciting place to wind up in this town, but they've got the aforementioned energy aids to wake a driver up, and they're right next to the highway, easy off, easy on. Matthew gets the green Ford parked between the white lines, locks it down, walks up the walk, into the den of fluorescent lights, candy, drinks, and hygiene items. A woman in a black Audi looks up, all glitter and graves, and she smiles a huge bleached smile, issuing a "Hello, honey!" and it feels a little like someone's glad to see him after a long drive.

"Figured I better grab some coffee or something," Matthew says while stretching his arms above his head. This is met with a frozen smile and eyes that seem to be paused while she tries to decode what Matthew means; can grabbing some coffee mean buying cocaine? Do johns ask for sex now by saying they're looking for coffee? What could this clown possibly be saying in street cipher?

"Oh, okay, time for something to keep you warm, huh?"

"Yeah, you know, or those little cans of the cold stuff, or whatever, I guess." And now Matthew is stretching his legs; to motorists a stretch, but to his new friend, all sequined and bleached up, another confusing cue to decipher, and so she asks him.

"Do you date?"

This strikes Matthew as a little forward, but maybe she's getting at something. Maybe it's obvious to the world that he's in the middle of figuring out what the hell is happening between marrying Kristin and meeting Tatiana. Or maybe it's one of those things where this woman is going to say that she read something somewhere about how people in a relationship are able to drive longer distances with less accidents than single people, because they have someone who cares about them waiting for them to get home, or something like that. You know, like that article you read occasionally that says people who are married live longer or are less prone to have heart attacks according to certain studies; maybe that's why she's asking. You can't judge people on appearance; for all Matthew knows, this woman goes home at night and reads *The New York Times* and listens to NPR and waits to meet like-minded people around town to discuss things they've both read or listened to. Matthew thinks about it for a minute, hems and haws on an answer, because it feels a little silly to say that he and Tatiana are dating. It feels even stranger, well, just plain untrue, to say he and Kristin are dating. But they are technically, legally, very much together. Matthew has been staring at this parking lot friend of his for a minute while he thinks of all this, and who knows what that telegraphs to her, who knows what that means in some circles. Fuck it, for the sake of conversation, yes, fine, he's dating. The intricacies of it are nobody's business but his.

"Yeah, I'm dating. Gotta grab some coffee and stay awake. It's either that or I'm waking up on the shoulder or wrapping it around a pole, right? Take it easy."

Jesus. This reply is loaded beyond what Matthew must realize. Yes he's dating, plus he needs to stay awake, and he might wake up on a shoulder, or he might wrap it around a pole. The woman's eyes are dollar signs; this guy wants drugs, he wants to pay for someone to stay the night until he wakes up, he wants the stripping maybe, the pole dancing thing or a blow job or whatever "wrapping it around a pole" means — holy Christ, it's a full-meal deal with this guy, it's a month's overhead from one tired driver in a Walgreens' parking lot.

Inside, the place is a long-drive paradise; eyedrops, yes, tall skinny cans, yes, little fat vials of jump, yes, and even a pad that heats when you shake the chemicals inside it, a sack of hot chemical reaction to place above the waist, between the back and the seat, right on the kidney. Everyone in the place looks like reality TV. A morbidly obese man and skinny little teenage boy, who look like they know how to make drugs out of almost anything, buy the big twenty-four-ounce cans of energy drink; the cans look huge in the teenager's hand, and tiny in the grip of the jumbo man. They talk fast about what to mix it with, vodka, or maybe really strong rum, they're saying. The garnish might be unpaid bills, court dates, and blood pressure medication. But what is one to do, this is a drugstore, after all, so their shopping list seems sensible in light of that.

In the checkout line, a couple of pretty young girls giggle and wait to pay for a couple of candles and stupid novelty hats; cocktailing or dealing, no doubt, starting their twenties and splitting an apartment somewhere around here. Matthew tries not to stare at them, wondering what years of this place will bring; the head racing with this refrain: *It starts off cute and then it gets ugly.* Out comes the little phone and email thing, the tiny keyboard on the screen takes the refrain, the thumb finds Matthew's email address, it cc's Tatiana on this, the index finger clicks on Send. Then, more cash to a cash register, via Matthew's hand and then the hand of the pockmarked kid wearing a red smock and trying to stay on track in this place.

Out the door with a little white plastic bag of fortified blood nourishment to keep the eyes open. Foot hits the mat, and the door jerks and hums open. Just out the electric door, the Audi is still there, but the bleached smile, boobs, and sequins are not in the passenger seat. That's because, holy shit, she's across the lot leaning up against the Taurus. Matthew does a fast and seamless U-turn without breaking stride, head down, bag in hand, and goes right back into the store. Upon reentering the store in the same breath that he exited, the security guard by the door perks up instantly, eyes on Matthew, and seems to be reviewing in his head whatever manual they sent him home with in night school; *Okay, I can't use unnecessary force because the perpetrator hasn't done anything yet, and I can't mace or Taser him, because I don't have probable cause to believe he's a threat yet. But he has just reentered the store with a bag trying not to look at anyone, and he's done this only seconds after leaving, so we've definitely got a situation on our hands. I can't believe I did crystal meth continuously from 1993 to 2003. I am glad I have this job. I cannot afford to screw this up.*

Matthew immediately makes like he's browsing, takes a minute of fake browsing to think, damnit, think: Why the hell is the hooker standing by the rental Taurus? He shivers at the thought of what thug must have the keys to that Audi she was sitting in; what twitchy reprobate is in this store right now waiting to take the driver's seat of that thing and hear about the john that led her on, then backed out and stiffed her? Between the bloody towels all over the hotel in Los Angeles, the hooker situation here in Reno, and the ghost of the marriage back in Connecticut, it seems like girls are nothing but trouble. There is giggling coming from the checkout line. It's the two girls buying the novelty hats, looking at Matthew, and laughing. Matthew looks down to realize he has basically, to anyone unfamiliar with his hooker situation, just walked out of a store, then run right back in, sped over to an aisle with every ass-centric product a pharmacy stocks, and stood entirely too close to the rack, terrified and staring at it, muttering the phrase, "What the hell am I going to do? What's my plan?" over and over again. He looks up at the girls giggling, he looks at the rack and realizes where he's standing, he turns and walks past the guard who is now slowly walking toward him, and he heads out the door again to handle this.

On the walk across the parking lot to the Taurus, the head stays down, and inside it, conversation reels and rallies up some sensible confidence, then undermines it; build it, burn it down, build it, burn it down: *Fuck it, it's your car for the remainder of the rental period, it's not like she's even on the contract, why are you so afraid to approach what is technically your car? Just ask her what she misunderstood; why she's waiting for you; what she thinks is happening or what she thought you meant. Yeah, but this could get really bad, this could come off like one of those things where it looks like you're trying not to pay a hooker. You see that in movies and television every so often, the thing where a guy is beat up, and it looks like he was trying to get out of paying a hooker. Look, it's not like you had sex with her.*

I know, but it doesn't have to be about sex. In the shows and movies, that's often the way it goes down; nobody had sex, but then the hooker tells some backup muscle that the guy's not paying, just taking up her time, and then the backup muscle guy starts beating up the confused man who didn't even have any sex. The head looks up in the last five or six steps of walking up and then it says: "Hi, so, I'm not sure what we arranged there when I was walking in."

"You said you're dating. And if you're looking for a date in front of Walgreens in this town, I'm it," she says with the stale cheer of salesmanship.

"I just meant I'm dating, that, you know, I have a girlfriend.

She's not my girlfriend per se. I think you're great, I'm not saying I . . ." And this is cut short by laughter. Matthew tries to join in the laughter, but is maybe too humbled by the experience of a hooker pointing and covering her mouth and laughing at him and slapping her thigh as she does it, as if this is the funniest stupid misunderstanding ever; all in the parking lot of a chain drugstore next to an interstate. It is, in fact, pretty humbling.

"Oh, sweetie, that's fine, that's all right," all these words making their way through a smile that's turned maternal. "You got more driving ahead of you tonight, baby?"

"Yeah. I've got a bunch. I'll see how much I knock out tonight before I get too tired to drive," Matthew says with too much smile and relief.

"You gotta sleep. That's the thing. You can't push it like people try to, honey."

"Oh yeah, I'm pretty safe about it."

"Okay, baby, you be safe."

And with that she walks back to the Audi. Matthew stands at the Taurus, a forty-five-year-old man having taken mothering where he can find it, a ten-year-old having promised a hooker to be safe while driving—thirty-five years just vanishing for a minute, and without the help of the Age Defying Cream with Botafirm advertised on the billboard towering over them on the near horizon. He unlocks the wintergreen sedan, crams in, pays attention only to ignition, first his own ignition by way of a couple of slammed skinny cans, then the car's, by way of key. He quickly opens the brittle plastic wrap on the heating pad and tosses the wrapper in the back, holds up the chemical pouch, giving it five or six fast shakes the way they do in emergency room dramas on television. He tucks it back between the right kidney and the seat.

Back on the road, and the eyes stay open until a ways into Idaho, and a night of sleep is in order at a motel someplace near Boise; one of those off-ramp junctions clustered up by absentee owners of the tiny franchises of big chains— Holiday Inn Express, a Dunkin' Donuts kiosk stuffed inside a Hardee's or Carl's, a Baskin-Robbins jammed inside a Subway, stapled onto the side of a Shell or Arco gas station. Someday in America it will all be one place, one brand, owned by one corporation—everything will be called McFridayBucksExpress&Things, and that's where people will go no matter what they need.

The full-size bed is just enough room for Matthew to fall asleep with a few false starts where he wakes up in a fast twitch, convinced he's dozed off behind the wheel on 80. The lull finally comes; a silent montage of Tatiana and Los Angeles; romantic little clips fading on and out with thirty-frame dissolves, the standard mainstream movie stuff until the interruption of bloody towels, which leads to sleepy, inexplicable thoughts of skeletons on fire playing bluegrass music on banjos made of trash at a combination wedding/race riot. Waking up in time for the free continental breakfast passes as having one's act together; a bright little linoleum room with single-serving oatmeal, black coffee, and orange juice. All of it is surprisingly good; it's easy to think one has been missing out all these years — how long has this stuff been sitting on counters in little rooms for free like this? And they're effective and substantial, these whole oats, this coffee, this orange juice. The oatmeal sticks to the ribs through Boise, through Mountain Home, up to the corner of the state as it turns into Montana. And the hippy snacks from Laurel Canyon last past that and eventually Matthew is pulling past Henry's Fork and then into the southwest corner of Montana.

24

Tic Tac, Modoch, and the Bearded Lonely Pervert

S UMMER IS IN FULL SWAY, swing, and stagger in most of the nation, but here in West Yellowstone, the season is characteristically a step behind and hung up in late spring; there are nearly melted drifts of snow from the last of spring's storms that were plowed to the side of Main Street. The place is littered with perfect American families in cars and campers buying little souvenirs made of turquoise and leather, probably made in Vietnam. The entire town is made to look like the Indians had a peaceful time of the country's colonization and simply decided in cheery fashion to open little gift shops that sell headdresses and tiny burlap satchels of chocolate wrapped to look like gold coins. Nothing is called a gift shop, it's a Trading Outpost, Mercantile, General Store — a concrete tepee in a gravel lot sells European coffee drinks and pastry. Every motel, free of heartbreak, never stained by the tears and nicotine of lonely salesmen or drunk conventioneers saddened by instant freedom from spouses and children — The Evergreen Motor Inn; The Stage Coach; The Cowboy Cabin; Pine Shadows Motel; The Kids Fall Asleep with Parents in Love Motor Lodge; The Mom and Dad Laughing and Kissing While Young Hearts Dream of Bison and Cowboys and Bright Stars in Gigantic Skies Motor Lodge Cabin Hitching Post. And there's Bud Lilly's fly-fishing shop where men with short graying hair and baggy tan Gore-Tex waders bullshit in the parking lot while they drink hot coffee and maybe wonder why the dream came true so late in life; they have finally made their money, they hadn't banked on it taking so long, and now going fishing includes plane tickets, expensive guides, and big tips forked over in gravel parking lots under bruised skies and sunsets. A text from Tim hits Matthew's phone and gives the final waypoints and directions to meeting up:

Hey Chief. Drive down main, make left at Imax theater. pass fat Navajo broads selling ponchos. @Chevron on left.

Matthew does this, and there, set away on the side of the Chevron, away from the traffic filling up their tanks, out of the loop of anyone getting anything done, is the monstrosity that Tim has been living in out here. What is this thing, forty or fifty or even sixty feet long? It's got a satellite dish on top, it has a huge eagle airbrushed on the side of it, it has a slight metal flake in the blue and red paint, making it pop against the white. Everything about it says the driver has cashed out the 401(k) and arrived in terrible style at the beginning of the golden years. How much does something like this cost? Fifty thousand? One hundred thousand? Three hundred thousand? There are stabilizers on the side that can apparently be deployed for when one is really anchoring in and doesn't want the thing to feel mobile in the slightest. Everything about the rig is an advertisement for insisting on high suburban comfort no matter where one is roughing it. It's like a cross between a multiplatinum country singing star's tour bus and one of those mobile marketing monsters parked in front of a shopping mall, doling out samples of diet cola, gimmicky fuel additive, or low-carb meal plans that promise to make and keep you thin. The make and model of the rig is painted in elaborate, airbrushed, prismatic, custom-color big letters above the back window. It is a Sierra Mountain Air by Forest River. Sierra Mountain Air, one must imagine, is probably pumped into one of the high-tech space-age HVAC units that sit atop the beast fore and aft, then heated or cooled as the pilot and his crew see fit, to make for a pleasant temperature that is kept consistent from front to back aboard the rig. The side door of the Sierra Mountain Air opens, slides left, and disappears in slow electric glide.

Matthew stays in his rental with the windows still rolled up from the long haul, and a silent-movie version of Tim comes down the stairs that seem to extend with each step he takes toward earthly tarmac; his lips move and it isn't hard to imagine what he's saying. His smile beams, his face and height still *Wall Street* handsome, but maybe *Wall Street* Part Thirty, the sequel to the sequel to all the sequels. Tim's looks won't go, probably ever, but he's showing the hard mileage he's undergone in exile; the last year has put ten in his eyes and face, even with the whole lower half being slowly grown over by a beard — a beard that doesn't suit him, by the way. He looks less like a bearded mountaineer and more like every piece of news footage one has seen of a former ruler being captured in his spider-hole hideaway by U.S. troops, or the domestic terrorist dragged by U.S. Feds from a lonely pervert cabin filled with guns and letters.

Standing in the doorway behind Tim is a man, maybe late forties, maybe late thirties, hard to tell with the costume, really. He's making no effort to explain himself with a smile or gesture, a tall black man with the gorgeous and stoic eyes of a killer or poet. He has strange and beautiful peaceful lips that don't rush to speak, and he's wearing what appears to be the skin of a bison — horns sprout from his head, the dried and wilted crown and snout sit above his eyes, curly rough fur drapes him entirely, down the back of his neck, across quarterback shoulders, down a broad back and hardened lean and chiseled arms. There are eagle feathers adorning the dead animal robe, and beadwork hangs from hanks of the bison fur as if the animal went through a spiritual phase just before being shot, then tanned, and turned into gigantic ornamental clothing.

Matthew pulls the Taurus right up behind the Sierra

Mountain Air situation and gets out to start the hello, to start figuring this out, or getting lost in it. Maybe this is exactly what Tim needed and maybe it's where Matthew should have been instead of sitting in parking lots and community center classes. Maybe spending time out here has made a man of Tim the way Manhattan never could have.

"Greetings, pussy boy!"

"Dude. Look at this, look at the man and his rig living on the land," Matthew rallies. They embrace with a hug of punches to the back. The giant black man/bison continues standing in the doorway silently watching over this.

"What the fuck are you driving, Chief?" says Tim, and this is the first evidence of the man in the doorway of the rig bristling. Tim notices this peripherally, and seamlessly makes a revision like a henpecked husband, "Sport."

"I don't know. It's a rental. I was in Los Angeles seeing a friend."

"Pull that fucking thing forward about five more inches and I'll drop the hook so we can tow it and you can ride in the rig."

Matthew gets back in, inches the car just a bit forward while Tim stares at the front bumper of it, then puts his hand up to signal a halt, then waves his fingers forward in a tiny come-hither series of three fast flicks to lurch the Taurus another inch or two, and then palms the halt sign again. The giant, black totem pole bison man walks down the steps of the rig and glides slowly into the little market attached to the gas station; two little kids in the back of an environmentally sound, small SUV giggle and wave excitedly at him completely unnoticed except by their parents, both of whom put a kind but panicked instant stop to the pointing and waving at the black man wearing an animal. Matthew and Tim head into the rig, and Tim takes the driver's seat; he starts toggling a switch while staring at the small video screen on the dash until the hook is deployed down and retracted a bit up under the frame of the Taurus. Matthew gets the balls to ask, "So, you saw that guy, too, right? Kind of dressed like a moose or whatever?"

"That's Crazy Daryl Acid. But we have to call him Modoch now. He's super into a Navajo thing about animals being our ghosts and all this shit. Him and Tic Tac fucking own the park. Vets, kind of fucked up from the first Gulf War; they basically live in Yellowstone all year long and I need them to get around the heat after getting banned by the asshole rangers who are basically communists. They're cool. I'm learning a ton of shit from these guys. Without Tic Tac and Modoch, I'd be sleeping in the IMAX lot over there and getting a parking ticket every fucking morning. They're like a free season pass to Yellowstone, you should see the respect I get from the rangers when these guys are on board."

"Tic Tac?"

"He's in the store. He's getting a bunch of shit we need. Traffic flares, cigarettes, beer, this kerosene fuel. It's for the camp stove, but we always get an extra gallon and use it for these meditation ceremony things Modoch's been doing to clear our heads. He'll probably get a couple hilarious, shitty tee shirts, too. He pays for the beer to make it look good and the rest comes out with him under his jacket. That's kind of the other thing—with my cash flow situation where it is right now, I need these guys to help me make ends meet. And they get to sleep on board instead of in a fucking beaver dam made of *punji* sticks, so everybody wins." And then Tim pauses, catching sight of Modoch and Tic Tac coming out of the store, before he adds, "Look at this. How fucking adorable is that? They, like, take care of each other."

Coming out of the minimarket: Tic Tac, mid-forties—a short man and all the harder for it, red, sinewy, lean, and generally looking like a piece of gas station beef jerky dressed as an eighties punk rocker still hanging on to a wisp of hair; a hairstyle that might be described as short if a victim were kind in relaying details to the police sketch artist. Steeled, empty, and determined eyes; tattooed forearms attached to a torso that will plow past fifty and refuse to believe it. Staring at Tic Tac, the head races with the word *black:* Black Flag, black boots, black friend, black eyes. Tic Tac's old denim jacket is so stuffed underneath he can barely walk in it, and Modoch is drinking a huge red Gatorade and whispering discreetly from the side of his mouth, saying something to Tic Tac that steadies his posture. Tim sits in the driver's seat, paternally shaking his head and smiling. "I don't even think the cashier gives a shit; seriously, everyone just looks the other way for these two. It's like Lehman Brothers in the nineties."

"So, I've been making these coffee mugs. I wish I would've brought some; with all of the crafts and souvenirs and stuff here, I could sell a ton of them, I bet. Especially if these guys keep cops off your back like you were saying."

"Dude, if you're making cash, speak up. Because I can get you twenty percent and that's after I take ten for the trouble. Everybody thinks we're in a recession, but there's mid-cap shit. Shit you can skim weekly right now, especially in bailout financials and tech; Citigroup, Micron, Netfl . . . a bunch of other shit I'm not gonna sit here and list off for free."

"I'm not making that kind of cash. I'm selling a few, but I'm not the guy giving you twenty or thirty to put in the market."

"This whole world cries victim — no offense — and puts their money in mutuals and ETFs like a bunch of little pussies — no offense — hoping for the best without taking a fucking risk. It's becoming the American way, to bear no risk then sit back and demand to be able to live like a fucking billionaire. Assholes — not you — fucking normal people. And what the fuck do I know about normal people?"

"You're, maybe, not exactly a portrait of risks panning out at the moment."

"What you're forgetting is that I only did as much damage as an *average* failure but I was completely strung out on the kind of A-list shit South American presidents are hitting. I was doing blow that left tribal chiefs psychotic and suicidal and chewing fucking coca leaves until their gums bled in huts made of dung up in the Andes. But people don't factor that in, do they? They don't take a minute to use reason and think: Well, let's see, yeah, the guy fucked up, but there are guys who fuck up that much *sober,* and this guy was out of his head on Christ knows what and he was still as good as a sober fuckup."

"Fair point, I guess. Anyway, I don't have that cash at the moment, but if I did . . ."

"Selling coffee cups . . . you're lucky I'm on a spiritual path out here with these guys, because the old me would've fully fucked up your mode for wasting time with namby-pamby pussy-whipped ideas like making money selling coffee cups. But now I live and let live, Chief. I seek to understand, not be understood, which is something Modoch taught me."

"Okay."

"Oh, real quick, that's kind of the other thing: ever since Crazy Daryl Acid became Modoch, shit's gotten a little sensitive, and saying Chief is apparently not cool with him, so you gotta help me lay off it."

"You went with Sport earlier. Why don't you just go with that?"

"I'm trying that, Sport's good, and I'm going with Genius when I want to give someone a little shit, because the only problem with Sport is that sometimes it seems paternal and positive when I'm not trying to communicate that. Sport's not as malleable as Chief."

Tim looks at the little side-view video screen, sees a tiny, bluish black-and-white duo at the door of the rig, and reaches to the dash to toggle a small electric switch so that the door of the Sierra Mountain Air slides open. Modoch and Tic Tac climb aboard.

"Hey, guys, did you get everything you need?" Matthew asks.

Tic Tac talks like a broken metronome, all fast and bad meter jumping the beat, stepping over the last of Matthew's question with the answer coming in too hot and soon. "It's fucking for everybody, it's for all members on board." And upon saying this, Tic Tac is instantly hunched and stooped with his head forward, hands flicking up under his coat like a tiny hyper and gravid crustacean tending to a bulge of roe just beneath its shell, gobs and grabs of bright wrappers and bottles and cans, all coming out, all dumping onto the rig's couch. A family-size bag of Spicy Hot Corn Nuts; a large can of lighter fluid; an aerosol can of hair spray; a large can of lighter fluid; panty hose; another large can of lighter fluid; a bag of assorted bite-size candy bars with Halloween not even on the horizon; a pair of bright orange work gloves; three large commuter mugs that don't even have art or a saying on them — corporate mugs, brushed stainless steel with a Nissan logo on them; a big box of kitchen matches. Tim is staring at the bag of Corn Nuts; he turns his head quickly to try to hide his lingering automatic flash of a scowl. Tic Tac rolls his eyes and reaches into his waistband and takes a red pine tree air freshener out from between his absolutely tiny, taut, muscular, amphetamine-etched lower stomach and waist. He whips the plastic wrapper from the air freshener as fast as a medic tearing open gauze or a syringe, takes two speedy strides forward, and snaps the thing up over the giant rearview mirror hanging from the rig's overhead console of controls.

"You ain't gonna smell a thing, princess, so don't get your period just because I got some Corn Nuts."

"Your life is not my life, live and let live. How I feel about your snack food is none of my business," and when Tim says this in the forced, languid pace of a man reciting mantras to keep from snapping, Modoch silently fixes a gaze of approval on him. Evidently Modoch doesn't speak, or maybe he speaks only when spoken to, and so Matthew tries, still new to the crew, and happy to see someone after the lonely car-bound hours that followed his exchange with the maternal Reno hooker at Walgreens.

"Hey, besides, I'll bet those Corn Nuts are gonna start looking pretty good after a long day and a good campfire, right Mur . . . dock?" Modoch stares. Matthew's eye contact shifts politely back and forth, first to Modoch's eyes, then up to the eyes of the bison head atop Modoch's long, furry robe, and back again. The silence lasts for what feels like minutes on end and is interrupted by Tim pressing a series of buttons that fire up the gigantic, strong, almost silent engine of the rig.

Tim speaks up and goes down a mental checklist like a pilot, "Doors good, generators off, hook's locked, all clear back and sides . . . and we're looking good for a long, wide left out of here. We'll come in behind that silver SUV, third in line, west entrance."

Tic Tac jabs a fast street-fight left at Matthew that flattens out into a handshake reciprocated. "Welcome, motherfucker! Nice to have new blood, so welcome!" and he starts laughing a speedy fast laugh that turns into a little dry coughing fit. Then he jabs the hand back up under his coat and yanks out a gift for Matthew, a pink tee shirt, a ladies' tee shirt. He fast-jabs it at Matthew like another sporting punch to the gut and Matthew takes it, smiling. Tic Tac wouldn't guess it, or Tim or Tatiana, or anyone else on the planet, but Matthew still gets a lump in his throat when someone gives him clothing. Someone gives you some stupid tee shirt or a slightly ill-fitting jacket that'll almost do the job for the season coming up, that's love. How many cardboard boxes came to those houses where he lived when nobody with his last name was left down here in this earthly fix; how many people doled out what worked best for each kid — that's love. No matter what you might fucking think, no matter how much it might look like the short shrift, it is love and it is gigantic because it is the only kind you have.

"Itty Bitty . . . Titty . . . Committee," Matthew says, trying to politely decode the tee shirt like a good sport.

"Don't say I never gave you nothing!" And the speedy laugh is back with the dry hack.

"But, wait, a committee is more than one person," Matthew ventures in sporting fashion.

"I didn't invent the shit, Professor, I just stole it."

The rig starts to taxi across the tarmac ready to make its left out of the gas station and into the line of vehicles waiting to enter Yellowstone National Park. In the little video screen on the overhead console of controls, the rental Taurus is there in blue-gray black and white, starting to creep behind in tow, then slowly and silently veering right, free of the hook, and creeping along in slow motion until it crashes gently into the gas station's Dumpster, ending its short-lived independence. Tim uses the word *genius* pejoratively. Matthew is still staring at a tee shirt made for a woman, but one that will fit him when he needs it.

25

Parklife

A T THE WEST ENTRANCE to the park, the right lane inches along as each car ahead of it pays, as each driver gets the free park newspaper and map and has to be told to put the receipt somewhere where they won't lose it in case they leave the park and want to enter again. Tim starts to sweat the slow line, starts getting tense at how slowly the rig is moving, how long the normals are all taking to get through the gate, but then Modoch shoots him a scolding look and Tim calms down, almost out of spite. Then he takes it too far, stops the rig altogether, sets the huge hydraulic parking brake, and turns the pilot's seat around on its swivel base to lock into a position that will allow him to flip through the channels on the flat-screen TV in the forward lounge area. Tic Tac is excited like a family dog to see the television turn on and instantly arches his neck almost straight up to watch the channels as Tim flips through them.

Modoch meditates pensively in the giant passenger seat, staring at the gap between the rig and the cars ahead as it widens, and after about four minutes of this, he speaks:

"This is a physical model of addiction; this is an illustration of the disease and how it takes any natural separation between the self and others and sits quietly as that gap widens."

Tim rolls his eyes, recommits his focus, and really tries to concentrate on the television; tries to ignore what Modoch is saying, even though Modoch speaks up so seldom that it qualifies as an occasion when his mouth is open. Tic Tac is just happy to be watching television, and says, "Oh, this one's fucking hilarious, it's about all these jerk-offs trying to buy houses in other countries and shit."

Out the windows, real mothers and fathers and children inch by in minivans and SUVs in the other ticket lines; Modoch is still staring at Tim.

"No sense being slow and quiet like a disease or . . . whatever the fuck you were saying," says Tim, trying to affect the tone of enlightenment or at least being resigned.

Modoch goes silent like a brooding boy used to being misunderstood. Tim looks like a man who was watching television but is now watching every thought crossing his mind. He huffs a huge huff, jams his hand under the seat, jacks the lever and spins back around facing the windshield, slams the seat lever back into place, mashes his right foot into the accelerator, and the Sierra Mountain Air lurches up like a kicked horse, closing the gap left in front by cars that have paid and entered the park; families look on at the huge RV rocketing fast right up to the ticket window then slamming on the brakes. Tic Tac never stops watching television, simply letting his body bump and lurch along with the rig absentmindedly while his stare remains chained to the screen.

Tim toggles the switch above his head that rolls the window down, the woman in the ticket booth, the ranger, smiles in olive drab and a wide-rimmed yesteryear ranger's hat, starts to say welcome and explain how much money it costs to enter the park. Tic Tac takes his eyes off the television and snaps to. Bounds up off the sofa, takes a couple of speedy strides forward, and stops by putting his left hand up on the back of the captain's seat and waving with his right hand. Before he can say a thing, the ranger sees who she's got here.

"Hi, Kelly," the ranger says.

"Hey, Joan." Tic Tac beams.

"Not even Fourth of July yet and you pulled a hop-on?"

"Yeah, you know . . . we got a receipt around here somewhere, but . . ." A pause hangs here long enough that Matthew can feel a whole life passing by, clocks dragging calendars through days.

"That's fine. Stay out of trouble, head on in, guys."

This small exchange takes place without acknowledging that there's a gigantic black man dressed as a bison riding shotgun. For the first handful of endless curves and bends on the road along the Madison, everyone is silent. Tic Tac turns his head the other way, back over his shoulder to look out the big side window as the river runs along the road with them. The early-season water is still carrying more than a hint of glacial aquamarine, before July comes along to render it gin clear and pristine, and well before August heat steals the high flow and leaves the river warm and shallow with a light amber stain like maple or nicotine.

The silence breaks with Tic Tac offering one insight: "And I don't wanna hear one fuckin' peep about my name. Joanie can call me whatever the fuck she wants. Any of you try it and you're waxed, grunts."

The park road unfurls in steady zags, a grayish white two-lane ribbon alongside rivers Madison, Firehole, Gibbon; occasional elk bedded down on the other side of the water where the grass widens into meadows. Signs alerting one to keep driving and not stop to look at the eagles nesting — this makes people stop driving in order to look at the eagles nesting. The rig makes good time, and so far the only sound out here in nature is the low din of a *Cheers* rerun on the Hallmark Channel playing on the flat screen, and the thin, flat narcotic hum of the HVAC system purifying and cooling the pure cool air from outside. Campgrounds pass by with names like the ghosts of the sons Matthew, Tim, Tic Tac, and Modoch don't have — Madison, Norris, Grant. The occasional traffic jam slows things for a minute — tourists pulling to the side, three or ten cars at a time. They get out of their cars, creeping up unwisely on bison, elk, black bear, and loading their cameras with images that would tell the grim and hilarious story of a beautiful and shaky last day on the planet should they be gored or charged. Matthew makes another stab at conversation with Modoch now that there's evidence of him being able to speak.

"Should they be doing that; getting that close to bison and stuff?" asks Matthew.

Modoch simply closes his eyes, takes a deep breath, and adjusts the bison head atop his own head.

Tim says, "Should who be doing what?"

And Matthew decides to abort his stab at conversation as quickly as he started it. "Nothing."

Tic Tac jumps in. "I seen a fucker, one year, get gored by a bison and thrown like a little rag doll right up into the top 'f one these pines. Funny as shit."

And then more silence, all the way up into the northeast corner. The Lamar Valley stretches out bigger and flatter than the whole country, huge herds of bison roam through it, wolves or coyotes are specks trotting the creek way out on the horizon of it, the whole scene a scale and sight so grand the head instantly reduces it to a painting, to an illustration in a grade-school history textbook growing up, to a mural on the wall of a trendy cowgirl bar full of lesbians from where Matthew and Tim were once ejected with force by a broad-shouldered gal. They entered the place already drunk, whooping and hollering, thinking they'd hit pay dirt — thinking they'd stumbled onto a cavalcade of women buzzed on

Buck's beer and whiskey; boots and tight pants as far as the eyes could see! And not a man in sight! In retrospect, this is what would make the whole situation seem like a baited trap. Anyway, the cruel, cruel lesbian bars of Manhattan are far from the Lamar Valley.

The rig rolls on, America's Serengeti taking forever and a day to track past, a sixteenth of an inch at a time, filling the entire side windows with living proof of what America used to be. Twelve or fourteen more slow-winding miles, and at Slough Creek Campground, Tim starts decelerating, starts sizing up the skinny, pockmarked entrance road into Slough like a pilot forced to land where he'd rather not be trying to land. To himself, or maybe to everyone else, Tim breathes words calmly and confidently.

"Looking good for going in on the left; that's my first plan. Trying to read past that pullout about fifty yards in. Everyone, eyes open for long spaces; sixty-plus and electric would be ideal up here, but we won't find it this far out. Going left, main road to that first shoulder right, then we'll see what our visual is for the best approach further in."

Tic Tac replies, although not with the calming copilot nomenclature that would have fit well here, "If you can get this fucker up there, I can get it out if need be to do the recon up ahead and report back. Full battle rattle, boss. It takes guts to get in, but it takes nuts to get out, bitch."

And just like that, Matthew's new family's residency at Slough Creek Campground begins. The rig is driven in, anchored to the one long, skinny space near the creek, which is basically the road, since the place doesn't look to be geared toward big-rig living. Nobody else is up here this early in the season, and the trees are still mostly bare, summer hasn't been here yet to chase away the isolation. There's no electricity, but a series of switches toggled on the console above Tim's head set generators into whir and hum and the rig goes about juicing itself. Another four switches depressed in fast sequence start the whisper of stabilizing feet coming down in all four corners.

Before anyone has stepped out onto this new planet, Tic Tac has made use of a small and rather unofficial doorway in the back lounge, an emergency exit in case the rig ever rolls. He jacks the red bar from across it; swings it open fast, shoves and shimmies his muscle and bone through to daylight; forgoes the little steel ladder; lets gravity jump him right down onto the packed dirt; and he's darted off to the side of the stream as fast and focused as a coyote on the scent of lunch. At the stream's edge he stops suddenly and seems to wait for waypoints and bearings to kick in — smells the air, sizes up his position relative to the trees on the far bank and to the mountain on the horizon. Without warning, his calm breaks as fast as it came; he wades out quickly, without reserve or ceremony, right into the middle of the stream. When the water reaches about neck high, he automatically pulls his chin into his chest and rolls his head down into an otter dive. His butt and feet come straight up and high into the air like Olympic form, his legs crossed tightly, he goes straight down underwater fast, stealthy and silent, creating no ripple on the surface.

Matthew stares on with wide eyes begging explanation, face weighed down by the kind of disbelief that comes with years of steady modern living. Tim and Modoch make no notice of Tic Tac's deft reconnaissance, and they go about straightening things inside the Sierra Mountain Air, Tim in charge of flipping up little doors containing meters and switches, seeing how much power is being generated, making sure the stabilizer legs have bitten in, peering out the windows on the starboard side to make sure there's clearance from trees so that the awning can be switched on and deployed. Tic Tac pops up after what seems like ten minutes under the stream's current, and he comes up in exactly the same place he made the fast muskrat dive, no matter that the currents here are strong enough to put any man off by fifteen yards at least. He pops up without a layman's gasp, just pops up silently, eyes and forehead barely above the waterline, like he could care less if he ever breathed above water again. He's got something in his mouth and he paddles like a beaver, just his head and mouth above the water, cuts a fast, efficient wake right to the exact spot on the bank from which his mission started. A foot or two from the bank he pops to his feet and is on land again seamlessly, walking right up to the rig and standing at the side door that Tim has now toggled and switched so that it opens in its silent spaceship slide. Tic Tac takes a big two-quart-sized ziplocked baggie from his mouth and unseals it, taking out two or three smaller packages from inside and smelling them each: cash, weed, a lighter, hash-ish, a little booklet of scribbled notes, a necklace, a knife, a coil of green cord and fishing line, the dried neck of a pheas-ant, two Twinkies.

"I'd love to see this world try and figure out where I keep my shit. Everything from tits to teeth is on loan while we're living and I don't need a fucking three-car garage to put it in, I'll tell you that. I'd like to see the enemy figure out where I've written all the shit I know. I'll be bones one day like the rest of us and the state won't be going through my shit trying to figure out what auction to stick it in, I can tell you that. Everything I own will be all around them and they'll never see it, and I'll be doing whatever ghosts do, moving people's keys around and switching lights on and off and shit like that . . . I'll be all hovering above my hidden shit, just laugh-ing my ass off."

Matthew howls through a smile, "It was amazing! I feel like if Tim didn't have us hooked up with this rig you'd be able to dive down there and get us a couch and television!"

Tic Tac, still calm and contemplative from being in his un-derwater world, states rather plainly, "Who the fuck throws a couch and TV in a stream? There's no couches down there." Modoch stays silent, and Tim is focused on setting up the lawn chairs and a portable table, but without even looking he manages to afford a bit of attention to simply backing up Tic Tac, like two parents who know enough to always pres-ent a united front.

"Matthew, you don't throw furniture and shit into streams — imagine what this place would look like if everyone pulled shit like that."

"No, yeah, obviously. I was just saying it's amazing what he has — how he's hidden stuff."

"Here, give me a hand flipping the table over," Tim says with a shake of the head the way a kind parent might shake their head in loving exasperation. Matthew grabs half, Tim grabs the other half, and they flip it over and into place, each arranging the four chairs around it.

Slough Creek is a desolate little northeast corner of kill-or-be-killed terrain, severe and broad. Matthew sits imagining the tents of late-season adventurers being stomped flat by grizzlies tired of tearing up thirty-pound stumps and logs for an ounce or two of grubs. The bones of an elk aren't far from the bumper of the rig, bones picked clean by everything that moves in after a kill has satisfied and left drowsy the wolves or bear that brought it down. The brain moves slowly here but manages the thought: *Another beautiful place where you can feel lives gone and whatever small trace they've left behind.*

The day fades down like a summer breakup song, goes from white-hot to burned and orange, to red, to a dark purple wound around a bright fang of a moon. When the day was still red and orange, Tic Tac made use of feathers from the dried jerky-shriveled pheasant neck. Spun, tied, and glued onto a small hook, fixed to monofilament fishing line, the fishing line fixed to the thicker, green floating-cord stuff, no rod, no reel, just lines and dead bird remnants. The feathers were sprayed with a little silicon lubricant from the rig's steel toolbox.

"This shit will stop the squeak in a door, get you high, and make this little fucker float better than a real bug—that's some bang for the buck." And with this, Tic Tac goes down to the bank again, lies right down at the edge of it, floats this tiny knot of dead bird downstream right near the bank, feeding the fishing line out from his hand first, then the bright green floating-cord stuff went right through the same two fingers, until the whole little tiny, precise assembly is eight or ten feet past his face at the edge of the stream. Hearty cutthroat trout swim along the surface and investigate the downed airship of what seems like coveted protein. Seeing no shadow at the bank or in the current, and sensing nothing awry with the offering, the trout poke their noses right up below the con job bug and suck it in. Tic Tac watches for a rise and take, and when he sees the fish suck it down, he quietly thrusts his hands down underwater, a fast punch at the earth to set the hook into the fish's mouth, and then quickly starts wrapping the line back around his hand, retrieving what he laid out. He never makes a sound lying there, doesn't even seem to breathe, he brings in three beautiful cutthroat trout, one right after the other, with the calm of an assassin far from home with a job to get done quickly and quietly.

Now in the part of the night that has turned from a bruise to all black and stars, the men eat trout cooked on the fire at their feet, served with rice microwaved in the rig looming at their backs. Look one way and it's otherworldly and untamed landscapes, almost lunar, black, filled with a thousand things one doesn't know about themselves yet — certainly roamed by wolves and bears out there somewhere; look behind you and the rig hovers there, sharp, shiny, ugly, comforting, humming, and whirring; a reminder that there are factories full of ordinary people making giant metal boxes that aim to deliver tame comfort on the most severe, lonely, gorgeous terra firma. This is land that leaves you sitting next to your own ghost at the end of the day, a fire at your feet, and just beyond the light of what's burning, animals real and imagined fearlessly feeding, fucking, farting, and howling hot breath into crisp air, living and dying.

After dinner, the night opens into a field of booze, beer, weed, and shoplifted snack foods. Tic Tac reads aloud from a weird little secondhand book of cowboy poetry. The genre seems to be the last American depository for Rocky Mountain men with names like Old Bill Bailey — sporting, spirited, vaguely racist dolts who pass their days shoving themselves inside of unsuspecting women or claiming Indian slaves to prank around with, all in a whiskey-fueled fiery boredom veiled as taking simple pleasures in a country that's up for making sport of a situation, all in good cheer. And what's even better about it is that it does all of this while being polite enough to unveil the legends in simple rhyme schemes that one can feel and predict even with a head full of beer, even after having the face and brain hovering over the vaporous maw of a paper sack soaked in aerosol lubricant and

stolen lighter fluid. Cowboy poetry is solid fireside enter-
tainment, it turns out. This poetry is to be enjoyed on nights
like this, far enough away from any intelligent society that
might rightfully set people aflame for celebrating it, much
less celebrating it with a sixty-foot-long Sierra Mountain Air
luxury coach off in the shadows, while getting high on what
your hop-on acquaintance shoplifted in town. Matthew sits
back and lets the brain bask in the silly rhymes of low he-
roes denuding cultures and raping kind and plain wallflower
women who never saw it coming. The heart feels heavy at
turns, but the head dances with the idea that these men took
the time to record their down days in funny rhyme and simple meter! The brain rallies that one's worst moments put
forth in elementary funny rhyme and simple meter may be
the point of living; that these cowboy poets may have had it
right all along, the rape and slave stuff aside.

"Why do people so often miss that point, you know?" Matthew asks.

"There isn't a point to that shit, it's just funny," says Tic
Tac. "That lady in the log cabin was just doing laundry and
when she turned her back at the sink, he gave her the horn
and that Indian had to stay outside feeding Bill's horse. But
the twist is, it turns out the Indian was smoking Bill's to-
bacco and drinking his whiskey. He fucked Old Bill Bailey
over since Bill got the lady! That's funny as shit, that's why
I was laughing so fucking hard. There's that part, what's it
say" — Tic Tac starts leafing fast through the tiny book —
"Right here: 'And my redskin friend had been doing to me

with a wink, what I had done all evening long to the fair miss scrubbing my laundry at her sink.' That shit's hilarious because usually the Indians are the ones getting screwed over in these things. This guy put a twist on it."

"Right, yep, breaking form," Tim offers with a pretty intense focus and speedy cadence for a guy who's supposed to be done with cocaine.

Modoch sits silently, clearly not enjoying cowboy poetry night. Matthew sits quietly, the head racing and always ending up wondering if maybe Tic Tac's right, that there is no point. The head ventures the theory that maybe we're just here and gone and maybe if we aren't ready to go, we leave our dirty little ghost roaming around with nothing to do but be seen by children and house cats. On the heart, a thousand little pieces of graffiti, all dead-end schoolboy doodles of Tatiana's name; the head tries to remember perfectly the details of her biological container, especially her stomach and face, the stunning angles, and even the weird angles, the ones we see people from as the years pass.

Something hits Tim, lights him up like it's 1998 again, and evidently it doesn't matter that there's no segue from what Tic Tac was saying. The way the men spring up and speak now is like the disjointed rant of rehab—random sharing, Tic Tac reading from his tiny book, Modoch in a vow of silence, Matthew playing the new arrival still fresh from the outside world. Slough Creek Campground feels like a psychiatric ward with fire and fish; a nuthouse with wolves and

bears and buffalo, all of it perched on top of some fiery bas-
tard of a volcano that will take it all back one day just as easily as it created it; and it warns them of this with the mild
sulfuric stink of nearby springs hot enough to cook a man,
and the giant hisses and distant geysers erupting even without tourists gathered up to watch from a safe distance. Tim
is up out of his chair, hot, ready to erupt.

"This world, am I right? I mean, here we are, in this park,
one big plateau surrounded by mountains of ice, and the
whole place sitting on top of a volcano that's gonna go again
one day and turn this place into one hot lava lake of dead
do-gooders on vacation, but in the meantime it charms families and fishermen with its beauty and grace. This place is
heaven but it's the devil's big fiery gut underneath it all that
keeps it going, fuck yes. And I'm the same kind of thing working the same con and grift, but they're trying to put me away
for it, Chief—Sport! Sport. The world paints a bull's-eye on
Wall Street because it's only the fighting, fucking, prosper-
ing, and starving they can see. The rest of it is hidden across
the country in national parks, and in every Plain Jane and
Joe Six-Pack work-a-day heart. Put on a fucking smock and
punch the clock at Walmart and keep the rape and pillag-
ing far enough away from your day-to-day grind and you're
a hero, but haul your ass onto a trading floor, whipped by
good noseful of burn from a hooker who's forcibly moved
into your home to sexually degrade you, get in there and buy
your buys and sell your sells, fill the day orders, fuck or be

fucked, bleed or be hung and bled out, and you're the bad guy. Make a lot of people wealthy and they call you a criminal and say what you're doing is illegal."

"Yeah, but what you were doing is, actually, considered a fel . . ."

"A guy like me, just trying to do something good, swinging the scythe through the bullshit that's gone to seed so he can find some green, make some money, sure, but leaving a lot of folks in his wake with more than they had in the first place. Sure, yes, fine, you move some junk at deep discount to make some Joe feel like a player in a free market that, hello, his country was built on. For that, they call you a criminal?"

"Yeah, but in your case, you . . ."

"Guys like me, Chief — fuck — SPORT . . . sports like me, Champ, we're not doing anything that the average grocery store isn't doing on any given day. Moving the milk that's almost bad up to the front, move the fresh stuff to the back behind it; take the money you made selling the milk and use it to pay the butcher instead of the milk delivery tab because the milk can be paid in thirty days when you sell a hundred grand in fresh meat, which you know is going to sell because you heard the weather's gonna break this weekend so folks can have friends over for a barbecue. Nothing wrong with it, but get a guy like me doing the same thing and people start yelling 'Stop, thief!' the second they think they should be richer."

"Yeah, but, I mean, for the analogy to work, the grocer

would have to be so high he's blind and wearing dildo boots that . . ."

Suddenly in a flash, Modoch is up from his chair by the fire in a huff, kicking up dust, stomping around. Tim's chest sinks right back to where it was before the puff and holler. Tic Tac stops staring off into the dark looking for an enemy that isn't there. Matthew stops cold and waits. Modoch's robe of bison undulates and bucks as he bends down in one single move, grabbing things from a duffel at his feet, looking past the fire for a place this can happen. The bison robe is hanging half off in disarray from the hustle of getting up and getting ready for who knows what. Matthew's head races trying to figure if it's a fight or mutiny, or an angry retreat to the rig for sleep, or a tension that was here in the muscle memory of weeks, way before Matthew got here, finally coming to a head; what is it? Tim snaps to a sober head like a teenager getting with the program so his dad doesn't fly off the handle and kill the weekend plans.

"Woops, okay, so, Matthew, we'll be back. We have to go do our . . ."

"All members. Everyone, all four," says Modoch/Crazy Daryl Acid, and he pulls the bison skin and head back into alignment so it fully covers him; so he's 100 percent Modoch again. Matthew gets up out of his chair at the fire, is ready to follow them, but doesn't know if he's supposed to be grabbing anything for the trip. Tic Tac knifes up and puts on a headlamp, snapping into action, all business, as if his whole night was just about waiting to be dispatched on a mission. Tim has popped over into the rig to grab some things. Matthew takes a stick out of the fire with a blackened end and realizes that's the stupidest thing he's ever grabbed when heading off to run some mystery errand in the middle of this remote corner of what feels like the last frontier in the lower forty-six or forty-eight or however many are below Alaska.

It's hard to remember much of anything in the waft of the tarred, sticky black chunk that Tic Tac has been firing up all night. A pungent opiate cut to smaller pieces with the knife from the same Ziplock bag, the one he hid underwater and fetched like an amphetamine-tuned muskrat with a sixth and seventh sense that his fellow upright land mammals lack. The head argues that maybe it's not the smartest thing to be following a man dressed like a bison into darkened dire woods — on a night that's bled a thick, pitch-black blind over everything but millions of tiny stars. On the other hand, the entire Milky Way seems an arm's reach away in a sky like this, so Matthew's got that to wish upon if he ends up in a bind tonight.

Off into the woods, single file, Modoch's big cape of fur and horns leading the odd procession. Tic Tac's second in the lineup on the path — his headlamp bounces a beam of cold blue halogen, practically X-raying anything he happens to look toward. Tim is in line after Tic Tac and proceeds tentatively at best; Matthew is last in line, and if there's anything bigger up ahead than a man in a buffalo costume, last would certainly be better than first or second. However, if the attack comes from behind, Matthew will regret being last in line. Five or six minutes up the path and Modoch stops cold, which means that the single-file domino effect has everyone stopped cold. Tic Tac has his knife out and is ready for action, but then again he's had his knife out and been ready to use it ever since the second or third hit of his underwater stash back at the campfire.

Matthew stands still in the black, watching what he can in the speedy, twitchy, every-which-way sweep of quiet halogen panic shooting from Tic Tac's head. Matthew's brain is certain something's wrong and that there's nothing to do now but wait patiently while Modoch is mated by a horny male bear or buffalo, up against a rock or pinned to the ground. The heart is beating too fast to argue thoughts like these racing across the brain: *That's what you get for wearing shit like a full bison skin; what were we thinking?; what if heaven is a lie?; now we die, and all because Tim ran west when things went south on him in Lower Manhattan.*

Modoch remains paused, then finally uses his/the dead bison's head to nod toward another path to their right; this is apparently the path he wants them to take now. Up the smaller sub path they go, like a drum corps marching roughshod over national park land, pushing forward with what's left of them after a recession, a war, hashish, corporate magazines, antihistamines and Vicodin, crafts and meditation, high-end whores and dealers, Republican urologists, animal-robe making and hide tanning, and every other slapdash stab at spirituality one can imagine. The battered platoon of modern living gone wrong finds a small meadow surrounded by a couple of rock wall bluffs that are maybe one story high. The meadow, all told, is small, maybe the size of a studio apartment in New York, or a home office in Los Angeles, or a utility room off the kitchen of any house in any place in this country. Modoch stops and nods with approval; this is the place, apparently. Tim and Tic Tac set into getting ready for something they've clearly done before; they pull a fat chunk of a stump over from the edge of the grass and right into the center. Tim aligns the stump and straightens it while Matthew helps Tic Tac empty out a small backpack stuffed with shoplifted stuff that is apparently about to come in handy.

Modoch fixes a gaze on Tim and Tic Tac to provide audience or witness, Tim sort of nods at Matthew, all business, looks at Matthew as if he shouldn't need to be told to take a seat to fill out a small semicircle of three men being addressed by a negro buffalo on a stump. Modoch speaks like he never does, because, well, he never speaks. But here in the meadow stump conference area, he fires an ad hoc combination of dressing-down of Tim, Matthew, and Tic Tac; a Frankenstein jam of rehab slogans, herbal tea box maxims, snippets of business books, maybe — the kind of buffet folks on planet Earth throw together on nights like this. Modoch bleats and spits like a jazz man feeling the time signature and falling ahead and behind and to the side of it, somehow in perfect meter and time.

"I see you making the same mistake, all of you, all of us.

I see you not being smart enough to know that you don't know. Thinking the goal is to find yourself instead of forget yourself. All of this thinking is happening but the thinking is upside down. How much food do you think is found by the hawk or osprey who flies upside down, back and shoulders to ground, eyes looking up instead of at the ground? You can't gain a thing until you give up. You can't find what you need until you realize you don't know what you need," and Modoch is only getting warmed up. Tim looks over at Matthew with arched eyebrows and his chin tucked down into his chest, with this sort of hey-I-told-you-we're-on-to-something-out-here kind of neighborly look. Daryl Acid/Modoch starts picking up speed now.

"You sit there hoping to one day know it all, but what you should be hoping for is that one day you'll realize you don't know much at all. Look around at how many people are looking for ways to avoid feeling pain. And see how much trouble not feeling pain brings; see how much more pain people cause themselves by running from pain in the first place! Running from pain hurts more than feeling pain, almost every time."

And Matthew sits there nodding like he believes, but suddenly the gray is rather soundly saying: *Ah, so, there's the catch. Almost every time. So how do you know which time is going to hurt like fucking crazy to feel? If we're talking about almost every time, and not every time, then clearly one can infer that it still pays to run from pain, we just don't know which time it pays. So, really, what we need is a spiritual awakening in the form of being able to pinpoint the times it's worth getting numb on the run. It's a good argument, this argument to feel pain, but it has a few holes in it.* This is what Matthew's head does every time help comes along. When someone like Modoch says stuff like this, it looks for holes in the argument. When someone like Tatiana buoys the heart and spirit, the same kind of smart skepticism races along with questions: *Why is she being nice? What's in it for her? Did she used to be a man? Does she have sex with entire football teams or anything that could hurt me upon discovery? How long until you say you love her and she disappears into the sky forever?*

Modoch continues on, "We, as human beings, we have this disease, this virus inside us, that makes us believe we're not getting what we want. The sooner you stop believing that, the sooner you start realizing how much you have. If people could stop long enough to think about it, they'd realize that if they would've gotten what they wanted in life, they would've been short-changing themselves half of the time . . ."

Again, the head races with clauses: *Yes, but which half of the time? The best plan, it seems, is to have one half of an awakening and one half of a realization and become only 50 percent fixed, because it seems in each of these maxims, the bad stuff is working fine half of the time.* And then the head is in such full-speed control of things that it starts revising and editing, interjecting right into Modoch's diatribe as it's unrolling from him. But the running commentary and loophole hunting stretches thin and something is about to come in, some kind of realization, but what, what, what, and why does it terrify the brain and make it race?

"Start taking yourself out of the equation of everything around you. If you're out of the picture, there's nobody in your way. Start seeing where the universe takes you instead of being so concerned with where you want to go. We are not so unique, and we are all looking for the same things before we're gone, so we ask the sky for the truth about why everyone we love is going to die."

Modoch is right about all of this stuff. It's all true, and Matthew sits feeling at least like his suspicions about living have been confirmed. The gray races through a sermon of its own inside of the head, and it reaffirms everything Matthew has spent years thinking: *We love people who will fade back to helpless, hunched infants in front of us or disappear in a flash too fast for us to have ever really gotten started on life with them, much less had the time to say good-bye. Some of the people closest to us, our only witnesses in what we've done with ourselves, just as we're theirs — they're gone after a phone call you had no way of realizing would be the last; and it was trivial and brief and rushed for what now will always be the dumbest reason to have rushed to get off the call. We get acquainted with doctors being calm, congenial men comforting us with a smile when we're young enough to still heal, and we come to know them as the somber men who confirm for us that this, what's going wrong inside us, is what time does to all of us. You feel loss, you catch on to what time does with all of this devouring of us, so you try to create more life around you. Fuck time and death, you'll start creating more life than death takes in your time. One day there's a marriage, one day there's the terrifying and heady news that you're now going to be three instead of two, after months of vibrant, radiant, beautiful swelling, there's the visit to the same doctor who has given you nothing but good news, but today the tiny heart on the blue-and-gray screen has stopped beating. The woman with the gel and wand who has been gliding over the slicked belly of life and chance and change is quiet now, because there's nothing to say that hasn't been fucking said in that instant when you all saw it still instead of beating and did the fucking math. And that was the day Kristin got a pass to do whatever might make her feel better about these days, and maybe that's the moment the whole marriage starts falling to pieces, the moment two people are silently giving each other permission to get as far away from a marriage as they need to, whether it's forever or for a one-night stand. And there's a giant world outside, but there's a little path called day-to-day life that most of us never stray from long enough to see the world for more than a week or two at a time. There are sudden suicides that were never supposed to happen in your little circle, and that day on the calendar can suddenly be seen coming from a mile away every year, same fucking day every year, tattooed forever on the inside of you. You take refuge in pets, and then there are pets that you love more than you thought you could, and the years go by fast, and suddenly you're standing there watching as they don't die quickly from the injection like the vet assured you they would.*

And you stand there feeling like once again you're screwing up the bigger plan that something up there must have, trying to snuff this innocent thing out quietly and quickly because of what happened inside of its liver, heart, and kidneys; because they said there would be only painful weeks left anyway; weeks of more breakdown and bad cell division, bleeding, dehydration; you couldn't stand seeing the pain, the blood coming up again, and innocent eyes full of confusion and so you said yes. You think you're being strong again, you agree, you bring her in, one quick little tiny sting and then it's off to sleep in heaven, if animals can get in. The paw is shaved, the little sting happens, you put her favorite toy down next to the cold, clear, thin hose full of a drip of who knows, the hose that has no idea what it's really doing today, the tube you keep second-guessing. But, go, just go, just go, just do this, fuck, nobody's ever going to explain it, do it, do it, do it. And suddenly she's full of life again, looking at you like you've made yet another mistake on this planet, how the fuck did this happen, how does any of it happen, cats, dogs, babies, parents, all turned to fucking angels living in a place you aren't even sure you believe in.

The truth inside of the head is done having its way with Matthew, and has darted off. Tic Tac snaps out of his haze, too, snaps out of sitting cross-legged on the ground, eyes dreamy, mouth open, looking up at Modoch like a six-year-old watching television. He's up, and in a flash he darts off into the woods. Tim seems fine with this, deep in thought about these things Modoch is saying; Modoch seems fine with the situation as well; Matthew is there wrought by the feelings and truth that have run roughshod right over him. Nobody is too concerned with Tic Tac darting off into dark savage woods on some cue that only he seems to have heard. Modoch carries on toward the big finish.

" . . . We ask that you watch over us in battle — the battle we fight within ourselves for no reason. The battle that will bring no gain or peace, no expansion or preservation, no spoils, but only pain and suffering by our own hand. And we ask you to give us a sign, Great Spirit, that you hear us humbly asking for strength and humility."

And just then, right at that line, as soon as Modoch says it, a giant streak of white fire shoots through the sky, right up into the ink-and-ashes black sea of it, right up from behind the rock bluff, which is about thirty yards behind Modoch and his preaching stump. Then another huge white streak of fire into the night, then another. Then what appears to be a paper sack on fire comes tumbling down the face of the rock bluff and falls to rest about halfway down the rock face and smolders rather anticlimactically. And then the sound of Tic Tac way off in the dark distance, "Motherfucker, ouch! Fuck!"

Modoch confirms the Great Spirit's fiery dispatches into the night behind him, "Our moment of silence is our humble thanks for your reply, Great Spirit!"

In return, from a distance, one can hear the muttering of a much more earthly reply. "That was me saying that, mother-fucker!"

Modoch's head bows in silence. Tim's head bows in silence. Matthew's head bows in silence. The three men start to shudder in silent lurches that give way and explode into laughter. The kind of laughter one remembers from being seven and eight and laughing with one's still-young mother so loudly, so uncontrollably, back when you got tears from laughing, and back when the laughter was so undeniable that an overworked and under-rested dad joined in — all of you, angels and equals and together forever and ever no matter what. If you've laughed hard enough with someone you love, or especially with someone you don't, it feels like there's hope for something taking you up and out of yourself; out of that head where things always have to turn bad; out of that heart that seems to scan life's horizon to find a way to be broken; out of that idea that life always has to include this idea that someone is against you.

Just then, on the bluff behind them, the smoldering sack catches, a small orange flame forms, grows a bit, and suddenly becomes a softball-sized fist of steady white-hot fire and hiss, turns night to midday all around it, and stays there burning white and then hot-blue, for at least thirty-five minutes. Matthew looks into the light, looks at Modoch and Tim, then back into the light. Not one of the three of them has an explanation for this.

26

Coda

THE NEXT MORNING, around the ghost of a campfire in desperate need of being restoked, Matthew and Tic Tac sit just a few feet from the rig in chairs still damp and chilled from Yellowstone's cruel overnight lows; Matthew notices the burn on top of Tic Tac's hand and speaks up.

"Sorry your hand got burnt. Man . . . last night was amazing. It's all pretty big, life, and, I don't know . . . forces and . . . all of that. I'm still not sure what happened when Modoch was doing his thing up there."

"Well, I'll tell what the fuck was *supposed* to happen. I soaked a paper sack down with lighter fluid and put the block off an old chain saw in it. Then I cracked two traffic flares and poured the powder inside, put cordite in there, just wrapped it around the block and tied it off—which was kind of a dipshit move on my part, since the load already had three sources of ignition. Anyway, what was supposed to fucking happen was, I would light the paper sack, it would ignite, I would wait for a count of, say, ten, until the magnesium in that block started to fucking go, and then I would chuck a big fucking white fireball into the sky so Modoch had his reply from the Great Spirit. But what happened was, I held the thing for a count of ten, the top of my hand got real motherfucking warm, and about four seconds later I realized I'm some fucking genius who runs into the woods in the middle of the night and sets his own Goddamn hand on fire. So the burn really comes on, I scream and throw the stupid bag, and it goes out in the air. So now what's supposed to be this big-ass ball of white light is just some paper sack full of engine parts and shit, tumbling its sorry ass down that big rock face. Then it stops and just kind of lays there, like the Great Spirit is just some asshole who throws a sack of trash into the woods anytime he likes what he hears."

"Right, well, but then . . ."

"But then, nothing. But then I'm standing back there with what's left of a cold beer, pouring the fucking thing all over my hand, screaming my ass off."

"It eventually caught, though. That's what I wanted to tell you; there was eventually a big white flame from it," Matthew tries to reassure him.

"Well, I wouldn't know, because at that point I'm dancing around with my hand between my legs wondering why the fuck me and Daryl — or Motrin or whatever the fuck I'm supposed to call him now — aren't just sleeping on federal land under a tarp or table like usual; like we do every summer, instead of being mixed up with magical mystery bus and the fucking weekly medicine man show."

"I really liked it. I think you guys are kind of on to something. At least you're doing something good and trying to be a little better each day." And as Matthew is saying this, Tic Tac seems to soften a little, staring down at the ashes at his feet in the fire pit.

"Well, I will say, that when it works right, it's a pretty fucking sweet thing. It's one of the few times I can feel a little . . . faith about things; feel like maybe I don't know everything, and maybe there's something bigger out there that does."

"Yeah!" Matthew agrees maybe too enthusiastically.

"Even though I'm the guy setting off the fireworks and shit that's supposed to be the bigger thing. So, I guess I'm kind of the guy behind the puppet show curtain who's starting to believe in puppets."

Modoch and Tim make their way out of the rig after a night's sleep; drag a couple of chairs over to the ash pit. Tim points sleepily to the edge of the burn, to the remnants of a trout skin that didn't get tossed all the way in.

"That's the kind of shit that brings bears. Like when that guy had fucking bacon grease all over the place. And then a bear comes, and then I have to come out and handle it, and that's when shit goes south like it did and I have rangers on my back. That's the kind of thing that starts it; that right there." Nobody really acknowledges the trout skin or makes a move to kick it under the ashes or anything. To Modoch and Tic Tac, parklife is a lot of things, but it's not a world where one has to swing Formica tabletops from an RV's impromptu arsenal at bears who would be on their way anyway after a minute or two of sniffing around. Late-morning small talk commences around a fire barely smoldering with a few orange hot spots in the cool gray of it. The head is up and racing now, and it issues the subtext of manly talk in foreign film subtitles on the lower third of the screen in this moment of three men talking.

"You gotta worry less about bears," Tic Tac says.

WE ARE HERE AND GONE IN A FLASH.
IT IS IMPOSSIBLE TO PREVENT.

"The bear market in lower Manhattan, the bear in lower Montana. Fuck 'em both, they're dealing with a white-hot laser; my plane, bitches, and it looks like we're gonna be in the Hudson. La-ser beam," Tim says, pointing to his forehead with three syllabic jabs.

FEAR HAS GOVERNED ME. I GET BY ON LUCK.
IT IS TERRIFYING.

Matthew laughs gamely, giving Tim a sporting nod.

I AM TERRIFIED, TOO. MAYBE I STOPPED GROWING
AT AGE NINE.

Tic Tac thinks about what Tim said, regards Tim, Matthew, and Modoch/Crazy Daryl Acid, shaking his head upon the survey of his surroundings and says, "I can't imagine any of you motherfuckers would know how to focus a laser beam if you did have access to one."

I CAN'T IMAGINE ANY OF YOU MOTHERFUCKERS WOULD KNOW HOW TO FOCUS A LASER BEAM IF YOU HAD ONE.

The conversation recedes and the subtitles fade. Tim mashes a nest for his coffee mug into a small, orange hot spot in the ashes of last night's fire in order to warm it up — even though it was made in a microwave oven, in a kitchen of finished dark cherry wood and stainless steel parked just feet away. In the silence, Matthew's head issues the standard litany of questions, but today, for some reason, there are answers. A new system! The system seems to be this: Issue answers to the questions, no matter how convenient, if only for the sake of having some.

Q: *How long can one continue to run?*

A: *A lifetime if that's what one wants.*

Q: *Why do we continue to struggle?*

A: *Because the least likely of days are wrought with small pleasures; moments or sights so small and sublime, accidentally hard-won, unpredictably forged, these pleasures and ideas and surprise endings. And on the days none of that occurs, there are the comforts of sex or loneliness, and cigarettes, and documentaries about the willy-nilly distribution of genius and the deadly rigors it comes with. If nothing else, the struggle is punctuated with billionaire idiots on television and the folly of singing contests packed with heartbreaking simpletons try-*

ing to impress wealthy, faded pop stars, and magazines loaded up with cultural bankruptcy, all of it making one aware of the practically Greek or biblical myth we're living in. To witness it at all is reason enough to continue on, really.

Q: *Will Tim just live here now, far from Wall Street, stuck between arrested development and a half-assed spiritual quest choreographed by two shoplifting hop-ons?*

A: *No, he won't. He will come to realize the music he has to face isn't half as ominous as he thinks it is, he'll face it, he'll return to making a killing managing a medium-sized fund or maybe demote himself to being one of those who grift the barely solvent out of what little money they have by charging them for get-rich seminars in shitty hotel conference rooms in the broken, recessive cities they live in.*

Q: *What will become of Modoch and Tic Tac and men like that?*

A: *They are probably ghosts to begin with, having more fun in the real world than the mortals stuck in it.*

Q: *Is Tim thinking the same kind of stuff at this very moment?*

Tim farts, takes one beat, and says, "Woops, it's about to smell like a Lehman Brothers ETF; hold your breath and count to ten, Chie . . . CHAMP."

A: *Probably not.*

27

Canyon to Canyon

DAYS AND NIGHTS go past the road and snakes its way south and west from Slough to Lamar to Yellowstone. Eventually, way back at town, the hook drops the Taurus and releases Matthew from the talon of this gang and groove. Night comes on like a summer breakup song far away from the highway Matthew is taking out of Montana and into Idaho. Somewhere way southwest of here, in California, in the Hollywood Hills, Tatiana's house is reasonably packed for a party. The guests move in circles, like fish in schools. The first circle, the inner circle, they are a mix of faces one recognizes from movies and they're schooled up with people one won't recognize but for their money and clear influence over the people in movies. The next circle out from that, the circle generally to the outside of those faces, those are the people who one recognizes but can't quite place; day-players and bit parts in too many movies, maybe insult comics that seem to run on an endless loop on cable; roasts and prank shows that flicker in the background of daily living, often with the word *Mute* appearing in the lower-right corner of the screen; maybe in apartments where people are talking or in bars that have a TV hanging from the ceiling. Then there's the circle outside of that, and those are the Remember When people — one has to look past the Hollywood hippie hair and weight to see the face that was on screens of varying size, say, a decade or so ago. All of the people in the first circle, the inner circle, they want to be loved — but what they don't realize is that it's hard for people to love you when you're everywhere at once. The people in the next circle, they want to be missed; missed because they aren't on screen long enough; missed so much that people demand to see more of them on the screen, but what they don't realize is that nobody can miss you when you're always popping up even if it's just to say three lines — nobody can miss you until you're gone. And the people in the far outside circle, the Remember When people, they want to be invited back into either of the other two circles, but what they don't realize is that you can't be invited when you keep asking if you can come.

All of these circles are in orbit around a fire pit out back, and ambling through a mess and maze of Tatiana's inconspicuous wealth, they're cornered (circle one) or breezing through (circles two and three) big lo-fi rooms that sprawl in a lazy meander; rooms that spill like a shallow waterfall of bittersweet molasses taking years to settle over different levels and lips of canyon ledge. One level of the deck out back has been built to allow two big trees to continue growing up through it. There's a gigantic solid table that was once a barn in Montauk or the teak casualty of a violent storm in former Burma, a ton if it weighs an ounce, as big as the swimming pool it points to, a long, skinny, dark horizon pool made to look more like a dark mirage, or brook, or long and narrow cold-water eddy. The table plants a long, thick, precise footprint that starts from the inside of the glass-and-redwood living room and lies right through doors built to close around it. Past the doors, the table continues on, like a long, skinny state, out onto a main section of deck that looks like the kind of place a coyote, or mountain lion, or the ghost of Jim Morrison might be spotted sneaking around if one were to stay up all night alone, smoking cigarettes in the warm Southern California air of jasmine, waiting for it to happen.

The anchors of the inner circle tonight are a gaggle of cute twenty-three-year-old guys with twenty-eight-inch waists who are Tatiana's only foot left in the business of managing people instead of managing things. They are the vampires that have provided the commission on royalties that basically bought this house and probably the apartment in New York; dangerous vampires safe enough for ten or thirty or a hundred million girls to fall in love with on tiny screens dragged around in their backpacks and pockets or on whatever big screens girls still make their way to, from Sunrise Mall to Sunset Boulevard, from Venice to Venice, from Paris to Lake Perris, and anywhere in between. On screen, this knot of cute mall-gothic bipedal leeches look for host bodies that will serve as the next blood meal, but at Tatiana's house with another summer smash hit in front of them, they are the most polite and timid guests; the cautious current winners of the biggest West Coast lottery.

"You guys good? Everything okay?" she asks through the smile, eyes, lips, life-and-death curves, and corduroy-clad hips, all somehow turned beautifully big sister or mom in a moment like this, which bleeds them of their speed and danger and they reply all over each other.

"Hey!"

"Oh, yeah, thanks for . . . thanks."

"Yeah, this is all so . . . yeah . . ."

And as twilight heads quietly into the night, there's some talk with a man named Neil about making sure the boys are staying out of the sun and pale before the upcoming rounds to promote the new installment of the franchise. Neil is a man who looks naked not sitting in a black Range Rover; a man who looks unsure as to whether he's talking to Tatiana or the little dipshit hands-free blue-flash-dead-tooth-jaw-squawk thing clipped to his ear. He's dark, tall, thin, receding, and determined to never get old, or at least die trying to make time stand still for every client he needs to keep young. Maybe Tatiana is not the manager of this lot, but the impression is that she's there in circle one, not recognizable, and so clearly has some piece of them some way or the other. Maybe she sold the film rights, maybe she licensed the merchandise, maybe she owns the words *blood* and *vampire* and is paid a dime every time someone speaks them, but it's something. One of the vampires is drinking from a coffee mug that says, *When the angry jerking about and spitting stops, the serenity starts.* This seems perfect for a vampire, assuming there's some struggle in getting a host body to forfeit a blood meal. Neil, the tall, dark guy who looks like he's running toward money and away from death, talks to Tatiana. Tatiana looks like she'd rather run away from money and toward death because of this.

"You still managing?"

"Managing nicely, thanks, Neil."

"You know what I mean, baby."

"I've got one of the three vampires and that's pretty much it. And you just said baby, which will answer the next question about why I'm getting out of managing."

"Your vampire's pretty much gone, which I shouldn't be telling you, but I'm telling you: We've got the other two and they're leaning on your guy pretty hard. It's not my thing, the agency obviously wants the package, so they've got everything on high."

"I don't give a hard, sweet fuck what you do, to be coy. If you guys took him today, I'm still paid on his last seven years of net plus worldwide DVD and a bunch of ancillary in perpetuity."

"Hey, plus . . . don't forget the cat books," Neil says, with every ounce of jeer one imagines it laced with.

"Yeah, I cashed royalties on three million copies of *No,*

Kitty, No!, plus I'll never wake up at three in the morning to a phone call from a wasted kitty threatening suicide because another kitty got more covers or was bigger on the poster. I don't get the call telling me that my kitty is blowing another kitty in a cabana at the Four Seasons and that it's my job to make sure every red state box office is selling PG tickets to families that believe the kitty is straight. I don't wake up at six in the morning to a phone call from an angry director firing a kitty because the kitty was caught banging a bag of junk in her trailer after it cost said director more than my client made for him on the last movie just to insure the set since she's turned into a junkie. So, yeah, I won't forget my cat books, Neil."

"Three million, seriously?"

"Two hundred and twenty adorable snapshots of people's cats doing silly things around the house, three million copies for the paying American public, one large loft in Manhattan for me."

Neil takes a sip of his drink. His drink is in a coffee mug that says, *God will help you find a gun if you're grateful.* In the second circle, the circle called People Whom One Recognizes But Is Unsure from Where, the guitar player from a band called We're Working on a Comeback Album but So Much Has Changed about the Business talks to a man from the circle outside of his, a man from the Remember When circle. He is probably better known as Guy Who Plays the Dad and he's a guy who is basically a poem that goes:

It's like what the fuck
I'm not even that old
five years ago I was still reading for the
   Hot Neighbor and shit like that
but now it's The Dad
hey, I don't even have kids
hey, I'm not even a dad in real life
hey whatever, I need the work
and anything that allows me to pay the bills
   and work on writing a screenplay is fine with me
that's the way I look at it.

But he hasn't written a screenplay; he hasn't written a thing. He stands and hears himself talking the same way he's been talking since he got close to having what these vampire kids have, back in maybe 1993, back when he was something, like, twenty-three. He keeps a good game face and thinks about how you get your shot, you get your taste, and then it seems one loses the right to hope for another try even after a decent little bite of it, even after years of waiting in line again. The world takes a look at you up on the shelf and thinks: *Well, he got his taste, had a shot, not a bad shake, got a lot closer than some, no love lost that he's working whatever job he's gotta take.* He thinks about how you can feel the world pull away when they aren't sure what to think of how it went for you, when they're not sure of what to say. He thinks about how you can feel it when it leaves for you; how you no longer have your little schoolboy prayers about how God must have some purpose for you and some work for you to do here; any of the little thoughts like that which may keep one going are gone after the first taste, because what if the little run you had was all God had planned? What if one seventeen-year-old just needed to hear the thing your character said in the sitcom you had for half a season back when you had your chance? Thinks all this stuff, staring at the vampire boys who are having it, having it, having it, and he says something gamely to the band guy about just doing the work because doing the work is all one can concern themselves with, really; says something sporting about how that's the real reward anyway. But the only work he's doing is working his way into a conversation with someone from the circle closer to the action, and closer to a chance at another shot happening for him. The guy from the band smiles as best he can, ducks away, writes some stuff down on a napkin with a pen he bummed from a girl working for the caterer:

> *The good days were one long kiss*
> *that came with one little twist*
> *all my teeth would fall out*
> *if I stopped to catch my breath.*

And about 707 miles north-northeast, Matthew keeps the midsize Ford Taurus or similar on course and straight, due southwest for another day at least, and the head is bored of singing, and trying to forget about home, and trying to run alone, so it kills time making anagram mash of whatever it can: The Heart Is a Lonely Hunter, a heathenish loner utterly, a heathenish rottenly lure. Three thousand miles east of all of this, in a bed not so far from the work training center in Norwalk, Connecticut, Chris is sleeping. He's dreaming of how Matthew hasn't been coming to pick up his mugs, how they're building up. In the dream, the boxes of mugs stack up higher than he's ever seen them, higher than the whole building, up through the roof, going higher than the sky, higher than clouds, as high as the moon. There's an astronaut floating around way up by the top of the stack, way up by where it gets close to the moon, and the astronaut looks over at Chris and acts like he's humping a box of the mugs. Chris starts laughing, starts coughing, wakes up staring at the ceiling, not quite able to articulate to himself that his eyes feel like they've been doing that heavy water thing that happens from sadness or laughing.

Eventually, Matthew is falling asleep in the sky against an expensive sweatshirt rolled up and jammed between his head and an economy-class window; Tatiana is sitting at her place in Los Angeles, drinking coffee, telling herself she's not going back to cigarettes even though her last pale actor in the knot of simulated vampires is as good as poached; Tim and Modoch and Tic Tac are still pounding Yellowstone's higher ground, the season will wane and they will start to tire of setting sacks of fuel aflame at night and hurling them into Montana's gigantic sky as reasonable facsimile of ghostly replies.

Every day Matthew spent on top of, under, and next to mountains has been a day of email piling up, and the night spent on a plane with a dead phone and no charger will be the same. Email stacks up high and unread, from Tatiana to Matthew, about how complicated things are with her; about how complicated it feels to explain; about oh fuck, never mind, it's simple and disregard what she was saying and who knows what's happening; about how she could help Matthew make a good chunk of money; about how millions of suburban girls who dumped their pony phase for a vampire kick will want a coffee mug that says, *It starts off cute, and then it gets ugly,* and that she's noticed that someone stole two of his mugs from her party; and how it was probably the same person who is stealing her last client making money. All of this is to say: The slow-motion drag of Matthew's days is about to turn a corner and hurl into the straightaway. Finally.

28

——

Living Like Your Food Was Drugged Is Fine Entertainment

MATTHEW WAKES UP SLOUCHED in a leather chair, the lighting dim and barely enough to cut through the smog of menthols drifting over from the little glassed-off corner where razor-sharp, small, and tanned men in suits are smoking them. The walls in here are mirrored gold and smudged, and on the little black lacquered table next to him, there's a small fountain with a little plastic dojo or temple or altar or something in it—it's plugged into the wall with a thin extension cord. Everyone is basically Chinese and staring at him. Mostly businessmen, well dressed, peering over the tops of complimentary copies of *The International Herald Tribune* and *Jakarta Times*. Oh, that's a hit waiting to happen. That's a mug waiting to be turned into a giant hit. Matthew picks up a small pad and pen on the table next to him and underneath the EVA Air logo writes this: *Everyone is basically Chinese.*

The head posits that waking up like this must be exactly what it feels like to realize you're in a Quentin Tarantino film, after someone drugged your food, after someone snuffed you with a soaked rag, or pistol-whipped you, and you're starting to come to. That woman back in craft class, Jan or Lynn, the one that bought the mug for her son because he likes *Pulp Fiction,* her son would love waking up like this. The head rants a little, shows whatever footage it has, think, think, Goddamnit, think a minute, the head screams tough, like some ham looking for work in those movies on network television. But, yes, right, okay, it's coming back in clips: made it back, the last fifty miles the pain was bad, those hills on 5, Santa Clara or wherever it is all the way to the Hertz rental return lane, that was a side-bent crunch of ureter pain and scrape; returned the car; upgraded to the big soft seats with a sad combination of two credit cards, cashed miles, and even wadded cash at LAX. This must be the layover in Taipei, this morning or night or whatever time it is outside of the airline lounge; last night, the legs allowing just enough go-again to get from the gate to this place and that's about all the memory there is, save for the fact that there was another long push of ache, a fucking blinding pain at the urinal during the interminable wait. Blood all over the white porcelain there, then a fast, fast, fast search online, on the tiny phone screen, for places outside of the United States that have hospitals that don't charge thirty thousand dollars to get rocks out of your kidney when they're too large to scratch and claw their way down and out.

Three grand or something dumb to get here on short notice, still a bargain compared to the States, one credit card smacked down onto the counter and then a second one to make up the balance still due on the fare, but it's easy to spend it all when there's internal bleeding and something that won't need a name or a college fund is clawing its way out and into the world. Doubled over in pain, leaning on the desk not batting an eye at charging up three grand and change. The pills made the pain of the cost go away, the pills turned LAX into a decent song or scene from a movie, the pills made it that much easier to lay the American Express Platinum, and then the less prestigious Visa Greenish Faux Marble, flat on the yellow and orange ticket counter's cool, flat Formica. The pills made Bali an option, but first there's this, the layover in Taipei, and the haze has left the head a cruel narrator in their wake, it's a fog of hurt to try and figure out where the biological container has wound up this morning. Jesus, stare all you want, you lazy sons of bitches, read your papers, peek up and over them, judge your fellow man, savages.

Up, up, up, and out the door to the last Starbucks one is likely to see between here and Denpasar. A Starbucks like any other except that they look sideways at anyone ordering with their hands crammed into the front of the pants in order to hold the nuts firmly so they don't bring jagged referred pain with each beat of the heart. The mouth smiles a little bit, because for once it's scaring the world instead of being scared by it, instead of smiling politely, instead of stretching thin with worry hoping that it has said the right thing. That's right, this is what it's like, you here standing at the gate to the west, you here making the grande iced coffee, this is what it's like in America at the moment, everyone staggering around like junk zombies, unshowered, mumbling about how everyone is basically Chinese, hands crammed down the front of their pants and holding on to their genitals for comfort, for reassurance, for dear fucking life! I'm telling you, Huang, it's a Goddamned jungle over there. Companies fattening people for decades then turning them loose in the streets to crush up lines of over-the-counter speed; to hoover up allergy pills and live in cars — you don't want it, man. You're looking at one of the lucky ones, this hot mess in your line trying to feed its blood something to wake its brain is the best-case scenario, and that's only because he's selling shit in parks and craft classes to round eyes who spend their days anchored at desks until the walking papers come.

Oh, the head is delightful, the head is having its fun this morning. Maybe the book about eating and praying is right and there's something to this getting up and getting out. The coffee comes, this fix goes in the face, the clock does its thing, and eventually a piece-of-shit plane, something pockmarked in the paint and described in handmade signage at the gate as a WET-LEASED AIRCRAFT, this dirty burst of fuel and metal, is hurled skyward for the remaining leg of this little spiritual/medical journey. Matthew tries his best to not leer at the flight attendant once the retired DC-9 reaches whatever cruising altitude it's capable of. Look at it in here, begs the stem at the back of the brain, look at it, this ghetto in the sky, this old horse that thought it was long enough in the tooth to go quietly into scrap and salvage, jerked back aloft, ready or not, shoved into service today. It's all but empty, maybe twenty or thirty people where there should be ten times that. Most everybody took one look at this junked old wheeze and walked back to the ticket counter to rebook. Is that the spirit, though?

Matthew thought about the question in a sort of mildly drugged earnestness and decided that no, no that is not, in fact, the spirit. It's still a jet, you pussies, it's a miracle, this old bag, it's nothing near as grim as thirty days at sea or in a wagon train waiting for cholera to stick half of your family in unmarked graves. It's a less aesthetically pleasing jet, yes. It's a jet that gives the impression of wanting to slouch its shoulders and succumb to a lazy high-pitched moan and ninety-degree downward plunge to a hard-earned retirement, yes. And sure, fine, the seats will weep stories of all the honeymoon asses that sat in them thirty years ago the minute you sit on them. The worn headrests and permanently oil-blurred and buffed windows will show you the ghosts of nineteen seventies and eighties California families still filled with hope; moms and dads digging a little deeper than they thought they could, in order to pull off a special international family vacation; the station wagon parked back at long-term at LAX waiting to get dustier than they'd ever seen it; mom and dad in the aisle seats, kids all wide-eyed in the middle and window on mom's side, their wide eyes glued to the window, looking down to see the dots of severe, untamed Indonesian terra firma in water as blue as it is in every pirate flick they'd ever seen in their suburban Cineplex; their most secret dreams appearing to just maybe come true if they were to believe everything that was unfolding underneath this plane back then.

And yes, there would be melancholy tales in every faded American aviation logo that couldn't be pried off by the after-market broker that sold this thing into service again, so for every eighties honeymoon the seats wheezed when you sat on them, the mind would sift through divorce statistics and wonder what came of it. None of it is any reason to walk away and book a later flight on a normal plane.

The heart starts to rally for Matthew to long for the wet-leased flight attendant, the head says everything to second the motion from the heart: She's cute and small, exotic and as doomed as anything under the sun on this side of the equator. She's all island skin, shoulders rubbed smooth from a thousand days in water and moist sand, she's one small waist and serious hips that scream, LIFE! FUCK AND CREATE LIFE! MAKE THREE LIVES FOR EVERY SINGLE ONE THAT DEATH HAS TAKEN! Her eyes smolder and her mouth broods. The head argues that she smolders and broods simply because she's likely been told this hunk of McDonnell Douglas shit trap is probably going to break into hot, rusty shrapnel after a week's worth of ferrying the desperate to low-season paradise. She looks so irresistible, the head posits, simply because she's struggling with the moral resignation it takes for her to follow the captain's rules, one of which seems to be: Under no circumstances whatsoever explain what a wet-lease is, no matter how many times the screwed-sideways, disoriented, daydreamy whitey holding his nuts asks. Look at her! That's the dare from the brain, look at how her heart is hard, her life dire, how she feels used up without ever being touched! All of this is projected, of course. Regardless, the minute the brain lays that last little portrait of engaging in some more emotional bankruptcy, Matthew decides he and the free-agent flight attendant have a lot in common and should talk.

Bad decision, too. Because the things in the blood that have conspired to make this woman look like a beautiful solution are the same things that have conspired to make Matthew look like a skittish middle-management reject drug fiend with a carful of guns, drugs, mildly profane coffee mugs, and discount porno in long-term parking at an airport in post-9/11 New York. He's covered in a thin film of about thirty-six hours of no air-conditioning, no shower, no real food he's recognized, and so strung out he can't take his hands out of his pants for fear of falling apart. But the brain is hardwired to try to get the biological container to create another container just like it before this one expires, so Matthew does his best to look suave, taking one hand out of his pants and pressing the flight attendant call button, which apparently stopped working right around twenty years ago just after the prime of this plane's life. Press, no *ding,* press, no *ding,* press, nope, and this goes on for about seven tries and then the brain seems to think that perhaps if it's PRESSED VERY HARD it will work. And so, really, that was how the button ended up working; not so much by making a sound, but by making the upper three quarters of the body writhe to reach up and depress it time and again, and harder each time while the head stretched skyward, cocked like a dog, trying to hear if the thing was *ding*ing anywhere, or just *click*ing about twenty-three inches above Matthew. But it worked, so in the end, that's all that matters about the dry-leased flight attendant call button.

Everything's disconnected on this plane, and it shudders at the oddest moments, it's quirky and worn like some des-perado acid-cult bus, but it's the kind of quirky and worn that feels like it could go into a hard dive into the water or ground at about four hundred miles an hour at any moment, and for some reason Matthew finds it all quite comforting. The gray tries to recall, the quasi-Wiki way it recalls, how it is that Ritalin is supposed to work. There's something rat-tling around about Ritalin basically speeding up the system of a hyper kid until the kid is somehow calmed by the fre-quency and speed of his biological water-bag-on-bones fi-nally matching the speed and frequency of his nerves and brain and thoughts and everything. And so maybe the plane is working on him in the same fashion, that is to say, maybe finally the stuff outside of Matthew feels like the stuff inside of Matthew; high speed and ramshackle, miracle and mistake, on lease until it has crashed and gone.

"Hello okay? Yes I can help?"

Oh, right, there's you; you're here now. Shit.

"Yes. I mean, right? It seems like you could. Oh!" Matthew's stammering start isn't made any smoother by realizing he still has one hand cupping his nuts in anticipation of pain.

"I wasn't, this isn't. I was just . . ."

"Put now on seat belt, sir."

"Oh, I know. Yeah, no . . . I know. And do you live in Taipei, or?" Matthew manages, while he puts now on his seat belt, sir.

But in the time it takes to fasten up, she's smiled kindly and left, back to her jump seat by the haunted and vacant boarded-up galley. Gone, just like that. In fairness, it's hard to surmise exactly how long fastening the belt took, especially with only one hand out of the pants and a head screwed on sideways more than it usually is. The noodle does dim math in the rich emollients of serotonin and the biological imperative, and decides flirting with the wet-leased flight attendant went well. Matthew, smiling kind of askance and looking like the victim of a discount dentist's generous prescriptions and gasses, jams his other hand back down the front of his pants, and waits for the improbable safe landing in Bali.

At the airport, the shitty station wagon lands hot and the captain slams on the brakes like a drowsy drunk surprised at how fast the curve in a freeway off-ramp snuck up on him. Matthew deplanes onto pale, soft, aged tarmac under a white-hot sun trying to X-ray his head, the day here is a laser drilled right at the eyes. The painful nuts, the fine elixirs in cans, the pills in bottles, it all leads to a slow-motion lurch into a blunt, round, ugly squat of a building; a sort of giant, low-slung concrete hat box that feels like an unfinished high school gymnasium turned armory.

If there's one catch to medical tourism's significant discount on Extracorporeal Shock Wave Lithotripsy, it may be that one has to stand, hands jammed into crotch, in a humid crush of about one thousand people trying to clear customs with no evident line or system. Kind and tame clock punchers from Phoenix in pastel sport knits; aged and fading bachelor warriors hell-bent on being laid back; middle-class families from Los Angeles with dads looking over a sea of heads damp with sweat, starting to realize the travel piece in the *Times* was a load of horseshit; a decent showing from the newly single thirty- and forty-something women that fall into the suburban-hot file, a contingency that certainly must have spiked recently on account of the book from the community center Put 'n' Take, which, Matthew surmises, must also be a movie by now, judging by the sheer numbers here. Or maybe the book was a movie first, the wilted brain imagines that this is how it works with books these days — first the movie, then the book, and eventually the idea.

The brain sits up there in its bone-hard sauna and figures that this is the way everything in the world works now, sideways and backward like this. First the movie, then the book; first the anthemic cultural catchphrase, then the pop song that incorporates it; first the divorce, then the self-improvement, then the marriage; first the mansion in the leafy upper-middle-class slum, then the plan to afford it.

The wait inches from fifteen minutes, to thirty, to forty-five, toward sixty. Matthew hasn't counted in fifteens since unloading mugs so many weeks ago, feels like years now, before the cabin, before westward expansion to Los Angeles and West Yellowstone, before pain forced any of this Bali shit to happen. There's no end in sight really to the way the weary crowd packs in and appears to make no progress. Officers of some sort patrol the perimeter. Matthew sees a skinny customs thug pressing by on the outskirts of the tight pack, and wisely takes a hand off the genitals to fold a twenty into a crisp thin triangle, a shock of Jackson's hair at the top of the pyramid, edges pressed razor thin.

When the man comes by Matthew says, "Excuse me. Hello? Is there a way I can . . ." And with this he motions forward with his head while handing the twenty over at belt level. The guard smiles and snatches it while maintaining eye contact, the way a crab on rocks doesn't need to stare at the hunk of dead fish it's just grabbed, and he walks on. Matthew follows, and the officer twists his whip-thin torso back and makes it clear with a bark that Matthew is to stay right where he is. Fuck Bali already, the head says. The heart, having developed a sensible love of lucre, says yes, fuck Bali indeed with its twenty-dollars-gets-you-nothing policy. A dad behind Matthew confirms that this is the way it works with these guys, that they smile and take the money like it's a hello, as if one has just had the brilliant idea to hand it over instead of keeping it for one's self.

"Yeah, tried that myself."

"Do they come back with a stamp or anything?"

"If they do, it takes more than a half hour, because that's when he took my money, smiled, and welcomed me to Bali."

Matthew and the dad take a moment to stand and confirm that the guard is all smile-and-con, a crooked vending machine sucking up money without surrendering a thing. A salve to at least have company in being taken, it somehow soothes the sting from the greeting. Jesus, no wonder people come to places like this and immediately hit the rum then stroll the streets in white-hot sex-blind boning fury. If one lands on an island and the hustle starts this hard and early, it seems only fair to walk the length of the place doing to the local stock what was done to you before you were fifty yards from the plane. The whole mess passes, the whole damp hothouse horde of second-guessing families; middle-aged, spiritually bankrupt desperadoes; young devil dolls from Los Angeles all gasoline blood, hot-rod giggle, and summer snatch that almost nobody on earth is having until the curtain starts to come down on these girls like it comes down on all of us eventually to level the field and narrow up the options. The whole parade made it through like time-lapse photography, through three narrow gates with glass boxes at the end with parrots like the one trained to snatch the bribe from your hand. The passport gets stamped, the

questions are asked. Why are you here? Vacation. And by
vacation Matthew means having around nine thousand tiny
sonic thumps aimed at his kidney until the rock shatters and
he's able to piss bloody sand on this seaside heaven then get
on a plane bound for American airspace. Straight along, the
dull-pain shuffle, lurch, and drag right past the suckers who
checked bags. Matthew's small backpack and carry-on are
targets for one last hustle-and-grin shakedown. Two rather
official-looking men run up all smiles.

"I carry, we carry, sir."

"I'm not a woman. Unfortunately."

"Thank you, yes, we carry, please."

"Fuck, the . . ." And this while yanking the fucking thing
right back from Nusa, or Naruda, or Akimbo, Gurn Blanston,
Mondo Paw, Tak "Jimbo" Fireside, Frond Jewel, or whatever
parents named these grifters when they were still angels
with dreams.

"Thank you. Please. To carry now for you."

"Fuck away. You dicking . . . up the shit?"

The one laugh the heart can count on is when the brain
and mouth jumble out a weird little rushed stab at casually
assertive profanity like this. Matthew tries to sell it with a
look, a look that tries to say, *Yes, that's right, you heard me,
and I mean it, mister: Fuck away, you dicking up the shit.*

The cabs outside make up for what one suffers to get to
them with prices so low they seem unkind to the man driving. The bags go in, smiles of tragic teeth, fair-price guar-
antees, and a greeting. A *slam, swack, kerrang,* as the trunk,

317

one door, then the second close, shut hard in a zip of getting down to business. Up the airport drive, out the exit, and on to what's left of the main drag, too skinny to take the punishment of the traffic. The proof of being far from home arrives around the first bend in this vein, in the form of the endless, smoky buzz-swarm of hundreds or a thousand mopeds and motorbikes, one metallic brittle that breaks and scatters like mercury for narrow bottlenecks and anything big that's about to drift over into its lane. The big snake of bikes scurries right along at pace with the vans and cabs, like a rain of flies following elephants.

Check in at the hotel resort situation, swarmed again, this time by beautiful local women with drinks on little teak trays, cool cucumber towels in little bowls made of bone. Not having health care is not that bad when you can make it to a place like this for routine shit like kidney stones. The catch is, you have to drink enough to pony up for the ticket on debt at LAX, but it is a health care plan, so very basically speaking, America's health care system is working just fine for Matthew. The paperwork comes over with keys in a discreet little leather binder that has no idea just how low the balance at the bank has dipped; the balance may be gone, in fact, below the line, in the red, in brackets, on to the overdraft protection with its interest, fangs, fees, and slimy coked-up, slicked-down, anything-you-need-now-you-can-pay-for-later demeanor. The binder is opened, the confidence is screwed up, the paperwork signed, and an entourage of orange sarong and tan skin takes Matthew to the room so he can check right out, now that he's checked right in.

Lonely from twenty-three hours of flights, and the preceding thirty-five years, Matthew goes about Googling diseases you can get in Indonesia, stopping only to refocus the eyes by peeking out the window blinds for a moment. The eyes relax into a long focal length to stare at a luxurious white sand beach littered with vacationers from America and the south coast of Australia. They lie in the late afternoon sun, enjoying drinks brought to them by waiters who stand by attentively in tuxedos abbreviated in the leg and length to accommodate the hot weather. It's easy to get the impression that Googling diseases and quietly draining the minibar alone in hopes of killing pain is not how one is supposed to spend their time in Bali, so before the haze turns to sleep, a call is made to the desk, and a shuttle ride is scheduled for tomorrow's ride to BIMC Hospital, Nusa Dua. There, now; that's more like it.

Things start slowly. Dogs sniff all over outside the van, men with mirrors on sticks sweep them down and under the van and look for anything they need to look for. Brain does the math of dogs and mirrors and recalls the blackened and splintered bombed-out disco was still there on the drive in yesterday. This world, fucking mad, or whatever the name of that film. It's hard to want the van to leave the chain resort where one is swarmed by women carrying booze; it's harder because, of course, the pain isn't here today. That's the way it goes with these things, get within a block of a hospital three thousand miles across the Pacific, the pain is gone. Get across the threshold, fall out of love, then right back in love with them the minute they're walking out. But it's there, it's there, it's there. The stupid films from the disc were sent, this was ages ago, after the dreaded price discussion, the one in which the urologist, the fan of Rove-as-author, took Matthew from the torture chamber and into the dark-paneled office to talk scheduling and financing the fancy USA top-dollar lithotripsy and stone removal. A conversation that went something like this:

"That Karl Rove book! I have to say, the guy's got a knack for . . ."

"Here's the thing, I don't have insurance at this point, so how much would something like this be in cash? Could I do it for ten or fifteen grand if I took it out of savings?"

"Hard to say. Could be twenty grand, could be thirty, could be more if it takes more than once, it's just hard to say."

"Okay, I'm going to do some checking around."

The subtext of the exchange was something like:

"*I'm one of those millions of people you read about in America.*"

"*No insurance?*"

"*Exactly. But I could swing ten grand in cash.*"

"*That's weird, I can't hear you for some reason. I see your mouth moving, but no sound is coming out.*"

"*Never mind, I'll just go to India or something.*"

The van is on its way. The paradise of tiny bottles, room

service, and window blinds fades into the rearview, and the road becomes less enchanted as the palms on the property end and the main drag of Nusa Dua begins. Painted plywood billboards cracked by beautiful days and the occasional hurricane blur past and advertise half-assed roadside bars made of cinder block and lumber and offering the chance to drink something strong from a bottle with a cobra in it. Or you can do a shot and eat the egg of a cobra, or you can get drunk then wander the warm roads and dirt paths at night until a cobra bites you and you die with a swollen black leg. The DVD shops show up in clusters like komodos to a kill. One offers a dozen Hollywood hits on DVD for $12.99, the next offers a dozen for $10.99, the next two offer a dozen for $9.99, and the very last one on the end offers a dozen for $12.99 — the same price as the first one, but they have more flashing lights than the first shop, plus there are pretty girls out front waving as you go past. Souvenir shacks blur past, too, but the souvenirs can barely be seen from way out here in the traffic pattern's snarl of vans and taxis. Motorbikes scream a steady chorus of *nen-nen-nen-neen-neen*, engulfing the shuttle van like a storm of red, white, and black locusts ready to strip crops of tourist green. The impression of the gift shacks' inventories at this speed is: small skulls of wood, cobra head key chains and paperweights, cobras in bottles of something, big lizards made of wood, small lizards made of wood, more big lizards made of wood, and certainly somewhere a cobra head glued to a lizard made of wood if one had the time to slow down and look for it. There are massage joints and spas, too, many offering something called the Bali Mystical Warm Stone Treatment, certainly a euphemism for something, the brain surmises. At any rate, strange the way the eyes key in on a sign that offers something so close to what the body needs at the moment. The body needs the Bali Not-So-Mystical Stone Removal Treatment and the hospital on the horizon has just that.

There's this thing the cab drivers here do, this moment where they know they're about to swing a hard right turn, and they slow a bit, almost close their eyes a little, as if to make peace with the fact that when the right is swung, the motorbike swarm may or may not part and that is up to something bigger than all of us. The choreography of it goes off without a hitch, a right turn that works like Stravinsky and the van is off the main drag and down toward BIMC Hospital, looking, so far, exactly as it does on the brochure; a building that was intended to be a low-slung, concrete resort hotel until something went sideways and a shipment of medical equipment arrived a few months before the grand opening. One checks in without the pageantry of area resort hotels, that's the first difference one notices. Outside, medium-cute girls, roughed up by the hours, smoke Djarums and steady themselves for the shift ahead; long drags and glances up at the cloudless vivid blue; the bedpan-and-gauze beat is better than dancing in front of a DVD hut or selling fake Cartier on the beach to tourists.

In the waiting room, a little window of glass frosted at the bottom slides half open and a woman, clearly no fan of ceremony, shoves a clipboard up onto the smooth, cool counter and more signatures are in order. Between clearing customs, crowds of short con men rushing up, being swarmed by women with drinks seeking signatures, and fast shuttle vans navigating throngs to arrive at the hands of bored administrative types waiting to usher you along discreet corridors, the head wanders to what it must have been like to be a Beatle in Japan circa 1967. Even more so since the pain isn't present in the nuts or back this morning. Clipboard one signed, all five pages, clipboard two signed, all three places, a locker key issued, a seat offered up in wait, dented and dog-eared gossip magazines of stars you've never seen. Soon enough the body is gowned and ushered along a purgatory of hallways and into the room, and then Matthew falls madly in love with a man.

This man is maybe fifty years of age, admittedly plain-looking at first glance, with an unremarkably benign bedside manner, but in full control of a little cart and rack that administers something that's been attached to the needle left in the left arm. The body lies staring at a ceiling and the brain wonders what daydreams are real, and the man smiles kindly at something; at everything for some reason, Jesus, enough smiling. The table has more brains than the body lying on top of it at the moment. The table has told the technician where the stupid black dot has moved to and Matthew is pushed a bit over to the left, asked to scoot down just a touch, bumped an inch or so back to the right, and then bull's-eye: The table's X-ray eyes tell the technician on Matthew's right that the little gel-filled electronic tit under the lower back is aimed at the money spot. The man/love interest on Matthew's left takes another look at his screens and flow, thinking about whatever it is anesthesiologists/lovers think of at times like this. The two men then look at each other and the table looks up at the two of them and nods, indicating that its screens, levers, and currents are ready to be cocked for nine thousand or so fast little weird ticks; tiny kicks that should cause subsonic demolition in the ureter. *Ureter. Ureter. Ureter. Ur. You're. Your.*

"Can you feel the machine, the ticking? Can you feel any discomfort there?" Matthew's future husband asks.

Inside the head, a refrain, *Say yes, say yes, say yes, say yes, say yes, say yes, say yes, say yes, say yes, say yes, say yes, say yes, say . . .*

"Yes."

"Okay, let me increase. You let me know when you're comfortable; we want to be sure you're not feeling pain."

Don't leave me. Ever.

The only thing that the head is trying to figure or explain is who the woman is who just walked right into the room and sat down to eat a plum and watch, like she had wandered from a kitchen into a living room. The lips tried to form the words. The head asked in silence a thousand times, *Who is that?*, but the mouth wouldn't have any part in getting the words to come. The beep on the monitor slowed, the warm flood hugged the veins, blood became love, and everything was fine for the very first time since before turning nine and getting the news that the parents weren't coming home from that second honeymoon, and hoping somehow that it meant the second honeymoon was going to last forever in heaven. The stuff in the blood is really working wonders on the past now, any rough spots in the road up to this point softened into mud; enemies melted into people who had only ever tried to love you and just messed up. Somehow the idea comes on strong that every day is sunny, even when it rains, if you just go high enough up, there will always be sun.

The woman sitting there smiling and eating a plum — she might be the source of all of this well-being and resignation, as far as the head can tell. The table ticks and punches at the rock in the guts, the machine to the left beeps steady measures of a heart still marching on in perfect meter, the woman looks up and her eyes squint a beautiful smile and her cheeks suck in a little at what must have been a tart spot in the plum. The lips are the ones; the nose is the one; the eyes are the ones; the breasts are the ones. People or machines could kick at Matthew forever, so long as this love smiled on him the way it is right now, almost vibrating like this. The heart speaks up plainly: *I'm ready; I'm done here now. It's been so hard since you've been gone and I've never said so. I've tried my best since the day they gave me away. I want to come home to you now.* The heart races at a weird full-speed arrhythmia while the two men flanking Matthew can be heard in some kind of panic about the new jazz-time signature on the machine, *beep, beepbeep, beepbe — bap, bee, p.* The heart races happy, sky swelling into the room from a giant glorious crack in the roof.

Matthew musters everything he has, cons synapses in hopes of gaming the system; to con the man in control of the morphine flow from the cart and rack. Matthew fakes a pain with a push left; arches up like it can't stand the feeling of the process even though it is numb and almost gone. The head tries harder than it ever has; pushes a grunt to feign discomfort; tries to make the men flanking the body think that there's not enough heaven in the room and that pain is still being felt, and that this is the truth. The light gets brighter, the music gets louder; earth is going to be gone for Matthew if this grift works; if this grunt and squirm tricks them, it's the end of this dull and sad dimension. Even the head had to admit that this is starting to feel like magic; somehow a nine-year-old is looking down at the longer, bigger, older thing it had become. The boy wishes and begs, in a sad fit of temper, to be done dragging this body through earthly days, to be through with spending the rest of his time disguised as this man on the table below him.

But it doesn't matter how hard you hope to never come to, they all rush to get oxygen on you, they call others in to slide the man from the table, to a gurney, to a bed, and before the head knows what hit it, they've moved the body and the brain and the heart into this other room to recoup. The nose breathes big, pure, silvery white clean hits of oxygen, the heart feels a world of warm yellow and orange turn all matter-of-fact and blue again, and the head tries to explain away whatever it recalls of the situation in the other room.

29

The Buffet Is Having Problems.
So Is the Business Center

MATTHEW HAS TWO SAVVY TRAVEL tips he can dole out to the first-time visitor to Bali. The first is that one shouldn't attempt to navigate the seafood buffet in the golden afterglow of minor kidney trauma, jet lag, near death, morphine, and Tylenol 4 with codeine. The head narrates the scene with the hysteria of a small-town neighbor talking about a house fire, but it might be justified here in the Club Level dining situation, the culinary equivalent of the VIP section, really. A stunning lattice of concrete pads that seem to float on ponds. Each square connected by teak bridges, the emerald waters beneath lush with flora of the region and bright orange-and-white koi, their colors dulled just a bit until they rise to the surface, for a silent chorus of hello kisses in this brilliant mirage of travel and leisure. The ears swore they heard a voice that was not Matthew's — a voice saying that life has been trying to show him places like this for ages now but that he seemed tied to routine and determined to resist.

It all seemed like a giant welcome to better living until a buffet table being politely descended upon by above-average people jumps up at Matthew like it's spring-loaded; like a prank reserved for rubes in here on a free upgrade. A giant wooden bowl of crabs jumps at the face and plants itself right on and into it. The head says: *Oh, shit, the pills have gained ground and turned the place into one big seafood fun house.* At first, the humiliation is too much to bear. The head wants to end it all, wants to disappear; it wasn't a bad idea, that idea in the hospital today of conning a sweet anesthesiologist into administering enough to slow the body down forever until the mortal shell was on permanent vacation. Then the heart rallies verve, understanding too clearly that days are limited and one day gone, and that it was absolutely a bad idea to hope to leave the planet early from that hospital today. Sure, the blood is thick with chemical debris fueling this spirited revelation, but there's also a certain inspired mood that comes of being at a seaside resort after a sunny day spent indoors falling in love with an anesthesiologist whose American name is Steve, while the beautiful ghost of your young mother looked on with her blessing.

And that's the mood Matthew is in, plus yes, Tylenol with codeine and a big Bintang beer — but the foundation of the mood, it has nothing to do with the pills and Bintang. The effect is that one is finally too exhausted to continue spending life's very finite remaining balance being polite and afraid; hold it all together long enough and one is finally cornered into confidence. And on that day, you may find yourself flat on your face in a bowl of tasty crabs. When this happens, eat the fucking crab! If chemical gravity and sway has landed one's face in the bowl, then it is no fault of one's own; it is simply the great, big, delicious mistake of science and medicine.

Will guests look on? Yes, they will look on; for that matter guests are looking on right now, right this very moment. Go ahead, pull your head up in between taking bites, and look at them; there they are, fattened by years of steady flow, staring back. Normal people are everywhere now, it seems. There must've been a time when it wasn't so. The head is through with worrying what they think: *That's right, folks, stare all you want, this is the splendor and horror that's available to you; hell, it's coming for you. You only have to wait; it's that easy to sign up. All you need to do is let years march on the way they do, slow in their brutality with you, forcing your hand, getting rid of all your stupid plans.*

Matthew stops eating for just a minute, turns and musters saying something to the man backing away from the buffet table, right to the water's edge: "Don't look so appalled, lady — you wish you were doing the same thing. You've been living for people you've never met; people who won't be by your bed when you take your last breath."

Another trophy man next to a trophy wife, this one at the very end of the long table, still piles a plate full, looks up suddenly at the commotion. Matthew hears himself saying this: "That's right, get a taste of that before I get over there. Because when the bear gets there, it's over. It's done, that shit's mine. I'll spend the first bite on your arm to back you down. This combo they've got me on for nut pain is savage and strange. I'm a bull, all kicked in the sack and agitated to the point of fighting; I never had it in me like this. I was always a flight guy, but you can't be and survive, not in America, not anymore. Maybe in your Australia you can turn the other cheek, get by in that desert of yours on rotten meat and dreams, but it isn't that way where I live. Around the world, thugs storm mosques and discos, so I'm taking this. Under God's sky, tiny hearts stop beating on ultrasound screens, or worse, kids are born with diseases that should've been cured a billion dollars ago. None of it's fucking fair — they don't tell you that when you're young, they let you catch on slowly, maybe by the time you're thirty. If you knew how stacked the deck was when you were young, you'd stab half the neighborhood in a fit, so they let it ride awhile, they watch you and see if you're getting it yet. They feed you sitcoms and cartoon strips about desperadoes with funny glasses and big bald heads and expressionless faces in cubicle graves, so you feel better about being fucked by days that you refuse to take as your own. So I'm taking this tortellini seafood salad as my own. And I'm taking your gin. Yum, yum, yum, the bear got into camp, motherfuckers. The bear was upgraded; the bear brought an American Express Platinum to a MasterCard Gold fight. And a bear's gonna eat, you know what I mean? I got here selling shit in parking lots. But I got here, didn't I? And now you have to face me."

What Matthew is actually slurring in a loud whisper is this: "This — the noodle . . . pasta thing? Fuuuuuck. Mmm."

The trophy wife is smiling — smiling! Her eyes lit with delight that she's trying to hide whenever it seems like the trophy husband might look her way by chance. She's the only person not frightened, inconvenienced, or disgusted, and nobody notices. So, right, the first savvy travel tip is about these buffet situations, and the second savvy travel tip is this: One should not attempt to print, sign, and FedEx contracts for coffee-mug distribution in gigantic American urban outfitting chain stores from a hotel's so-called business center under the sway of a long, strange day. Because even though it all works out just fine, there are myriad humiliations awaiting, including but not limited to having a cute young woman wipe drool from the margin of a contract you are signing. Aside from those two tips, do as you will while in Bali, mystic land of enchantment.

There was so much email. Weeks old, even older, some of it. Replies were attempted and some even sent — a nap between the buffet situation and the visit to the business center had made things a little easier to navigate. There was a woman in there too, bored to tears, stuck in paradise manning a hotel's business center. Not much was said; the mouth had done its work for the day, and a sterling performance at that. There was the business of hellos exchanged and the woman didn't say anything past that, really, just looked at Matthew and looked away whenever he glanced her way. The post-buffet stretch was tough to read, and either a language barrier was at play or she had heard about Matthew's new approach to resort dining and was unsure about saying much to Matthew and triggering an episode of some sort. It's nice, though, to have that kind of distance from people when trying to think straight; one can't be too hard on oneself for creating a little space on vacation like this; for putting a few layers between one's self and the upper-middle-class riffraff.

There was an email from Tim, a personal advisory of sorts. Tim's life-coach act, when he lapses into it, is now undermined by living in a park with a leathery, shoplifting, amphibious hashish fiend and another man wearing a dead animal for a robe and giving the world the silent treatment. The message was a bold chorus of one man, though, and it was a big gesture, Tim likely having taken the time to duck into some concrete Injun Trading Outpost and Café staffed by white people to send word on an ancient charged-by-the-hour PC. It's not the first time Tim has said to move on from Kristin, but mostly the ears and eyes have been trained pretty well to not register Tim's previous suggestions in the arena of love. For a month or two after his head was shaved by the sex worker with the violent disposition and the suitcase of prosthetic penises or whatever she brought to bear on him, Tim was pretty quiet when it came to advising anyone in matters of the heart. But now he's back to having elected himself the harbinger of personal growth. The email from Tim was the usual stuff, but maybe not, at least in that things seemed to be wrapping up.

Greetings, Fellow Doomed! Guess what, I'm tired of being lost in a park that's supposed to be so goddamned simple. If nature is such a perfect system, why can't it make it clear what the hell state I'm in? One person tells me we're in Montana, the next person says Idaho, the next swears up and down that it's Wyoming. I am starting to get the impression one could drink a bottle of fortified strawberry wine, get in the rig, and do a doughnut that would swing her ass end through terra firma belonging to all three states. So I did just that, on sort of a dare from myself, Chief. I've generally been getting my act together but I allowed myself one lapse into the powder and booted it up with some strawberry wine thing that Tic liberated from the minimarket a couple days after you left and we went out of the park to refuel. Modoch is pouting about my behavior, big surprise, but Tic Tac tells me, LAUGHING HIS ASS OFF, that I was literally, technically, swinging the ass end of the rig through all three states. It was loud. Things got loud after you left and I allowed myself one last dance with the demons inside me to get a few things straight with them. Anyway, I was drinking and searching for some answers, and had jumped in the rig to do doughnuts and blow off steam. And that's when the heat rolled up strong with their beef again. The same guy that crawled all over me for defending myself against wildlife up at Canyon Falls when I accidentally smacked the neighboring camper (again, his fault, snuck up on me) but he's with a new guy none of us have seen. They cooled off real fast when they saw the company I'm keeping these days. Modoch assured the ranger that I've been making spiritual progress of sorts. Tic Tac made some crack to the new guy about how he might want to go back to his shed or barrel or wherever they kept him. Then Tic stood right there and told me to get back in the rig and do it again, do another doughnut in the thing, but I felt pretty lousy after they had to strong-arm and scare the park screws, who were just doing their job, so I said I wasn't up for it and that we would tone things down for the rest of the night. New ground for me, am I right? Modoch saw the progress in my feeling remorse, I think. Tic Tac just got drunker and very silent and sad. He looked, believe it or not, like a little boy whose birthday party had been shut down early on account of bad behavior. Like a little kid who was told he was getting nothing but coal for Christmas. My heart broke, it really did. So I said, "Oh, what the fuck," screwed up my nerve, gave him a wink, and fired the steel horse up and let 'er rip all over that field again. And, get this: I ROLLED THE GODDAMN THING! Little bit of a bind, to say the least, Chief. The boys kept me out of the worst of it. They told me to get all of my shit out of the RV and stuff it up in whatever rucksack I had, and Tic made an anonymous call to the ranger from the park call box, and then we all hid on the other side of the river there. When three guys from RV Rents USA came into the park along with a big diesel tow truck to winch the beast off her side and drag her back up onto the road, Tic Tac jumped up out of our little foxhole over on the far side of The Madison, his face was all camouflaged with moss and barbecue charcoal and shit, and he power-walked across the river the way only former military assassins can. It was worth the price of admission, even though I haven't had to pay admission since picking these two up in July. No clue what Tic Tac said to the RV guys, but they decided to kindly drag their goddamned top-heavy, overpowered RV out of the park before it killed somebody, tow it back to their lot in Bozeman, and that would be the end of it; no harm, no foul. Anyway, look, I've spent too much time bullshitting here. Here's the thing: it was great seeing you but now there's something I haven't said since the day you got married: don't do this. Don't keep hanging on, Chief, move on, she was never the one. I can say that now without getting the hassle I got from your in-laws when they MADE AN EFFORT to overhear me when I was telling you the same thing DISCREETLY at your wedding. It doesn't matter what went south, doesn't matter if you were married too fast or looking for a mother, it doesn't matter if the boy got married but the man stayed longing and looking for trouble, it only matters that you stop living like she's still at home with you, because she hasn't been for a long time. You've been alone in that house too long, probably still convinced she's upstairs or in the other room. Take down some of the pictures on the walls, change your screensaver, quit calling her your wife in conversation, it's been over a year. I bet if I got you up on fire mountain with Modoch doing a ceremony I could get you to admit it's been two or three years, but I'm done here and by the time you dodge two more of my calls, I'll be headed back to Manhattan to face the music. And by music I mean the Federal Fucking Trade Commission and a long list of people who would probably like their money back.

Signed, the only family you've got, whether you like it or not —

T

There was more mail from Tatiana saying essentially that things are complicated in her life, but that maybe they're not as complicated as she thinks. A still relatively young man has to count it as a plus when a beautiful woman doesn't run screaming from the hotel in which blood is urinated onto her by accident. And not only does Tatiana not run, but she lies on the bed to watch television documentaries about geniuses and says she has a hunch that the man has a touch of brilliance, even after this terrible mishap in the shower that would seem evidence of the contrary. This is a solid partner in crime, this is not some Miss Minor League Come and Go. Aside from positing the idea that life was complicated but maybe not, Tatiana's email spoke of having business to tend to for herself and Matthew. Because when a cute vampire actor uses Twitter FaceLink to post a picture of a fellow cute vampire actor drinking coffee out of a mug that says, *It starts out cute and then it gets ugly* across it, there are millions of girls in millions of bedrooms in front of millions of computers trying to find that mug in a mall, even though most of them probably don't drink coffee. There is email from Jim Montgomery, executive director of The Norwalk Developmental Work Training Center. It is a note saying, basically: "It is the future I got wolf blood powers Jim is full of shit."

This must mean that Chris figured out how to email Matthew on Jim Montgomery's computer. But there won't be much time for hijinks, there won't be time for much more than producing and boxing mugs and mugs and mugs. Chris will be thrilled to learn that there is a rush on for millions more now that there is a distribution contract and the matter of this Internet picture situation. The head reels at the idea of it all. The kind of money that Tatiana is talking about in the contract is crazy money. It is the kind of money one works in the middle-management maze of a place like New Time Media for two decades or more to amass. That's a lot of money today, but it won't be in the future, it's a fortune now, but what if one lives to eighty or ninety? Still, there is no better way to be flying back to America than with one's mug in every magazine on the newsstand, and someone in Los Angeles making sure it is credited and getting more press, and making sure it is licensed and in line for a big advance.

There's no better way to be flying back to America than to have left going broke, marginalized, unemployed, low-spirited trying to get high, and now this. But for now there's the same economy seat and anonymous quiet of life before it was all spun around. Alone now over the Pacific at night again, done with the Denpasar-to-Taipei leg, done with Taipei to Tokyo, halfway done with Tokyo to San Francisco, and then only San Francisco to JFK will remain. Maybe upgrading is in order for the last leg, but for now, economy, sleeping against a sweatshirt against a window, hopefully through with eating pills and pissing red sandstone.

The window rattles and chills the head and it's a little easier to feel the fight fading from the chest way up here on a night like this; a little easier to see that maybe all of these lives have one thing hidden in the fine print, that they've been closing in on the end from the day they began with a slap. All days numbered and ticking away, all clocks doing their sneaking by, all calendars spitting up squares until the grid is done with us—the rush of having it all ahead of us gone, the body aged past the promise of what any stranger might've assumed was within reach, time doing to all of us what we've seen it do to everyone.

Then again, a jet! A fucking jet! Up here, seated and fed, up here moping around in air we wouldn't even be able to breathe in! And that doesn't even start on the miles of sky above this thing, miles that go way past where gravity has any card to play. Men have stared at the moon and figured a way up. And pilots sit in the nose of these planes, steel and fuel and fire, seven or eight miles above the Pacific all night, and they touch down soft as angels without incident every day! Tatiana is somewhere up ahead, a thousand miles off the nose of this thing tonight, maybe even smiling. Chris is out there dreaming of boxing up mugs like there's no tomorrow. Tim is coming down from the mountains, surrendering and heading back just in case he sees a chance to try and take Manhattan again.

Maybe it's not so hard to have a little faith. Maybe it is time to be done with every bad decision that has prolonged the pain of transition — guns, half-assed drugs, drinking, that thing where one is thinking they have everyone fooled, never realizing everyone saw what you were going through, and you were the last to know and everyone knew it. Milton is down there alive and waiting for the next session, right? And wait until he hears just how much progress there has been. Sure there are catches to starting one's life all over again; this is going to hurt, this is going to be the heavy lifting, this is saying good-bye to the gun before getting the hang of it, and saying good-bye to drugs and drink and to the lonely pornography from under the driver's seat. Well, maybe not good-bye to the porn, maybe don't quit everything at the same time and go insane. But yes, let's get rid of some of the crutches; let's ask for help when it is needed; learn to have a little faith that there's still time, no matter how much was wasted. Maybe whatever life one gets is more than we were ever owed to begin with. And all that time wasted on the job thinking one was getting over on the bosses, well, the end is going to come, and in the end, we will all realize the time we thought we were clever for wasting was ours all along.

So, what are we waiting for? Keep this free bird pointed east, Captain! Bring it down gently right at the minute the first half of the big mug money direct deposit from Los Angeles hits! Come on, let's live, there will be time enough for everyone to find their loves and friends and family as ghosts in the end, and maybe then everyone can meet up again. In the meantime, the sad songs are gone; the cigarettes and anthems of the downtrodden have fallen by the wayside in the shadow of a hospital and hotel; there will be new songs now, and they won't be songs about things going wrong. There's nothing to lose but what time's already planning to take.

ACKNOWLEDGMENTS

—

Thank you, Mom, Dad, Trish, for getting to earth and every single kindness. Thank you John Murphy. Thank you Maria. Maria! Thanks James Levine and Daniel Greenberg and everyone at Levine Greenberg. Thank you Larry Kirshbaum, Ed Park, Carmen Johnson, Julia Cheiffetz, Maggie Sivon, Justin Renard, Alexandra Woodworth, and everyone at Amazon Publishing in New York. Thanks to George Dawes Green, Joan Firestone, Catherine Burns, Jenifer Hixson, Maggie Cino, Catherine McCarthy, Robin Wachsberger, Kate Tellers, Kirsty Bennett, Paul Ruest, Daisy Rosario, David Mutton, Brandon Echter, and every single person from Stories at The Moth in New York City, past and present — Joey Xanders, Lea Thau! Joshua Wolf Shenk, thank you as always. Thanks to Pamela Koslyn, Esq. Thank you Christopher Monks, Jordan Bass, Jory John and everyone at Mc-Sweeney's, 826 Valencia, and The Rumpus. Thanks to Raha Naddaf. And to Jim Nelson and Michael Benoist at GQ. Hello to Michael Patrick King and thanks for making me laugh so damn hard after a crazy beautiful strange gig so far from home. Thank you Amanda, Ben, Janine, Nat, Dave, Eric, Peter, Lotta, Atkins, Doug, Loren, Cam, Sheri, King, Juliet, John, Susan, Jeff, Norm, Scot, Ravi, Courtney, Alex, Karen, J.C., Leroy, Aaron, Dan, Paul, Linda, Kevin, B. Frayn, London, Lyle.

MANIFEST AND WAYBILL: 20 pages in 2003 on Wall Street, stopped, started again in 2006 on 35th street, stopped, started again in 2008, stopped, started again in a cabin in upstate New York, August 2010. Finished 10/21/11 on West 11th St. Daniel Greenberg emailed that it had a home and contract on 03/12/12. I mention this because I have said that writing is easy work one too many times and it finally bit me in the ass.

File under: Pressure.